I0597469

By R Frank Davis

Across the Line
Love Gods Magic
Love in Lockdown

Published by DREAMSPINNER PRESS
www.dreamspinnerpress.com

LOVE GODS MAGIC
THE BLACK PHARAOH

R FRANK DAVIS

DREAMSPINNER
PRESS

Published by

DREAMSPINNER PRESS
8219 Woodville Hwy #1245
Woodville, FL 32362 USA
www.dreamspinnerpress.com

This is a work of fiction. Names, characters, places, and incidents either are the product of author imagination or are used fictitiously, and any resemblance to actual persons, living or dead, business establishments, events, or locales is entirely coincidental.

Trade Paperback ISBN: 978-1-641-08782-7
Digital ISBN: 978-1-641-08781-0
Trade Paperback published October 2024
v. 1.0

AUTHOR'S NOTE

THIS IS my first venture into the genre of Afrofuturist magic/fantasy MM romance, and as a former journalist, I feel the need to provide some attribution, as in what truths are in this novel?

For as long as I can remember, I have been fascinated by ancient cultures and mythology. Edith Hamilton's classic, *Mythology*, was my introduction to and my bible for the Greek and Roman gods. Other sources retold the Norse legends. But I couldn't find a definitive text for ancient Egypt. And when I was young, almost nothing was written about the Kingdom of Kush without placing it deep in the shadow of the Egyptian pyramids.

What a difference a few decades can make. As I began researching for *Love Gods Magic*, I found many internet articles on the Nubians and their varied roles in civilization along the Nile. Two of my best sources were *The Kingdom of Kush*, published by Captivating History, and *Ancient Egyptian Magic: A Hands-on Guide*, by Christina Riggs. And there are numerous YouTube videos about ancient Nubians and current museums featuring Nubian art and artifacts.

Many of the names and locations in this book are taken directly from the historical record: Taharqa was pharaoh of Kemet, the "black land" of both Kush and Egypt. Abar was his mother, and another Kush pharaoh/queen was Amanirenas. Gods' names, both Egyptian and Nubian, are called upon, as are some of the gods' powers. The cities of Kerma, Napata, and Meroë were real.

I am, however, a creative writer, and much of the Nubian and Egyptian history is still being uncovered. This means I present the reader with the *bamiya*, stewed facts and lies cooked up to create a digestible dish. Taharqa's ennead is my creation, along with the modern story that is the meat of this stew. Much of the rare-earth science is speculative. And then there is Stevie. (Note: Stevie stories, which appear in three of my books so far, have totally separate narratives.)

My interest in Kush is personal: I have a great desire to see the nations and empires of Black Africa given some of the attention European mythologies have had for centuries. The kingdoms of Axum, Mali, and Ghana have stories as heroic as any comic book fantasy. Who knows, maybe some imaginative author will take up those stories as well.

Until then, I offer to you *djed medu*, the words to be said, to make the magic.

R Frank Davis

To all who participated, online or in real life, my deepest thanks for helping this book become reality. And, of course, to my love and champion, Roger. Here's to decades more of us together.

Chapter 1

Intercepted missive: For the pursuers—What you don't know won't hurt us, so go dig for clues, blues! For all others—Enter our adventure here.

Taharqa

I OPEN the dormitory door and I am in his eyes. Large eyes, ebony black, shining out of a broad brown face.

In a small room, all white—ceiling, walls, grayish tile, fluorescent glow—he is the shining star, physical and confident in a well-filled T-shirt and sweatpants marked with Pardell University in the school's colors of black and gold. I have entered a jewel case, and here is a red-gold treasure on display. Already my heartbeat tweaks.

I see the American in him, the differences that come because most American Blacks are at least a quarter European, or so says DNA. His skin is not dark like mine; his nose is more Roman than Bantu. But the shining eyes, the close-cropped hair, the high cheekbones are African enough. By appearance he could be a descendant of one of my people, the seemingly long-lost Nubians.

What is most American Black male of all is his body: a coiled spring. Even while relaxed, smiling up from the bed he is leaning back on, I can see the tension in the (ample) muscles, the forever-tight, be-prepared-for-anything posture of people torn away from the homeland and for too long made to defend their right to exist. This anticipation of antipathy is a strain and a strength, as I have learned. American Blacks can be the least trusting, most trustworthy people on earth.

Of course it doesn't hurt that he is a young bull: strong chest, thick arms, and legs like tree trunks in his baggy pants. His six-foot frame sits up, and he extends a wide hand toward me.

"Wassup, bruh," he says. "Welcome."

"Hello to you, my friend." I lean toward him, offering my hand. He rises and grasps my palm, surprising me with an African handshake—the common grip, then a turn of the hands to grab over thumbs, then back. This *fahim*, this intelligent one, knows more than I have come to expect from the modern ones in the States. And I'm wearing a rap-music T-shirt and jeans, so how does he know I am African?

"I'm Branden," he says. "Branden Hickcock."

"Taharqa Nimiery." Now he certainly knows I am not American. "*Oof!*"

That *oof* is the result of my being shoved out of the doorway from behind. I turn to let in Ahmed, his tight-muscled arms loaded with my TV. Looks like my new roomie will get a gander at how well-off I am.

"Damn," Branden says, "is that a sixty-inch flatscreen?"

"Sixty-five."

"Puts to shame my little thirty-incher."

"We shall share."

Ahmed is still standing, the heavy load in his arms.

"Oh," Branden says, "I didn't know which side…." His hands are pointing around the room.

"Just put it down, Ahmed." I say. "We can sort it out later."

"Very well, effendi." Ahmed adds a little head bow and a hand twirl of obeisance. "I shall bring the rest."

"And knock off the effendi, bruh," I say. "We're not playing *Aladdin*."

Ahmed nods again, coming up with a big smile, crossing his arms over his chest. "Wakanda forever!" he shouts.

"Y'better watch out," Branden says, laughing. "We take that Wakanda shit for real around here."

Little does he know how much Ahmed and I do too, though in our own way.

Ahmed turns to Branden. "No offense, effendi."

Branden nods back. "No shade, really." And Ahmed leaves.

"Quite a dude, Taharqa," Branden says. "Is he always that way?"

"Many times worse," I reply.

"But Taharqa?" he asks. "Like the Nubian Pharaoh Taharqa?"

This Branden is truly fahim. That interest in me that had shown at the first moment of our meeting is back again. "How do you know this?"

"I'm the son of two history profs," he says, "and they made sure I know African history. They made me take Latin just so I could learn more about the Romans fighting the Kingdom of Kush. Taharqa was pharaoh when Nubians ruled Egypt during the twenty-fifth dynasty. His name is in the Old Testament. Man, your folks must be so proud to bring the name forward, what, forty-odd centuries out of the past? Taharqa. Wow."

I nod, because what else can one do. "We keep the stories alive. And I'm known as Archie here in the States."

"Archie, sure." His expression turns quizzical. "Why Archie?"

"A bit of a story. I had a teacher in Key Stage four, your high school level, who spoke Mandarin. She had some difficulty with my name, and when I wrote it out in syllables, she used the Chinese pronunciation of *q*, which is like *ch*. Taharqa became T'archa, and soon enough the Brits had me named Archie."

"Dope! Oh man, I am so glad I asked for an African roomie."

Yes. But that takes my hopes a bit down. I had asked for a gay roommate.

"So are you from there? I guess it is Sudan now, or South Sudan?"

"Sudan includes much of the land once known as Nubia, and it was once the land of the Kingdom of Kush." And for us Kush will remain, no matter what national tag or location the moderns may wish to hide us under.

"That's a long way to travel to attend a farm-country cow college," Branden says.

"Cow college, you call it?

"Pardell is the state agriculture school, so it gets the cow-college nickname. How did you learn about it?"

"Oh, we researched US universities heavily. I attended mainly European private institutes, and I was looking for a good engineering school in the States." A good, not-so-high-profile, serious place where one might experiment without prying eyes and one could find the ways to succeed in our great stratagem. "I understand Pardell is digging deeply into climate change and energy issues, something of great import at home."

"Sure is. That's why I'm here." So maybe that's why we were teamed up—common interests, likely common majors. "That and to join the wrestling team. I heard the Nuba have an ancient culture built around wrestling. Still true?"

"For some Nuba clans that is still true. I, however, am not much practiced in it." My clan has very different rites. But those rituals, like our secret mission, are not to be known by moderns. There are some even I don't know. How much more will I need to conceal from my new friend? "Today's Nuba are a collection of ethnic groups in Sudan, but they are not Nubians. And today's Nubians are split between southern Egypt and northern Sudan." Excluding a few not to be mentioned—at least not yet.

"That's confusing for a Yankee," Branden says. "Still, it would be great to have you watch me wrestle, give me a few pointers?"

Watch you, handsome man, flexing muscles in a skintight singlet? I would drop a sacred praise of thanksgiving, and religion is not my strong suit. Well, not the religions most people would know today.

"Certainly," I say.

A bustle at the door: Ahmed has returned with a double armload of trunk.

"And where shall I place your cask of gold, silver, and priceless rubies, effendi?"

"How about up your ass, buddy," I reply. He drops his load, nods, and then beats his chest and gives out a feeble Tarzan yell. He exits to our laughter.

"Buddy?" Branden asks. "Bruh?"

"That jerk? I guess you could say he's my best friend slash servant. Ahmed and I have been together since we were kids, so we're more like brothers. He's helping me move in."

"Is he going to school here?"

"Yes, but no. The home folks think we're together, but he's too interested in the arts to waste time at an engineering school. So he's actually going to the Indianapolis School of Design. We had to do a bit of work to get his tuition paid through me, but it's not hard to fool the home folks when they're seven thousand miles away."

Branden seems strangely pleased. Hmm.

"Have you ever been to northeast Africa?" I ask.

"Not really."

"Don't worry. If you've been in a sandbox, you're not missing much."

"My mom got to go to the west, to Gorée Island, the Door of No Return in the House of Slaves memorial in Senegal. She said she cried and cried."

Gorée Island is a place, one place of several, where chained, defenseless Africans were taken to be sailed across oceans in the hellish innards of slave ships, to die or to defy death without home, family, culture. There are such infamous places, even older, in the Horn of Africa. The Arabs were slavers in Africa's east before the Renaissance Europeans came human-buying in the west. The ocean was Indian instead of Atlantic, but slavery's cruelty was the same. So when thinking of these ports of shame, cry, as must we all. These are the words to be said.

Now Ahmed is suddenly back, banging through the door with stereo speakers, a box of CDs (I'm only slightly old-school), and a box of books somehow balanced in his arms. I help him put things down, then realize there isn't much walking space left in our shared living quarters.

"I think I brought too much."

"Well," Branden says, assessing, "We have two TVs, two stereo systems, too many clothes."

"Ahmed," I say, "you take the electronics."

"But they are brand new, Archie. You just bought them."

"And you can have them. There's no room."

Ahmed is greatly appreciative. "Thank you, bruh. I'll put them in my car." He looks heavenward. "Amun be praised," he whispers, then leaves.

"Here," Branden says, "let me help. And anybody hungry? Let's go eat."

Chapter 2
Branden

Amun be praised? Guess I'll ask about that later.

I know I got at least part of my wish when he arrived. I found the African in America I dreamed of meeting: Taharqa, named for a pharaoh of the Kingdom of Kush, ruler of all Egypt in his time. He is regal in stance, aloof, tall and dark and delicious.

Dee-licious. Gorgeous and well-formed, tasty, attractive—no, beautiful. A man of black marble, like the carved museum idols you can pull up on the internet. And he's my new roommate, Archie. Yeah.

What would it be like to have this man as my own? His precise, accented speech is itself a turn-on. His openness, even with his regal posture, has me yearning for his approval. And what I see—strong chest, broad shoulders, a muscled waist and luscious hips, have me breathless. Hell, I'm thirsty! When do I get to have him? Be with him? Love him?

We met less than an hour ago. Maybe I'm rushing a little bit.

The three of us are having dinner at a hamburger joint across from campus. Already I am learning things. I know Muslims don't touch pork, but is Archie a son of Islam? He surprises the shit out of me by ordering bacon for his burger. Maybe he was raised on the Christian side of the border?

"Pork is from pigs," he declares. "Bacon is from heaven."

Yeah, and so is Archie.

We laugh and talk—no, we laughed and they talked—and I greatly enjoy listening to them. They are this strange mix of best friends and brothers and fair boss and faithful servant, African men and international youths, and they seem to have shared all those roles from infancy. They remind each other of events from their family village to their homeschooling to a private academy in England—one of those snobby places where two African boys survived only because they had each other's backs. And Ahmed does a terrible posh-Brit accent, stiff upper lip and all.

"The wuhld wuz, ahfter ahll, their coupe of tee-ah," he drawls. Now the globe, I sense listening to these two, seems theirs to protect.

"So much at risk in the world," Archie says. "Of course, its salvation must come from somewhere yet unknown."

I'm strangely at ease with these men. Even as they relate times only the two of them have lived, I am part of the sharing. We are three with visible differences—Archie very Nubian black, Ahmed more Arab tan, and brown me. Are all African brothers as welcoming to the children of the diaspora, or have I lucked into a special nation?

History says Kush, separated from ancient Egypt both by color and by the cataracts of the Nile, was known and accepted by its lighter-skinned northern neighbors, and each learned and profited from each, even when they were at odds or at war. And if much wealth and Egyptian power lay north at the Nile delta, Nubian power and religion lay south at the shrine of Jebel Barkal, sacred home of Amun Ra for both civilizations.

Meanwhile in the too-bright light of the storefront burger joint, I'm also checking out these two: very hot men in a way different from the rangy White boys and sweetie-pie brothers of my past sexual experience. They are new, and a turn-on not only because they are new. There is a health and a strength and a confidence, even for Ahmed, the thinner, smaller of the pair. Does Archie prefer that physical type, quite different from big-boned me? Still, I get to live across a room from him and not halfway across the state like the pharaoh namesake's friend.

Afterward we walk Ahmed back to his car—a year-old Audi that Archie bought him for his birthday—and Ahmed drives us over to where Archie's car, which isn't allowed on campus because he is only a freshman, is being stored. Another Audi, this year's model.

"Don't worry," Archie says. "Mom's money will get me a parking sticker when I get a chance." Man, what kind of royal African money did I move in with?

Ahmed takes off for his one-hour-long drive to the state capital and the design school campus. Archie and I walk back to the dorm over tree-lined streets and through the sweet heat of a late summer evening.

It's a wonder we don't get lost, because I can't stop looking at him. Dark, dark eyes out of perfect skin. His features are a handsome mix—the ancient eyes of Horus, the lips and cheekbones of central Africa. Idris Elba has nothing on him. A well-proportioned body with moves that are elegant, graceful, balletic. Yes, I have no more than an inch of height on him, and that makes him just the right size: the right size to hold, the right size to snuggle. And sex? Yeah, that too.

Will Archie at least snuggle? I have no gaydar signs that say he is gay or gay adjacent.

We fall into a silence a couple of blocks from the dorm, walking together, hands not touching (achingly). Archie stops walking, looks up, speaks.

"Brand," he says—we got to Brand and Archie over dinner—"I don't want to… to surprise, or, uh, disappoint you. I couldn't say this with Ahmed there, but I'm afraid… I'm afraid I'm gay."

"What's to be afraid of?" I let my laugh, too loud to be false, show I am not disappointed.

"What, uh… I thought you were straight."

"Lotsa people do. Lotsa people are wrong."

"Oh," he says, almost jumping. "Oh. Oh. Okay."

"Okay?" I ask.

"Okay. We're both gay." He picks up his step. "That's what I was hoping for. A real gay roomie. Things were so frigid, locked down at secondary school. There was one guy there, well, maybe two… but it was all so surreptitious."

"Surreptitious can be fun," I say.

"Sordid."

"Sordid? Sordid eventually stinks."

"Yes, and you question whether it's the sex that stinks, or do you." He pondered, then suddenly, "Oh, not that I'm assuming we are going to have sex."

I trip a bit on my next step. Because I assumed we were, and soon.

"I mean, we can share our experience, our views, because we are outside of the straight world. Outside and looking on, not looking in. We can be real friends."

I *knew* it, *knew* it was too soon to be making bedroom plans. (Dorm beds are notoriously narrow.) Not even one day and I'm getting tossed into the friend zone?

We walk quietly. Campus lights loom ahead.

"But," Archie says, smiling, "we can't assume we're not going to do something."

And we continue on to our dorm room, talking, anticipating, plotting.

A swift, red-flashing-light, sudden break here.

From whisper to clacking cacophony, a missive roars out across Unreality. The ether/echo is transcribed on hot, breathing wind. Here there is sand speech, the grit of substance that blinds the mind. Here is...

Intercepted missive 001: Blimey! Interesting times—the scarcity market's gone N.U.T.S. (Needs Universes of This Shit.) Who put the dental floss in China's tasty applesauce? Is it Istanbul or Constantinople? Upper South or lower North? The hounds must sniff out this rare-earth pile. The solution to the world and the destruction of the world all exist in the world. Doesn't anybody have a clue? The story starts. Love has locked eyes; soon the plot pops out.

Whatthefuque?

I know messages like this (and there will be many) must spark confusion, and that is the intent. Cliché, anagram, song lyrics, alliteration, false allusions, inside jokes, subreferences, repetitions, natural conflicts— the missive scribe throws these all together because of his audience. His audience, not you audience. They are the bad guys and the worse guys and the very worst mofos. They are the pursuers, and they are falling all over themselves seeking signs and portents, traces and translations that will help to accomplish their goals.

The missive scribe's goal is to lead them into inadvertent slipups and major mistakes, and to keep them as far away from their goals as possible.

Know that these "missives" are filled with clues meant to be frustrating, tempting, and even insulting to a group of Keystone Kop-itals desperate for some truth. You who follow the story that follows—the tale of Archie and Brand, love, gods, and magic—will see that these facts are not buried but quite visible in their meaning as the adventure progresses.

So for your very own shits and giggles, read the missives, interpret the signs, then check off the boxes as you read on. The writer of this doggerel hopes that you, the most honored reader, will find fun in these games and laughter at the expense of those who "got no sense a yuma." You and I will meet, sooner than you know, and you may smile with me at their fates, our friendship, true love, and the mythology that only imagination can make real.

CHAPTER 3
TAHARQA

WHEN ONE gets what one asked for, one may learn that one shouldn't have asked. This I ponder as I turn from my chemistry book, sitting open on the desktop, and watch my most handsome roommate *who I have not touched since we met two whole weeks ago* towel off after his sports practice and shower. Watch, want, wait… don't take.

Gymnastics is known as the sport of the body beautiful, but for young men, wrestling cannot be far behind. Consider this: One works and sweats—hefting barbells, flipping tires, wrangling thick ropes—until one's limbs, chest, and back swell with muscle. Then before an event, one limits all intake, even water, while sweating some more until the weight is at its lowest level to support that bulging meat. Then one throws one's self against another one who is equally strong and fabulously cut (and barely dressed, crotch watchers agree), for six or seven minutes. About the average time for a man to ejaculate. Hmm.

Oh, there is more. A joyous nature, my young Brand has, with a laugh loud enough to echo down dorm hallways. He loves history, yes, which is good enough for me. But he loves popcorn and debating world politics, and he can name flowers and trees without reference books, and he binge-watches dark thrillers, action comedies, modern musicals, and gay romances, which can make him cry. (Okay, tear up anyway.) Everything in his appearance shouts "Man!" And everything in his actions whispers "gallant," "sweetheart," "swain."

Add that his heart is open, welcoming, eager to express itself. Brains and brawn, they used to say, were a rare find, but brains and heart, emotion in smiles and silences, this is the bio-alchemist's apogee.

Put more simply, Branden is a wet dream in coffee with cream. I would call him *bomani* (strong soldier) and *habibi* (my love), if I could. Instead I find myself anticipating, not acting; leaning in, not touching; laughing with, but regretting; sitting on my hands until he's not in the room. (Then my hands find other things to do with me.)

Too often I wake mid-night. I look over to his bed—barely a cot for his athlete's build. I hear his breathing, soft and regular, watch his chest rise and fall when he's pushed the covers to his waist. If he turns over, I catch the curved rise of his well-trained butt. I want to disturb that breath, explore that ass crack, spread fingers across the warm brown skin, heating it to passion. What would it take for me to creep across the floor, wake him with a kiss that spilled into lovemaking? And what would it take to turn lovemaking to love? I could so love this lovely man.

But I dare not. Branden is pure heart and open arms, and I must be a closed, secret door.

(*Look out, folks, here comes the plot.*)

I have to be separate and secretive: for my empire, for myself, for my stratagem, and quite likely for the world. I dare not trust anyone, and if I love someone, like that fresh-washed hunk across the room, I will be pulling him into the danger, threat, likely torture that I face for my people and the future.

No, I am not from Wakanda. No one real is. But where I am from is as cryptic and mystic and clandestine as that imaginary, invisible kingdom of comicdom.

In the old language, Nub means gold, and Nubia means land of gold. The Nubians have existed for nearly 4,500 years. Their empire of Kush neighbored and fought, prospered and reigned, withstanding time for fourteen centuries near the Horn of Africa, the birthplace of humankind. Their imperium was erased from today's maps by conquerors and colonizers, its holy temples sunk beneath a damnable Nile dam, its worldly traces left half buried in deserts miles away from the nearest Sudanese towns.

Modern Nubian families live in southern Egypt and northern Sudan among Arabs and Egyptians and numerous indigenous clans—ethnic groups that barely recognize them. But these are not my people.

We descendants of ancient Nubians identify ourselves as Hu, ancient Egyptian for the seed spilled at the world's creation. We are the inheritors and protectors of eternal Kush. The Kushite Empire lives, silent against today's religious warfare and the cycles of postcolonial politics. We are hidden among hillsides where no road exists, taking actions no one notices, following plans designed only by ourselves, the descendants of warriors and clerics, kings and queens, pharaohs and *qores*. We Kushites prepare for our return to world importance, the rebirth of the Kingdom of Kush.

I won't bore you with more history and mystery here; Brand is the better historian, Ahmed the storyteller. It is the present and the future that is my fortune and my stratagem.

But for now, here's a side trip into science.

Take a look at a periodic table of the elements. Go on, it is online. It's that confusing organization of chemicals, ones you'd never give to a rat you were planning to feed to your pet cobra. Confusing groupings, yes, but organized. Look at the first two long rows, the third squares in; the names filled in are scandium and yttrium. Who has ever heard of them? Then there's that odd asterisk showing where scientists would slip in another row of fifteen tongue-twisting titles. They are listed on that line just below the main table.

I don't want to turn this into some Russian novel of appellations one can't pronounce, much less remember. But know that from scandium to lutetium, these are the rare-earth metals.

"So what?" one might ask. Some of these chemical metals are used in cruise missile systems, nuclear medicine and other high tech, everyday products like smartphones, batteries, lasers, and computers. They are very useful elements in high-demand products. And that adds emphasis to the word *rare*.

You see, rare earth isn't rare. These elements are well distributed across the planet. Unfortunately, that distribution has them well mixed in with other matter, some of it radioactive, some otherwise toxic, and it takes a desert full of mining and refining to get a small amount of useful metals separated from each other. So they are not rare, but very expensive and ecologically damaging.

As our economists still try to teach us, rare supply and sky-high demand mean exorbitant prices to buyers. Also great profit if you happen to have some to sell. China, possessing its own Gobi Desert and badlands— and the ability to demand production no matter the environmental cost or human danger—provides 97 percent of the world's rare-earth metals. Other nations, including Canada, Australia, and the US, have tried, are studying, and/or have failed in making the current refining processes pay off.

But what if one could evade the claws of that mine/refine monster? What if one could present a well-separated supply of metals that would cost less? Injure few? Damage less? What if somewhere rare-earth distributions weren't so random? Climb one hill, grab some ytterbium unmixed with yttrium. Take another path and pure praseodymium crunches under foot. Roll down a mountainside of erbium, nuke-free. Holmium hell-mium! One would have a mountain of cash waiting for one!

What if one doesn't like dancing to China's authoritarian tune; if one despises the odor of the old British colonizers; if one distrusts the promises of US minimoguls with dress-up clothes and phony-friend smiles. What if one could become the piper and call forth the ancient, mummified tune of the Kingdom of Kush?

The sphynx itself might rise on its stony haunches and walk.

I am here in this Midwestern research university to test samples—some in my luggage, some to be carefully shipped through convoluted paths from home—to see how well these pure mountain ores work, and to see if they will do even more than we know. I am here, at the behest of my sister-in-fate Darisis, now the qore/queen Amanirenas, to do these things and to learn more as secretly as possible. I am to return with our successes and to take my position, as yet vaguely described, as we unleash salvation on the planet. And that will make that giant stone kitty strut.

But to be able to afford this foray, we had to sell some supply, thereby exposing us to great risk. The hounds of great nations and the jackals of great corporations—often the same—are sniffing about. So we tell China they are buying surreptitiously from Australian raiders, and we tell Australia they are buying under the table from Chinese smugglers. The Pacific powerhouses think they have one-upped each other, while Kush takes some profit from both.

Our location in the Nuba Mountains in south central Sudan is unknown and secure, but those of us outside its stern protection are in the wind. Our recent secret deal was performed more than 750 kilometers away in the haunted, hated ruins of Suakin. In America I am always aware of the tingling sensation that warns I may be watched, and not just by the cute guy in the next bed. I exhibit trust, but I trust no one, not even Brand. Though my heart says I must. Can I take a chance?

These are the words to be said: I am not here for fun, I tell myself, not here to lay my body open to that thick brown cock, to wrestle passionately with this wrestler, to find a way toward love. I am not here for love. But he is so fine, so welcoming, and so warm. His lips so inviting, his arms meant to hold, be held by, and be caressed. My breath halts with the thought of him. How can I let this secret go on, knowing I will likely never find a potential love so fitting, exciting, and near?

He has even asked if I mind if he dates. Would I mind? I'll cut off the nutsack of the stranger who dares to wink at Brand! I'll mince it into ham salad!

But how can I play cockblock when the main cock I'm blocking is my own?

Wee-ooo! Wee-ooo! Wee-ooo! Another missive break:

Intercepted missive 011: Methinks we're sniffing down the ferret hole. Phew! What say you? Is it fair-oh to say our leader's secret life is past life, past lives? Hickcock so far is a Wild Bill. Get ready for an Arch of a march. But outside the motherland, the deal has gone down; Ozzie and Chine-iot on an isle of coral ruin. Whoever's on the tab for this, bitch better have our money. Nuba sits silent; Nubia glows in secret; Kush calls the tune. Where will the song be sung next?

CHAPTER 4
????????

THE DORM'S steel-and-glass back door shuts silently due to Taharqa's careful catch and slow shutting motions. It is as if he fears Branden catching him, though there is little chance of that. The roomie he crushes on is probably on his way back from practice, so Taharqa leaves a note—*Back soon. Cyah*—on the back of their door, then slips down the staircase on the other end of the building to get outside undetected.

Except by me.

Pardell's campus at dusk is both abandoned and busy. The class day is over, so the hourly flux of students to and from and between buildings has ended. But a few dorm windows, closed to the early October chill, still rattle from the blare of stereo speakers as residents cool their brains after cafeteria dinners. Soon enough, neighborly complaints will push the listeners onto earbuds, but some open-to-the-air music is a rite Spotify can't always replace.

Taharqa, in contrast, is moving silently as a cat. Perhaps he has a stratagem.

American colleges are historically seen as leafy and tree arbored. Pardell, built on farmland in a nearly treeless middle of Middle America, has little natural cover, only the sharp shadows from buildings blocking the setting sun. Taharqa, ever careful, must use these as points in his path, whether or not they are on a direct line to his destination.

He is so careful, I observe, yet his body tension is kept in check, ambling loosely like any other Pardell undergrad on an evening stroll. He passes no one, and no one passing would notice him. Black T-shirt and jeans, battered sneakers, he is ubiquitous and invisible.

Good.

The chiaroscuro of sharp dying light and sharp black shadow makes the whole maneuver mysterious, at least to the observer who wants to watch. There is blank mystery in this journey from somewhere he's expected to be to somewhere else, a place where he doesn't want others to know he is.

From shadow to shadow, objectively seen as strolling but inwardly creeping toward his target, Taharqa's progress is careful, steady.

Interrupted. A touch comes from behind.

"Hey, neighbor! How's it hangin'?"

It's Reggy, one of the dorm dudes he and Branden share a bathroom with. Then again, Reggy is more than a dude. He's a campus hero.

As lithe and muscular as a jaguar, Reggy is the football star of this year's team. Playing wide receiver, he is the center of Pardell's gridiron success. If the ball's thrown, it's most often thrown his way, and if it's coming his way, he most often catches it for yardage. A rangy six foot three, café latte colored with a bloom of black curls on top, he's athletic, attractive, and hot to trot. He'd be an alluring distraction for Archie to avoid his Branden fetish, except that there can be no distraction. Also, Reggy is straight, as many a campus female can attest.

"Oh, hello," Archie responds. "I did not see you there."

"Just chillin' my dillin'," he says. "Got a study date with Amanda."

Archie may not know Amanda, but as Taharqa, he's aware that this location is quite a distance from any campus library. It's probably a dorm-room meeting, and dorm rooms have desks, door locks, beds, and often a horny visitor.

"Have a good session… studying," Archie says slyly. Reggy gets the message and grins like a Cheshire cat. They move apart, two separate goals to reach.

Night falls like a ceiling collapse, or maybe like a conspiracy. In this sudden blackness, Taharqa moves with determination but not speed. Perhaps he knows that what he is headed toward will be there waiting. Or is it that speed will betray the import and secrecy of his journey?

Now his challenges have switched from sunset and shade to night and streetlight. In the frequent dark, he is less concerned with discovery, but there is something else. He seems to sense that difference. Is there a noise, a footstep, or a rustling of fallen leaves? The wind whips up, dies down, and it carries and distorts sound. His demeanor shows he is no longer sure of his safety. He starts to run.

At the one busy street across campus, he lounges back at the traffic light, almost blending with the pole. Cars pass. He is frozen. When the street clears, he sprints across toward the student bookstore (there are three), the barber shop, and the sandwich store, all well-lit. He slows to a walk. Be casual, his steps say, don't draw attention.

Another spurt of traffic flashes by, and Taharqa looks back toward it as if to recross the street. He steps sideways, but as the last auto passes, he twists backward and slips quickly behind the retail building, up an alley, and to a back street.

Is there something there? Something behind him? He pauses, listens. If ears could be stretched, at this moment his would rival a rabbit's, look like space antennae, catch movement soft as a whisper. He pauses a long time. He does not see what he sensed. Finally he moves on.

He walks up a tree-lined residential block diagonal to the main avenue he had crossed. Soon he finds a new alley, and taking up most of the block is a large building. Redbrick. Scalloped roof. Three stories.

He is at the back of the new physics/chemistry/biology laboratory building. Walking to its far end, he finds the door—the solid steel, usually locked back door. This is his goal, one part of the stratagem, and unseen access is what he needs.

The alley has no streetlights, a cost-cutting measure that saves nothing but his ability to stay undiscovered. He reaches for the door, sure that it has been left unlocked by someone. Actually by him, earlier today after all the students, teaching assistants, and professors had cleared out.

He reaches for the door. There is a tap on his back.

Taharqa whirls around, a surprised animal ready to run or fight. Then he stops. He sees me.

"Oh. It is you." His tension drops. "Come, let's get this done."

Intercepted missive 111: Was that a trip, or what? All the little spy worms can't get to it, but they taste the scent around it. Is this a one count, or a three? Guessy, guessy. No news is more to speculate about.

Hey there, readers. We're gonna put a little romance in the pot here. I mean, that's what you signed up for, right? We'll let the guys get physical, animal, sexual. Let the plot pot boil.

CHAPTER 5
BRANDEN

WHY DOESN'T Archie like me?

Slap at arms. Scramble left.

I mean, he likes me enough to be friends all right. He likes to talk with me after we finish homework. Sometimes we do homework together; we are in most of the same classes, though too often at different times.

Lock arms. Push the opponent's head outside my bicep. Scramble right.

I'm okay for him to work with, to eat lunch with, to argue with over the entertainment value of soccer. So often he is joking and close, but almost always he is above, stoic, that royal bearing that would be insulting if it weren't so natural to him. He knows no other way. In secret and to myself, I think of him as my idol, a godlike man with a killer smile. But really he is Archie, and a really good friend. He doesn't want worship, and I shouldn't violate that.

Dive for the ankle. Watch out for the reverse!

He hasn't stopped by to watch me practice either, though he promised to try. I even tried a little psych on him, said there was a big bad senior on the squad who was looking tempting. I mean, there is, but he's straighter than a telephone pole, so what would he do with me?

Dive for the leg. Twist the shoulders. Press! Press! Press! Pin!

I'm getting really good at the practice scrimmages, and coach says I should get to start when the season opens right after Halloween. Gotta keep my weight in control. I wonder how many calories there are in candy corn? How many calories in Archie's cum? Oops.

Shit! I got distracted and got pulled under. Need to use all my strength and concentration against this practice mate to pull myself out of this one.

Still, not a bad night for me. I trot home from the rec center, hoodie over my wrestling singlet. I want to take my shower when Archie's there. He likes to watch. So why won't he touch?

There he is at his desk, calculus calculations on college-lined paper. He smiles as I enter. It's like he's relieved to see me.

"The calc is a sneering asp tonight."

Archie has his own system for categorizing the difficulty of our homework. "Sneering asp" means tricky; "golden spider" means complex;

"soaring falcon" means easy and freeing. And I know, depending on category, he'll help me see the way through.

"Thanks," I say. "I'll get with you once I shower."

"Great," he says. "Can I watch?"

He always says that. Damn him!

"Sure. Door's open."

I strip quickly, tossing my jockstrap far back under a pile of laundry in my half of the room's closet. I turn my naked back to him and move into the bathroom. On with water, in with my sweaty self.

I follow carwash rules when bathing—start at the top and work down. So my head is full of shampoo and my eyes are closed when I hear a click out past the shower curtain. Hmm. It's not our bathroom door opening. More like the lock on the other door, the door to the dorm room that we share our bathroom with.

Good. Male vanity or no, I'd rather not be a surprise picture for our neighbors, a White guy who can't keep his eyes off me and his straight football-jock-bruh of a roommate.

I'm rinsing my curls now. The hair has grown longer than I'm used to since I don't trust anybody around Pardell to cut it. Lost my fade for sure.

"Hey, Brand," I hear, "gotta question."

That's Archie all right, but not from the dorm room outside. He's gotta be in the bathroom with me, maybe even sitting on the toilet. Interesting. It's not like him to be in any kind of hurry to use the facilities.

"You okay, Archie?"

"Sure, why?"

"You're in here."

"You invited me."

"You invited yourself."

"And you graciously accepted. How could I refuse? And I have a question for you."

What was with all this banter? He's in here, and close. Anyone familiar with modern dorms knows there's nothing but close inside a shared bathroom. And this old dorm building was retrofitted; it has even less space.

In my mind's eye I see him, princely figure casually leaning against the bathroom sink. Legs crossed at the knee. Blasé and buff. So attractive. Perhaps bending to be heard above the shower water. So he's near. Near enough for my penis to notice and jump.

Shit. Gotta wash that stiffening hard-on down offa me before he sees it.

"So, uh, what was your question, Arch?"

"It's really a question from your question. About dating. About my minding."

"Yeah?"

"If you have someone, someone you want to date, why do you need to ask me?"

"Well, uh…." Is it time to be this honest? Sure. "I don't really have a particular person I've asked to date. I just wanted to make sure it wouldn't bother you."

"Bother how?"

"Well, we spend a lot of time in the room together," I say, washing across my chest like I'm making a vow. "I won't bring a… a date back to the room if it puts you out, makes you uncomfortable."

"I appreciate that you care for my comfort," he says. "That is very kind of you."

"I'm taking care," I say. "I mean, we get along real well."

"True, very true." I hear his feet shuffle outside the curtain. "And so?"

"And so?"

"And so, why look outside the room for someone to… date?"

That makes me drop the soap.

"Would you want… want… to date… me?"

"I surmise that would be a good thing to do." And I hear a smile in his voice. "Even better would be to have sex with me."

I drop the soap again. I sputter, not able to put my thoughts, and my hardening cock, into words. *He wants me.*

"I have considered this for, well, some time," he says, "so I think we can start with one, then see about the other. Or opposite. Or both."

"Are you kidding me?"

"I do not kid." And he sounds serious. "Look at me if you don't believe me."

I pull back the water-soaked cotton curtain—just enough to stick my face out (as if I'm not seriously hoping to expose my eager self, touch his dream-inducing body and drag him, clothes and all, under the showerhead).

And what I see is this: Archie calmly leaning on the sink, fully clothed, ankles crossed, with my stinking jockstrap over his head. His eyes are on either side of the ball sack. The leg elastics go over his ears. His mouth is bare below, his proud nose covered under, well, sweaty dick smell.

"Does this please?" he says.

I laugh so hard, I slip on the wet tiles and nearly fall.

CHAPTER 6

???????

(A BIT of history while Archie and Branden get it on.)
Let's talk a bit about this place called Pardell. Let's call this the *Cow College Confidential*.

Pardell University is its own contradiction. It's mostly Victorian, three-story piles of dark brick under green, scalloped, clay-tile roofs on the old campus, and redbrick, block-on-end high-rises in the newer areas. It's all set out over several acres in the middle of fertile, featureless, flat Indiana. Think (1) spooky-movie mental hospital, (2) 3D-copied into identical horror halls, and (3) more recently surrounded by faceless ten- to twenty-story modern dormitories. It's way more IBM than Ivy League.

Pardell is also its own town, a college town, which means it's filled with twenty thousand educators, administrators, researchers, and their families in cloned modern suburban houses, along with ten thousand unhappy service providers and set-in-stone working-class members trying to hold on to their grandma's frame house while it stands.

These people exist to teach, serve, work with, and envy the forty thousand registered youths—those typical, lovable, hormonal post-teens who have been set free at last to live without supervision. The students fill the dorms or share the remaining battered, off-campus, fifties-era housing stock, which has been busted up into multiple bedrooms and one pizza-heating kitchen. These young (dare we call them) humans are just old enough to be held responsible for their feckless, intellectual, stress-filled, sex-crazed actions—meant to end after four or more years with a well-recognized university degree and entry into professionalism (and its feckless, intellectual, stress-filled, et cetera, activities called adult life).

By now our two young men are quite wet, but only one is naked. Two smiles stretch across two young faces. The water can't compete with the heat rising in each set of dark eyes. Archie, having caught Branden midslip, pulls his buddy close, one hand on the muscled pectoral of Branden's chest. Brand slides closer, close enough that their noses meet, forehead touches

*forehead, and breath mingles with hot, eager breath. Brand begins to fumble
for Archie's buttons and belt. Archie helps.*

Founded and funded by federal land grants that began under Abraham
Lincoln, Pardell opened after the Civil War, concentrating not on the
highfalutin' liberal arts or super-practical teacher-college skills, but science,
engineering, military science, and agriculture. Yeah, a cow college. And like
almost all of her land-grant sisters, this state school has become a massive
public institution teaching everything, including those highfalutin liberal arts
and classroom instructional methods. At least that's what the diploma says.

*Wet clothes litter the bathroom floor. Kissing has begun, slow and
searching at the beginning. Each seeks what the other likes; each finds for
himself the excitement of shared excitement. Wet hands caress necks, slide
down torsos, reach for sensitive zones. Soon enough Archie has Brand's
eight thick inches in his grasp, while Brand's fingers have glided behind,
toying with Archie's ass crack, slipping down. Breathing is heavy, longing.
Kissing continues.*

Set inside an outer belt of small-town Hicksvilles and basic-skills
factory sites—which themselves are extensions from the greater Midwestern
Rust Belt—academic pursuits place an invisible wall between Pardell and
the townies outside the college campus. Townies don't enter; only daring or
careless Pardellians spend time in the neighborhoods. And big cities—one
north (Chicago), one south (Indianapolis)—are little more than a one-hour
drive away.

The land granted to the university is itself a confrontation to its
surrounding duller environment. Head off one interstate ramp toward
campus and you enter a river valley shaded by oaks and elms grown thick
during times past. (Don't try this move too early in the spring. Water can
cover the roadway because the river's span, normally no more than twenty-
five feet, doubles in size from ice melt and runoff.) Come out of this lengthy
arbor and one soon is dwarfed on the right by a high cliff, maybe three
stories up. And along this cliff Greek letters abound. This is the frat row,
which got the best seats in town. And don't they always?

A steep drive uphill and a right turn brings you to the campus itself,
boundaries fully demarked by the age-darkened classroom buildings. At the
north end of campus are massive football and basketball stadia. Yes, this is
a college-sports powerhouse, even if it hasn't won a national championship
this century. And these two arenas created their own steep hills for their
edifices to sit on.

Bookstores camp at the outer edges. Sandwich and pizza palaces offer the most tempting foodstuffs—that means anything the dorm cafeterias don't spew out. These "restaurants" also do quadruple business after fall football games. Clothing stores are merely fanwear shops. Movie theaters (who needs them?) have faded away to the outer rim of the town. There used to be a music record store, but as the kids say, "Records? What's that?"

You'd think by now this pair would have moved from the dripping shower to where beds await. Instead they let the shower bathe them. Perspiration from body heat mixes with water temperature, and they are wet with want. Brand falls back, his shoulder blades against the gloss-painted wall, as Archie presses in. He strokes Brand's cock, a steady pace, and he lets his own dick, a truly royal rod, brush Brand's thigh. There is soft moaning, and a gasp or two.

But it's probably all those high-hormonal youths that are of the most interest here. As a science-engineering-agriculture school funded by state budgets as well as student tuition, its student body is overwhelmingly pale male, nerdy, farmboy, and Midwestern conservative. A Pardell female was once heard to say, "Five miles of cock on this campus, and I can't get five inches."

Don't let that fool you; there's more than enough panky to wave a hanky at. Here, as in most of young America, students have come to decide that 1) their sex lives are their own business, and 2) everyone else's sex lives are none of their business "unless they want some of my business."

Bodies wet and slick to the touch come together. Breath races. Slick flesh encourages sliding, parts against parts, warming, arousing. Is it the shower water or tears that come to Branden's eyes? Is it demand or desire that has Archie crushing in, pinning his roommate to a chilly shower wall while all the heat two men can create melts them together?

Pardell makes at least some effort to diversify. People of color make up about twenty percent of the student body, women about thirty percent, and foreign students, drawn mainly by STEM degrees, about five percent. Very few Africans, which is why one certain East African chose this place.

Who knows how many LGBTQ students there are? Some still hide out. There's a Gay Student Alliance, but there hasn't been a Pride Parade ever. Still, boys find boys and girls, girls.

Within all this animal attraction and mammalian action, a small but reverent branch of sex seekers carries with it a story, some say a myth. The myth is about a strange young man, narrow and energetic, with black-rimmed glasses and red-orange hair. This man, those in the know say, is surrounded in the aroma of human love, and he promotes sex positivity in a very personal way. He has his own fame among people who have met him and those who have been touched by those who have met him. But no one knows where he'll appear, on campus or off, or how long he's been here. All they know is he teaches lessons in love and the natural human joys of sex. And his name, he says to those who meet him, is Stevie. (Brand and Archie don't know it, but the jock next door will have a transformational fuck with Stevie come Christmas break of his senior year. Another student learns of poetic love under Stevie's influence. And a student journalist uncovers a meeting of Stevie-aholics in a student union basement.)

Another note about this campus: Next to a low building repurposed from the college heating plant stands a tall, massive redbrick chimney, four feet in diameter at its tip. Everyone on campus knows its legendary nickname, derived from a local farmer who gave up the campus land at the founding. They all call it John Pardell's last erection. Hah. Hah.

So is Pardell any different from fifty or one hundred other university campuses? Not from this raconteur's perspective, and that similarity is its appeal for some of us foreigners who don't want all that attention. It's big enough to do interesting, leading work and unheralded enough to avoid news-story prowlers and science-secret thieves. Certainly those whispered rumors of joyous sex and open love bring Pardell a furtive sort of fame, but the truth about Stevie is rarely shared and hard to find. Readers here may have some familiarity with his tales. But his role in this narrative comes later.

Coming. Later. But let's hear how the boys tell it.

CHAPTER 7

In the minds of two boys together…

THESE ARE the words to be said: The odiferous headgear doesn't stay on past five seconds.

Archie leads, fully clothed, rushing into the shower water, while Branden, still laughing but braced from falling by his roomie's quick hands, removes the jock strap from Archie's head and tosses it into the sink.

"There you are," Brand says.

"As are you," Archie replies. "Good to see you."

Struggling to stay upright on the wet tile floor, Archie tries a deft, tricky maneuver around, but this time he loses his balance. Brand catches him.

That's a friend-zone violation.

He's going to kiss me, Archie thinks. *I need him to kiss me.*

I've got to kiss him, Brand thinks. *I can't stop from kissing him.*

I'm going to kiss him first, Archie thinks, and does.

That kiss is short, but the break is shorter, and the next kiss lingers, opens to tongues, moves with hunger between two young men. Archie feels arms around him, warm in the hot water, so warm and so hot.

Touch me. Want me, Archie thinks. *I can't have you, and I won't be without you.*

Brand's grip slides open so he can pull Archie's clothed body to his without pain. Archie feels the wide palms and long fingers on his upper back, pulling him into the kiss, then slipping down his back to his hips.

Archie also feels arousal. Brand's penis is hard against his lower belly. His own member is straining against his pants front, and Archie is twisting to find something of Brand—here his muscled thigh—to push it against.

I don't know what my body is doing, Brand thinks. *It needs to get closer. Closer.*

The joy in their kisses has them grinning. Attraction opens the door to delight.

"Brother," Archie says, squeezing water from his shirt, "I'm all wet."

"Dude," Brand replies, "let's get you wetter."

They stop, step back. Branden grins like a madman, pulls at Archie's waterlogged shirt, fumbling at the buttons, so Archie joins in. That gives Brand the opportunity to reach for Archie's belt, jerking the loose end from the belt loops and then pulling loose the buckle. He opens the snap and watches the heavy, wet slacks fall to Archie's soaked socks. But what he really looks at is the shape pressed into Archie's briefs: a stiff, broad cock, pole-erect, perfectly outlined by the black cotton cloth.

Archie looks down, and Brand does something that makes his shower-slick hard-on jump, pop up like a flipper and bounce. Archie looks up into Brand's eyes and laughs out loud.

"Something is happening, roomie," Brand says.

"Yes," Archie says, gently sliding a finger up the exposed shaft. "I can feel it."

Archie is moving, moving Brand farther back into the shower. The noise of splashing water seems amplified. Everything is amped, fresh, wonderful. His hands spread across the young man's chest, pecs carved from granite and nipples hardening in the human heat.

Brand touches Archie's muscled torso, even more cut than his own.

"Someone's been working out on the sly," Brand whispers. "You shouldn't hide this."

"No more hiding from you," Archie whispers back, pulling Brand's hands across his own pec muscles and to and over his nipples. They are already hard too.

Brand thinks this is more than sex. This is more than heat and body and lust.

This is love, Archie thinks. *This is our love, our need for love, and our need to love. This lovemaking expresses love.*

The boys break as Archie chucks off the wet socks, kicks his soaked pants from around his ankles. Now they can look at each other unimpeded, with desire and gleeful passion.

Oh yes, Archie thinks. *I like this brown boy!* He notes the broad shoulders, strong chest, defined arms. V-taper to his waist, where the abs are gentle hills, not carved valleys. Thighs and legs muscled, sleek as a racehorse. A wet face, warm and inviting, with a looser curl in his black hair. And his scent, fresh sweat mixed with fresh soap. Enticing.

And Branden thinks, *You are so beautiful! Your tightly curled hair, cut close, has a springiness to it. Your body is perfect—everything in perfect proportion. Your blackness, a dark chocolate with a smooth glow, covers all, from just above the soles to just outside the palms. Ebony statuary, comforting to the touch. And the knowing, cavern-deep eyes assure me I'm with a man, a real man who wants me like I want him.*

Oh, yes, and…

Archie: *Nice dick, thick and veined. Do you reach out for me? I'll be glad to shake hands with you. And I do.*

Brand: *Wow. This is the motherland's gift to her children, carried across the seas. He's even thicker than me.*

Hands and lips and bodies and body parts meet, press, slide, hold. Brand's hands are on Archie's hips, touching, moving. Archie's hands hold Brand's penis and support his balls.

They move, finally, from the bathroom into the main room. They stop, stand between the two beds, which are only slightly longer than traditional twins.

Archie slips down to his knees, still holding his prize. "I want you to know I'm not a slut who fucks on the first date," he says, then immediately (like a pro) inhales the cock in front of him.

Brand inhales too, more of a gasp, caught in the warm, wet grasp of Archie's mouth. He moans a tiny bit, adjusting his breathing to the steady pump of Archie's head gliding back and forth on the dick while gently cradling the balls. Every third stroke or so, Archie might swirl his tongue around the head or squeeze ever so gently so that the balls might slide against each other. Either of these moves sends shivers through Brand's spine.

"Wait! Wait!" Brand wraps his hands over Archie's ears, holding the head barely out of reach of that glistening prick. "Wait. That has to hurt your knees." He lifts Archie to his feet, kisses the full lips then and there. Brand then bends down and pulls one mattress off the bed frame. "Anyway, I want my turn too."

Now he lifts Archie into his arms, Archie's legs around Brand's waist. Brand turns, leans forward, and plops Archie on the thin mattress.

Archie shifts to lie back full length while Brand comes in for the kill, stretching over him to take Archie's black-iron cock into his mouth. Well, as much as he can at first. The thing is thick as a tree branch. It takes some work to get that past the teeth and down a throat. But Brand is known for his wide smile and deep voice.

And Archie is on the move again, reaching for Brand's butt, only something is happening: Brand has got the hang of it (pardon the pun), and the rhythm and the pressure and the warmth and the *Oh shit this is too good and I should suck him too but damn that is hot and he's right oh fuck I don't but I love it but I'm not but I can't but it's oh and its oh and its….*

"Habibi, I'm gonna come!"

Brand, not breaking the beat, chuckles with his mouth full.

"Please," Archie whisper-shouts, "Please. Please. I'm gonna."

"Give it to me," Brand says, pulling off but not backing down. "Give it."

Brand pumps with his hand, and it isn't long before Archie, with a shout, spurts forth, the first shot leaping over Brand's face to land in his sweat-wet hair.

There are other bursts before Archie, gasping, relaxes. His eyes close softly, then open with his smile. And then a curious look.

"What's that in your hair?"

"That's your splooge."

"My… splooge?"

"Your come. You shot right over me."

"Oh, sorry."

"No prob, guy." Branden slides his hand across and up with the spot, making the sticky hair stand on end. "I could be that girl in the movie."

"No you can't," Archie says, and grabs Brand's cock again. "You've got other acts to perform."

As has been said, it takes some doing, especially in dorm-room beds that have little space for maneuvering. But soon enough Archie has Brand where he wants him, on his back and thrusting ever-so-slightly up as the companion blow job works its magic.

Soon enough, it's Brand who is hard and sweaty and panting and out of control. Archie brings him to shivering climax as Brand's splooge shoots down Archie's eager throat.

They are spent. They are satisfied. They are friends. They are two boys clinging, two men together.

Intercepted missive 123: B&A, glad, glad, glad. Please don't mind the slow spin, the plot's surely revving up. Nations and corporations, spies and stalkers, magic and myth: They are all in the offing. And the off-stage players shift and stew. Love heats up too.

I couldn't resist throwing a little more romance-novel scenery in there, even when the interceptors have no hearts or the ability to understand them. So this one is for you, reader; not a lot of clues there, but hopefully some encouragement. We want our boys together.

CHAPTER 8
TAHARQA

IT'S TIME, I think as I survey the near-empty cafeteria. Time for the talk. Who knows, maybe past time.

I'm so (happily) tired.

Over there is the perfect place, a table as far from the breakfast stragglers as possible, in the too-bright light from the east-facing windows.

Branden finds me, places his own tray on the table, but squints at the glare.

"Jeez, bruh," he says, "you missing home? This place has more sunlight than the Sahara."

"Please, sir, sit." Why do I always sound too formal when I'm trying to be serious? "We should talk."

"Okay." He sits quickly, looks down to his breakfast plate of late-morning leftover eggs and bacon. I have opted for oatmeal, and, yes, bacon. I need to let my bowl cool, but he picks up a bacon strip, bites, then looks up at me. The sparkly eyes have gone soft. Does he think I'm going to scold him?

Well, in a way I am. I say, "We need to go to school, habibi."

"We're in school," he says, grinning. "We're learning about love."

"I meant go to class. Brand, since we started this two weeks ago, I have been to one class session. One."

"You got past me for that one." His "sorry" look adds a silly smile. "I got a perfect record. Zero."

"And that, Brand, is the point. You know I love all the things we do." I pause, pick up my own bacon strip. "But we are doing them entirely too much."

"You started it."

"I did not."

"Did too. And you do. At least half the time, you do."

I can't argue with that. From that first night, I've reached for him and he for me again and again. We go at sex like it's about to be repealed. Until we fall asleep and wake up and go at it again. Unless we stumble to the cafeteria, gorge like ravening beasts, and race back to bed.

We tell ourselves we are learning about each other, but that's not it. It's much deeper, much worse. We are learning how to make love to each other and, well, still learning about love. Lust with emotion, a most dangerous thing.

Do our minds understand what our bodies are doing? Do our hearts? And is there even time for this, what with classes and wrestling (and secret stratagems to save the world)? I grow closer to him each passing hour, and yet I lie to him too often, maybe just to be with him longer. (I am lying to the ones back home too, the ones depending on me to fulfill my role.)

This is wrong. This is *wrong*. The mission is primary; my penis is not. But my heart? Everything says I must shut this down. I must do it to save my secret—Nubia's secret—and I must protect Brand as well. Strong and sweet, he is not made for this technopolitical skullduggery. I need to put my love away.

Can I lock down my heart? Can I? Do I dare to try to answer that?

Whatever else, we have to get our minds directed and grades up for the semester.

"We should contact some other classmate and see if we can borrow notes," Brand suggests.

I wake up from kicking myself.

"Have you met anybody at school besides me?" I ask. "Not counting the breakfast cooks and Reggy the jock next door, I only know you."

"Yeah," he says, "you're right, bruh." He pauses, takes another bite, looks up at me. "So you wanna break up?"

"Not in seven million stories from Abu Simbel," I say, and I mean it. "You're not getting away that easy."

I guess my heart avoids brain prison this time.

"So?"

"So we need to better use our time," I say, "or we're going to be out of here on our arses. Midterms must be near, and I don't want to be back in Meroë—I mean Shendi—before December, and you don't want to waste that wrestling scholarship. So let's set some rules. Okay?"

"Okay." He starts the plan rolling. "No skipping class unless you're sick or the prof stinks, and no skipping my practice."

"Yes," I say, "and we'll keep up with workouts. And no copulation until homework is done."

"Aw, gee," he says, pouting.

"Homework and the reading for the next class. That has to happen."

"Cuts into our sexy time quite a bit."

"We're lucky we're still walking with all the sexy time we've been having."

A pause.

"I want to hold you while we read, babe." It is Brand's straightforward demand. "I want to."

"Then," I say, "that is how it will be." I pause, then remember. "And physics labs. We can go together."

These are the words to be said, and so it is done.

WE HAVE had a couple near misses early on, but we're sticking to it.

Sticking. Mainly.

There is one night Brand and I are seated on the mattress we keep on the floor. He sits in front of me, my legs are outside his, we are naked back (his) to clothed chest (mine). And this is enough.

He is talking, animated, arms moving and head emphasizing. I hold him close, riding on his body like a sledder down a frosted hill. He is so happy, and I am happy to be happy with him.

"The guy is so hard, so very hard," Brand says. "And heavy. It's like we're rooted together, straining."

He is talking about a wrestling opponent, a match I saw but am glad to relive, because I'm living it through him.

"And then I feel it—a tremble. Just a little tremble, and I *jump* on it. I pull together all my strength and *jump*. And suddenly he's tumbling, falling past where he can recover. And I land on him. And they're my points! He doesn't quit, even then, but he can't recover." Brand stops, smiles, sits back into me. "And I win."

"And you deserve to win."

We have been doing this for days now, not actually shagging, simply enjoying each other. We talk, touch, hold, and talk some more, so comfortable together. I speak of Sudan and what Kush, Egypt, and the Nile once were. He talks about his hometown and today. We revel in the present, our private little point in time outside the past and safe from the future.

I do so hope he is safe.

"Archie," Branden asks, "why do you like me?"

"What do I say to that?" I have to think about it, then reply, "Why do I like you, or why do I love you?" Yes, we've said that word as well as done the deed.

"Both."

"Well," I say as I adjust my hug, "I like you because you are a person who would ask that. You are open and confident and full of feeling. From our first day, you have made me feel, well, important to you. Interesting. Worth knowing. It is good to know that someone wants to know who you are."

"Is that it?"

"Oh, there is so much more. How you can be silly and loose, serious and strong. I like you because you are so damn likable. Not like the Brit grammar-school boys."

"I don't think I'd like those grammar boys." We have talked about my secondary school days. A lot of aloneness, being unwelcome. Without Ahmed there, it would have been stultifying, toxic. Instead of only being a bore.

"I'd think not," I say, "yet they would like you. I can't think of anyone who wouldn't like you."

He seems at first satisfied, and then, "And love?"

"Why do I love you? I love you because you love me—that is a most important element. I love you because even when we disagree, we can't argue, because our first thoughts are about each other."

"Yes."

"And then there is the fact that you are the best rodger on the planet."

We both chuckle at that.

My turn. "So, Branden of the Hickcocks, why do you like me?"

"Like or love?"

"Like. I feel the love. I don't question it."

He grins. "That's the realest, bruh. The realest."

I grin right back.

"I like you," he says, "because, well, because of my folks." We have talked much about his parents, but this turn in conversation was quite different. "I told you that they love history, and they love African history. They turned ancient times into magic and myth for me. And here is a man, a real man, sprung from that myth. And despite centuries and a continent apart, abuse and slavery on both sides, you welcome me as one of your people, your brother."

He pauses, putting his cheek next to mine. "And you are so smart and help me understand calculus and know so much and share so much, and you're like a bottomless fountain of, well, care."

A tear welling in my eye slides down, touches his cheek.

"Plus, you fuck like a god!"

There is so much we give each other, and that means there is so much we need from each other. So we are magic time. Who needs questions?

These are the words to be said, and days and nights like this will fill months and seasons. We don't get thrown out, and I am on the way to making first semester honors, and Brand competes in the conference wrestling championships, and the first semester goes acceptably.

Meanwhile, a world away, secret deals get done, and even those who think they are in on the secret are wrong, so very happily wrong. I know there are missives flying, and I laugh quietly, knowing how crazily the words conceal the truth.

But Christmas vacation looms. Brand urges me to stay at his family's house for those three weeks, but my own people have not seen me for more than a year, and they are adamant that Ahmed and I return. Every second becomes one less second to be together, every responsibility another thing to regret because it takes time away from Brand and me.

The only good thing is that the Hickcocks live in Chicago, and it has one of the busiest international airports. After our last winter class, I drive us up to the city's northwest side and meet his joking, probing father and very open, loving mother, who feeds us well but beds us in separate rooms in their two-story brick Tudor across from a large public park. (We don't stay that way; Brand wakes early enough to sneak to his room before they can "wake" us with breakfast.)

Ahmed arrives the morning of our flight, and leaving his Audi to be picked up at the Hickcocks' by a Sudanese consulate employee, we all go to O'Hare International Airport.

It is too sad how terrorism and fear and fear of terrorism have ripped airports in half. Those leaving are pulled into the slow-motion maelstrom of ticketing lines, baggage checks, and the long march through security. Then we are left to wander nervously morose because airlines want us at the terminals hours before takeoff. What was once a shining glass portal of transport is now a bifurcated jumble of hustle and wait.

Meanwhile, those seeing us off have seconds at the drive-by drop-off as cabs and cars jostle to pull in and out and around us.

With Ahmed there, Brand and I give our best "bruh" goodbyes: arm grabs and smiles and man-hugs, serious attempts not to kiss or caress or cry. But Mrs. Hickcock surprises me with a kiss on the cheek and these words: "Taharqa, I know you are good for my son. Branden can be loose and, well, knuckleheaded, and I know you had a lot to do with his knuckling down at college. So come back. Do come back and stay longer."

These are the words to be said: May Amun make it so.

Been a while since we've ruminated together in the plot clues, eh? Romance does demand stage time.

Intercepted missive 145: Christmas season. Snow and sand. Guess you'll "get" this once love reigns supreme. And speaking of Su-preme, how'd y'all foreign deal-stealers like that silent city of crumbling sea reef? You know, where it all went down, and no one but everyone knew? It's the FOMO of IRL. The game masters gather their chips and slip out of view. The roots nourish themselves. (The plants are mere distraction.) Underground, the son of the godly sun progresses and reports progress—even gains he cannot yet assess. Another term is to begin. What truth will anyone learn in class then?

CHAPTER 9
BRANDEN

IT'S A not so merry holiday here. Barely any snow for Christmas, but plenty cold. Then an avalanche dump the day after. Mom went off the rails buying gifts for "her boys," and I worry how she and Dad are gonna be able to pay off those credit cards. Her college dean delayed her tenure, and Dad took an unpaid research leave from his school, so the money's not flowing like before. And brother Ben and his wife have been bickering since Christmas Eve. The "big man" even thinks he can bully me because he's older and so very straight.

"Did you ask Santa for a dolly this Christmas?" That is his idea of a joke. I only know that because of the sneer on his balloon-round face. "No? Or maybe some stiletto heels, bruh."

"Hope so," I reply. "They'll fit perfectly through your eye sockets, bruh. And meanwhile, why don't you go harass this wife. Or can't you pay alimony for three exes?"

Even his stupid sneer is weak.

But worse is that I haven't heard from Archie. A good part of that silence—I hope maybe most of it—is my complete cluelessness about what's happening with him. I worry. Taharqa Nimiery is thoroughly Westernized, probably pining for bacon, and he's gay and in a very fundamentalist place. Or is he?

Archie's conversations about his home are as confusing as a pharaoh's riddle. He speaks carefully about all people, Black people, the peoples in Sudan and its mountains, and his people, who he tells me are distinct from all. Never, never do we use the word "tribe." That word is hardwired in the West to something less than civilized.

"Tribes are told they are to be stepped on," Archie says. "People are not carpets. And communities, nations, empires are propelled to rise above."

Sometimes he slips and uses names from ancient times, like the third Kush capital of Meroë for the nearby Sudanese town of Shendi; the second Kush capital of Napata for today's town Karima; and Amun, not Jehovah or Allah or Vishnu or God. Amun Ra, sun god, god of the gods of the pharaohs. Do Archie's people still venerate the sun?

Archie is with family and, as far as I know, not out. And getting outed in some nations, Christian or Moslem or other, could be fatal. So very fatal, I fear, that I shouldn't call. Instead I'm hoping he will.

And then there's me. I'm hornier than a brass band, and I've gotten hooked on having our sexy time. Oh sure, I could cheat. I've been with girls. I've been with boys. But I've never been with someone I love like Archie. I want to have him, but I really need to hold him.

I mean, it is this bad: Mom's in the kitchen wrestling with a New Year's ham; Ben and wife three are out shopping or returning what someone shopped for them or more likely arguing over what they didn't get and "Who should pay for that, negro?" And I'm in the upstairs bathroom with a hard-on so skintight I'm near tears.

No kidding, this is a throbber. I mean, I do have more than most boys, and it's swelling a lot more than that. I'm sitting on the closed toilet lid, pants around my ankles, and it's bobbing like a fishing rod with Bruce the *Jaws* shark on the line. The room is small, and my boner seems to be taking up all the space.

I take it in hand—two hands, really. It feels hot. Really, really hot. And really, really hard.

I'm uncut, but swollen to this extent, you'd hardly know it. It's a big brown pickle, and I feel the blood pushing, pushing, with nowhere to go.

"Archie," I whisper.

The advantage of being uncut is you don't need lube for self-pleasure. The skin slides back off the more sensitive tissue underneath. And slides back over. And slides back off.

"Archie." I sigh and close my eyes. I stroke myself, imagining it's him, my Archie, my Taharqa, my love for true. I imagine him on top of me, feel his hands on my chest, his hole riding me, hear his gasps and moans.

"Oh, Archie, Archie, where are you?" Sounds like a cartoon song. Sheesh.

I find myself switching roles: I am bottoming on the bottom. I can make myself feel him thrust that hard black stick inside me. It's as big as a baby's fist, and it reaches part of me too deep to control. It punishes and pleases, exposes my sorrows and releases my love.

"Oh, sweet love," I whisper. "Take me. Take all of me."

The advantage of self-pleasure, once you know how to last, is you don't have to last long. And I'm going for a record. I've kicked the bathmat to the side. One leg is propped up, the foot on the rim of the bathtub. My white T-shirt is pulled up. I start to pinch a nipple. Just there. Ah. There.

"Branden?" Mom's shout hits simultaneously with when my first ejaculation arcs out, landing short of the shower curtain across from me. "Branden, can you hear me?"

I have to struggle to get my composure back. "Yeah, Ma," I croak.

"Branden, could you come down and help me? I'm at a loss here."

Yeah, I lost something here too. "I'm in the bathroom. Down in a minute."

I don't hear her "okay" because I've turned on the bathroom sink. I rinse my member real good, clean up the goop I shot, wash my hands again. In the mirror there is a sense of ease on my face, along with some regret and a dose of sorrow. I'm released but not relieved.

I head down to the kitchen.

Mom has spices, herbs, and cookware strewn from one end of the kitchen to the other. This space, with the same yellow paint and brown Formica counters I grew up with, is more often Dad's domain. But on holidays, Mom moves in like it's a sacred rite. That doesn't mean she knows where everything—or most anything—is. Tonight she is trying to remember her spiced ham recipe, how many cloves per square inch. The thing is huge, way too big for us even with Ben's kids. And as I dig out the formula from where she always forgets Dad hides the recipes, I tell her so.

"So much meat. Are we catering the Bears' game?"

"Oh, it's not just us. Adele's folks are gone, and there's no reason she should be left home alone. And I invited Donna and the kids, and Helen too."

Oh joy. My mother, who will never remove a chair from the family table once someone has sat in it, has scheduled a New Year's Day bash with both my brother's exes, his kids by wife one (I love them), and one of his former mothers-in-law.

"Does Ben know?"

"Yes, Ben knows."

I am gleeful at the prospect. Nasty big brother Ben forced to be polite to so many lives he has fucked over. And miss college football on TV? Priceless.

"He doesn't like it, but he knows," she continues, followed by her last comment: "Serves him right for running off with someone who can't cook."

Choices.

We bond as usual in the kitchen, me helping my mother get the chaos under control. We laugh and joke, dance over the tile floor, and I lift the monster hog thigh, spiked and scored, into the oven. I guess in the pause my thoughts of Archie slipped in.

"Look, Branden, no need for a young man to have to stay home and entertain his mother. Isn't Claire holding a New Year's Eve party tonight? I'm sure she invited you."

Yeah, Claire invited me. She's nice enough. We even have some history—two times. Then it was her turn to fall into the friend zone.

"Go out. Have some fun. I think your friend Taharqa would want you to."

That put me in a strange emotional bind. I want Archie, Archie would want me to, and I don't want to without Archie, but I do want. All mixed up and not sure what to say.

So she says, "Go put on your coat, take the car, and have a good time. I'll probably have the eggnog ready by the time you get back. So be careful about drinking."

And still twisted up inside, I take her keys and go.

The car starts up fine—not a guarantee in temperatures near zero—and I head out. The city streets are almost never empty, but this frigid, snow-stalled end to an old year is doing a good job of keeping traffic to a minimum.

And the city's streets and sanitation priorities are hampering my progress. Years of bad weather and upended electoral fortunes have taught our mayors to first keep major streets clean and make the alleys passable. Chicagoans never forgive being unable to commute to work or failure to get their garbage picked up. But that means the residential blocks can stay snowpacked for days. Worse yet, the freeze-and-thaw pattern is hell on often-patched pavement, so as I near the party, I get a mini-roller-coaster ride of pothole, ice bump, pothole.

Finding parking on Claire's block isn't easy, so I guess she has a good-sized crowd, and I can hear recorded Christmas carols and happy voices when I get to the door.

I ring the bell, but "Come in, the door's open" comes from inside. The place is warm and warmly lit. A fieldstone fireplace, polished wood floors, midcentury sofas of blue and tan, and a huge and heavily decorated Christmas tree grace the living room. A large crowd clumps into conversational groups around a family room decorated in red and green bows.

My guess is that Claire's folks are welcoming the new year with her granddad at the nursing home. They really must trust her.

Claire comes over and takes my coat, and I get a few "Hey, dude" acknowledgments. It's strange. I never had one clique I hung with at high school; I kind of circulated between jocks and nerds, power girls and cheerleaders, and bookworms. They all had something about them that interested me, and because I could move among them, they all seemed to like me.

I stop by the b-ballers in the kitchen, who always understood why I never made the team (I couldn't hit a basket with a bazooka), and the gamers. My favorite young scientist is in serious discussion with Claire's tween and serious brother. And there are the three virtues of high school: Hope, Faith, and Wanda. It is good that Claire got along with the cliques like I did.

I get an eggnog (spiked by someone), do some of that "just back from campus" catching up that will fade the more time we all spend away from each other and experiences spread us apart. I guess I was comparing dormitories with a Northwestern student when Claire roped me out of the herd and over to a quiet spot. She handed me a fresh drink.

I'm sure our talk started out with something like, "So, how're you doing?" and the usual questions about what my school is like and whether I like it. But I'm not much of a drinker, and by that second nog, I'm not exactly sure where our conversation is taking us until I feel her gentle hand on my thigh.

Claire is truly a beauty—dark skin. soft hair, and large, dark eyes. And she's had a thing for me since fourth grade. More choices.

"Oh, girl," I slur, "we been through that and out."

"Sometimes feelings change," she says. "Love can come back."

And I look at her and love her and say, "Claire, we gotta get you a guy."

She moves closer. "You're a guy."

And I smile and say, "No, I'm a gay. I'm a gay guy."

There she is, totally shocked, and I suddenly remember I was never out to her. Hell, for almost every face in this room, I'm not out to any of them.

That status changes immediately.

"You're what?" she shouts over speakers playing "Hark the Herald Angels Sing." "You're *gay?*"

All conversation stops; everyone turns toward me. And I think of myself, I think of my family, I think of my Archie, and I say, "Yep, I'm gay."

And I hear "Good for you." And "'Bout time." And "We got ya, bruh."

And the only snide remark comes from a football player. That team and I never got along. They all figured that at my height and heft, I should play fullback or something. Fullback with them? Not likely. (And I didn't want my brains turned to mush after a season full of tackles.)

"Hey, Brandy girl," the jock says, pulling at his crotch, "I gotta pigskin for you. Wanna suck?"

I laugh. "You think anybody could find it without tweezers and a magnifying glass?" As he starts to puff up like a poison toad, I add a little something. "Then again, from what I heard, Terry, you got no problem finding the other end of the pole."

I know cocksucker is meant to be an insult to the gay mafia, but its negative force really applies to certain straight asses.

So he finally blows a gasket (as I said, not the only thing he has blown) and starts toward me, but Claire is not about to let this bulldog damage her parents' place, so she collects a couple of guys from the crowd and they block the Terrier, back him up, and get him out the back door.

Figuring I've created enough joy this evening, I collect my coat and head for the front exit. Claire stops me.

"Oh, Branden, I'm so sorry. I didn't mean…."

"Not a problem. It's very good that people know, especially good for me to know that people know." I touch her shoulders. "So have a happy holiday and think of me as your newly liberated gay friend. Okay?"

She leans forward for a hug, and I add a kiss on her ear as a bonus, then head out to the car before that meathead football jock can gather enough brain cells to figure he can catch me on the way out.

I drift a bit on the way back, letting the night air sober me as I swing around city blocks filled with World War II era housing stock. A spot along a curb, shoveled clean, holds two lawn chairs linked by a two-by-four stretched between them. It's an example of the grand Chicago tradition of dibs: The homeowner digs out a parking space in front of their house and uses detritus to save the space. And the devil take anyone who disrespects dibs, only Satan might not want them after the homeowner gets through with the violators.

And I'm thinking as I drive, *So I'm out*. How do I feel about that? At first, like nothing. Very much like that nothing I felt with my first boy. We were all sweat and juice release, but there was nothing personal about it. Next? I feel a bit of shame—shame that I did not come out sooner, that I let others assume rather than confront their assumptions. But I can't change that, and I have already corrected it. Tonight I came out with my old classmates, and I feel good. I feel authentic. I feel free.

Back home, Dad is nodding in his easy chair. "There's nog in the fridge," he says. "Did you have a nice time?"

"Dad, did I ever tell you or Mom I was gay?"

"You never had to. We never cared about that either way."

"Thanks," I say, and I get some of the eggnog. It is well liquored, and that makes me well snockered. Guess I hadn't sobered quite enough, Anyway, I need to go to bed.

I drop right after the Times Square ball does.

But I never rest well if it's an alcohol-induced sleep. Which this time is a pretty good deal, because at 3:17 a.m., my cellphone rings.

"Happy New Year, habibi. It's Archie."

CHAPTER 10
TAHARQA

I AM terrible with daily time, especially about the hours between one time zone and another. But I know it must be sometime during New Year's Day where Brand is. I need to call and let him know I'm alive and I love him. I let my thoughts roam through the weeks, thinking of events I must keep from my lover.

This is the most bumfuck, mixed-up-crazy, choose-your-hate season in this splintered nation called Sudan, and it is that way most years. Muslim holidays rarely happen in winter, and their new year comes in the West's midsummer. So the nation, which converted to Islam over a period of six centuries, has no reason to be in a holiday spirit. Except that not every Sudanese is Muslim; there are plenty of Christians, most of them converted through the religious racism of colonialism. Then there are adherents to even older indigenous faiths.

Ahmed and I have spent many an hour decrying this land the West declares is our birthplace, yet we will not be its citizens. He can go on for hours.

At least I am not in the tense capital of Khartoum for the "festivities." I make trips all around the country, but I spend much of my visit here locked away under hillsides where my people have our own lives—and some working cellphone towers not even the Sudanese government knows about.

Darisis, who has been my sister-in-fate since we were children, has welcomed me to our hidden home as a blood relative would. But forthwith, as Queen Amanirenas, the high priestess of Amun designated to be qore and coleader in our stratagem, she has had me quite busy these three weeks. Busy meeting contacts. Busy plotting schemes. Busy covering tracks. The metals we sold to China and Australia last year made us a tidy sum but got the rest of the world asking how the beleaguered Chinese were able to suddenly fill such a hole in the long-standing shortage of rare-earth material, especially the heavy metals. And why did the Aussies find this batch was so much purer than anything previously available in even a dark-web transaction?

Now that I am in our Kush, we stage another foray at the abandoned port city of Suakin, a repeat of the distracting drama our "rude mechanicals" performed for the Chinese and Aussies.

Suakin is a place washed in myth and infamy. Tied to legend from before Cleopatra's salad days, King Solomon is rumored to have imprisoned a djinn here. Ivory, gold, and gems were traded there. And it has a more heinous history as a port for slavery, sending people in chains to the Middle East and Asia.

One could say hard surfaces led to the city's downfall. Coral reefs grew in its harbor, and though much coral was used in building construction, the reefs expanded until ships could no longer approach safely. The end of the ivory trade, and slavery before then, left Suakin to tumble into ruins. Four-story buildings made of ghostly coral blocks and white plaster have crumbled into rock piles. The cryptic spirits of Arabian Nights fairy tales, pachyderm slaughter, and human bondage walk its narrow paths.

Suakin, therefore, is a perfect place to redeem through our secretive successes.

For this new scam, our players, hired from the Sahel (the area between the African savannah and the Sahara) and under my direction, convince both a Saudi-American cooperative and a Canadian startup that the other is selling them pure goods, for which we make a modest 90 percent profit. (Remember, we can harvest these materials with minimal effort and expense.) Meanwhile, we know their various spy networks are tripping over their tongues trying to explain how the materials were sourced from unknown locations in the Yukon, Mohave, or Rub' al Khali.

Our covert caper is hellish hot, sweaty, tense, and exceptionally remunerative. I observe it all from a safe distance, but this is no place to feel comfortable or secure. Still, the swap is so successful our targets are left unaware of the deception involved.

I take the well-gotten loot and convert it into solid international investments. I think about our customers, that maybe they are looking for the real in this deal. Good luck, fellows.

However, even our completed caper isn't enough for the regnant queen. In her throne room—dark stone glittering as if splotches of candlelight flicker in the gloom—her displeasure glowers. A haughty face under the double crown of asp and falcon turns on me.

"What have you been doing at that college of yours?" Her question was as imperious as her royal robes. "Ahmed says you have a friend."

"My friend is not a problem," I tell her, and it's true. Brand is no problem at all. "It takes time to assess whether the Americans have the right equipment for our tests. Then I have to gain access to that equipment, preferably with unsuspecting permission. Then there's calibration, simulation, evaluation. We schedule testing when no one is looking, record and confirm the data. Only then can we make decisions, test further, try out the final applications."

I turn brotherly in addressing her. "But you know this takes time, Darisis. Why else are Ahmed and I registered as beginning university students? It will take years."

The sister in her sighs, but the gold trim of my queen's sky-blue robe twists with her frustration. "Yes, I know, brother Taharqa. But I know we do not have time, and less of that each month this drags on.

"You were named son-prince to complete your duties. Lord Ra has spoken, and all the priests say His will is to allow our kingdom to return to glory. The great treasure He made for us shall make us saviors of all peoples. We must not be distracted. We must not fail."

I know my vow requires royal respect, and I address her in her transformed name, the name of a historic, heroic Kush ruler: "I will not fail you, Queen Amanirenas."

These are the words to be said. But distraction? Branden? No. He is love, and love is essential, never a distraction. He is how it must be.

"There is more in your future than you know," she says softly. "A new name awaits you, brother-in-fate. Thus you must be ready. We all must be."

Even now I'm not sure what this future talk will mean for me, but after that confrontation, I know I am ready to have a little talk with that tattletale Ahmed. When he and I meet to confer on future plans, I have to upbraid him for his disclosing my relationship with Brand. I take him outside our stronghold to a dale between the ancient hills of Nuba, a place where we can have privacy.

"Why would you do that, friend? You have put the stratagem in danger and encouraged Qore Amanirenas's wrath for no cause."

Ahmed's eyes are cast down on the scrub grass around us, but his grin betrays him.

"Beg pardon, young pharaoh-to-be. It was a slip. And I find it hard to resist love-item gossip." He is quite cavalier about the matter. "I wanted people to know you were happy. Satisfied... and happy."

"Happy I am, and dedicated as always," I say. Despite the snark, it is hard to stay angry with my friend. "As for you, how goes the computer access?"

Ahmed perks up; he is all gesture and motion.

"Oh, bless Horus's all-seeing eye, these Americans are so blind—and arrogant in their blindness. Pretending to be a novice intern programmer is hindering my attempts to straighten their asses out."

"You know the cover story is necessary," I remind him. "They have to think they discovered the way. They cannot know we led them to it."

"So I understand, effendi," he says. "We stay quiet until the Avengers assemble."

Ahmed is such a joker; I wonder how the ever-serious Amanirenas puts up with him, though the Darisis in her loves him as I do. He is the unquestionable friend, even when I find his humor questionable. We end our conversation with a handshake and a hug.

All that is memory. When it's nearly noon here, I find a good signal strength and reach out to America.

"Aww, babe, I miss you," Branden says, his voice slurring with sleep.

"And I you. I miss you every day. But what is this you call me?"

"Oh, sorry." I can hear embarrassment in his voice. "I mean Archie."

I tease him, "You turn me into a child? Am I not adult to you?"

"I'm sorry, Taharqa. I'm just sleepy, that's all."

"You may call me what you like, as long as you call me love. And now I can at last call *you*, habibi."

"Have they been locking you away?"

"Worse. My people have been running me ragged, meeting with others, learning their families, studying their politics. We contact different peoples every day, over mountains, through deserts. Then I'm meeting leaders and advisors and cousins of both. Our African families are entirely too big."

Branden actually knows almost nothing of my family—or at least little that is true. I say to him that my Muslim father has two wives, which is acceptable under Sharia law as long as he provides equal homes for each. And he has children by each wife. I say I am the second son of the second wife, in a decidedly inferior position.

In truth, I have no father, no father known to me. My mother, Abar, was a vestal virgin of Amun's temple. Her pregnancy was a scandal, and I was taken from her to be raised in the priests' quarters of hidden Kush.

I recall our only meeting: After many years' separation, I at last get to see her, a tall, slender wraith of a woman in a dark purple chador. Even then she does not embrace me. "You are a son of god's choice," she tells me without emotion. "I was his vessel, and only when I proved that truth would they allow me to see what the god had wrought."

"How could you prove this, Mother? Amun's way is mystery, and you were a child."

"There is a power in me." Her whole manner rises, stiffens, hardens under the flowing cloth. "That power cannot be challenged, and I displayed that power. Soon enough, such a power may come to you, should the gods be willing."

I have never made much sense of that conversation. In my early teens, I was chosen to be trained for work with Darisis and Ahmed, trained in ways Western and occult, trained as brothers and sister, sons and daughter, pharaoh, vizier, and qore, and leaders apart. I know political systems, computer programming in three languages, modern ways of persuasion, incantations, food spells, and hex signs. Yet the only magical effects I have seen with my own eyes were the work of Harry Potter's gang on the movie screen.

Still, I can sell sewer gas on social media. For a profit.

I can observe religious ritual and not believe in any religion. I can live the life of an African prince (who wouldn't?) and sicken at the excess and falsehood while so many Africans face a fate not nearly so fortunate. Worst of all, I can fake living as a good Nubian for only so long, because my life is as a gay, not "good," Nubian.

I have to think that this knowledge is what has let me learn that I am not like them, even as I am part of them. Being in schools with Western secularism, I am able to know myself as gay and not feel I am failing the people, their culture, or myself.

All this I keep from my beloved Brand. But I can make phone calls to this, my lover, when I get the opportunity.

"So where are you staying?" Brand asks. "Are you with your folks?"

"Yes and no," and this is both truth and lie. "Much of the time I am in what passes for hotels, small buildings with a few beds."

"Do you ever get to Khartoum?"

I think he is trying to picture where I am. Where I am is like no place he can imagine. And I can't tell him more than "No."

"What do they want from you?" Brand is awake now. I hear concern for me in his voice. "Are they, like, prepping you for something?"

"I say I am preparing to be an engineer, but they smirk and say I must know these traditions as well. And it's not just me. Ahmed was with me much of the time. On many occasions he seemed no more pleased with them than I."

"What does Ahmed say about this?"

"Ah, vipers! That's another thing."

"What? What's wrong with Ahmed?"

"They have taken him away from me. One day he is there as always. Then our leader calls him over at the end of a meeting, and Ahmed goes off with two security guards. I have not seen him since."

"Did your leader say—"

"She says Ahmed has new duties, as I have. And that's all."

"Oh, Archie, I'm so sorry."

"Not your fault, and not Ahmed's. I don't know what has happened."

A pause on both sides.

"But Brand, I do have some good news. Can you pick me up at O'Hare next week? I'll be flying home to you."

Intercepted missive 202: Do you know the way to that Sudan bay? Something wicked that way comes. Wait for it. Meanwhile, this time the Maple Leafs say the dealer takes two; the Saudi–US deal is in the cards, so read the tarot, pharaoh: Really, the whole cabal needs to be Amalgamated (patent pending). Now on sale: More rare-earth exports just for you.

Pick over that one for a while, readers. And get ready for a surprise appearance!

CHAPTER 11

SURPRISE!

Lord Taharqa Nimiery is a prick. He's my best friend, main conspirator, and semi-demi-hemi-god, but he's still a prick.

"Pharaoh Taharqa, the beautiful face protected by Ra." That's what the magical Kushite cartouche of his namesake says. And it is a beautiful face, and a fine form that this many-generations-later possible descendant struts around in. Which makes me want him. Which reminds me I don't have him. Which makes him a prick.

Why did I bust him before Amanirenas about his little romance with a roommate? Is it really all that important? I know at this point he would probably call it a dalliance, not worth worrying about. Only it's not a dalliance; I know that. Archie and I had a dalliance. Taharqa and Branden have the real thing. Those two rodger their todgers.

Branden. Is he, like movie legend Marlon Brando, a great performer? He's not a film star on the videos I get from the mini-cams I secretly stashed in their room. But he is a master lover, and not just with a todger. I can tell, filtered through the optical technology and transmission equipment, that he loves and revels in love. With the attention and screen time I give them as I'm watching in my digs down here in Naptown, aka Indianapolis, there are real hearts at play, and the both of them are going all in. Damn them.

So that leaves me, Ahmed, back in the Indytown cold this January.

What? You didn't know this was me? I'm the one who's been commenting *in italics* on all those intercepted missives that were passed along to you. I'm the one who buried you under all that Pardell University research we had gathered before selecting that place. I'm the one who shadowed my buddy across campus to the lab building (you know, Chapter 4).

It's me, Ahmed Abboud, brown guy, wiry build, ripped frame, hairy chest, big mustache. And a bit about my name. You can't see the Middle Eastern "kh," but it's there in the pronunciation. AKH-med, like challah or allahu akbar. Just don't call me Awk.

I know Archie told you all about our stratagem, but he's only told you what he knows. I'm the real expert here, which is why the royals and the religious cognoscenti have me keeping an eye on their prize prince. He has a path to walk and a name to earn, and testing rare earths is not the half of it.

Of course, that doesn't mean I'm now going to spill the pekoe on what goes on in this story. God's balls, I'm not that stupid; we are not even one third along the way.

So here is what I can tell you, effendi mine: Taharqa's playing with fire when he brings his lover into the stratagem, and don't worry, he will. The danger triples, especially if the son-brother-pharaoh-to-be is distracted or unprepared for his challenges.

In chess terms, he must leave his most precious Black pawn unprotected among conniving bishops and marauding knights of opposing forces. He cannot allow distractions. He will need to have his mind unfettered as the protectors of ancient belief test his mettle. Only then will he gain his true power and bring its effect to the world. He will become protector, castle, and rook, and from the Persian word *rokh*, Kush's war chariot.

He may even lose Branden as he assumes his fated power and place. (I wouldn't mind picking up the pieces from that one. Even a heartbroken Branden would be someone I could give my yearning heart to.)

How do I know all this and Archie doesn't? Well, unlike my fatherless, practically motherless friend, I am an Arab son of Kushite priests. My father and the priesthood serve the hierophants and the seers and the avatars. Father has been to Jebel Barkal, Amun's own home on earth in what was neohistoric Kerma. My father knows there are special duties for Lord Taharqa; he is the returned soul of a pharaoh, a pharaoh's soul is a god, and gods only return to benefit humans. The son-brother-pharaoh-to-be and his sister-queen-qore-regnant will apply those special abilities to do miraculous tasks that father would not describe to me. Yet I know they will be true and will be magical.

So you thought you were reading an ordinary old Midwestern gay fuckbook, huh? Instead you've signed up for a magical, mythical adventure. Remember back there in my commentary on the first missive, I promised love, magic, and gods? Well, they are coming, along with extraordinary Midwestern gay fucks. And not one mention of dissociative personality disorder. Or Oscar Isaacs's canceled streaming series. Or comic books.

But *not* enough about me. I have been Archie's friend, assistant, pseudo-brother, and guide from the time we toddled together. We play games with each other, but my solo game of silent watcher is a pain. I try to stay meticulously honest with him, yet I observe, encourage, and help him find direction in his life under the unacknowledged tutelage of the priesthood. From playing in the valleys of the Nuba Mountains to lessons in the hidden caves to private conferences with Queen Amanirenas and secret missions in Suakin, we've been side by side. Once we were even closer than that—mouth on mouth—but my smartass comment afterward turned a kiss into a stupid mistake. My mistake, and my duty, is in letting him go.

So I sidekick my way through life, his life and mine. We laugh over priests' pronouncements (even though I am sure they are true). We learn the hieroglyphics on walls and the computer code in complex programs (and both are useful). We play servant and master, older and younger brother, friend and forever friend. But never lovers, at least not for me.

I am down here in this most Hicksville of hick capitals, a place that seems to think professional sports is an industry. Local names include Whitestown, White River, White Castle—you catchin' my drift? I am not one to shout bigotry (though some of the residents here are), but what can you say about a place above the Mason-Dixon Line where citizens call nonresidents "Yankees."

I keep my narrow brown arse in safe zones around the design-college campus here. I can pick up a little action at the art school, so it's become a place of solace. (Especially when my jealous soul sees that my long-distance surveillance targets are done with their homework and have switched to their bed work.) I don't sneer at the Hoosiers who ask me if I'm from Mumbai or Iraq or New Mexico (?!?). I move on, sliding through town in my Audi—which seems to draw sneers and awe from homegrown Indiana boys—to my job and my secret task at a minor computer firm called Burriers, Inc.

This place, we Kushites discovered during months of technology research, creates special computer programs and apps for its small number of clients. Because it has been around since the early 1960s, it's had computer programs that MS/DOS, the backbone of computer science, never got to. And Burriers was never happy with giving up its proprietary work to join the PC revolution.

Result: This is a unique location where programs on mass-market operating systems are jury-rigged to work on an OS no one else in the world has. It gives Burriers customers some of the most hack-secure services anywhere, since what hacker is going to waste time trying to decode something almost nobody uses. And it gives secret Kush spies a way to program, test, and wipe from memory the projects I design with Taharqa, and no one is the wiser.

So I come in to Burriers as a mild-mannered programming intern and art student to help them create an image design suite for a very special customer. Actually, creating that very special customer was easier than getting me hired as an intern. Money talks, and money from rare-earth swindles can talk loudly and in computer languages.

My work has become very important to them because the "customer" is paying in installments as the development progresses. I emulate a form of the ancient Penelope scam. During the day I do work for the "customer." At night I use my door access code to slip in, do work for Kush, and undo some of the work I did for the imaginary design customer to give me more days for doing Kush work. I'm such a dedicated worker, they tell me, it's too bad I keep having to redo my work for the "customer." But, well, he is paying, so they guess he's happy.

I think I'd be happier closer to Archie. We were buddies, allies in the war against the toffs at grammar (English upper-class) school. And I really like Branden, both from the time I met him and the time I've watched him. He's a charmer, so open and eager, even with his American Black reserve. (Yes, this Sudanese Arab notices. There is a distinct difference between those who have always had their own country and those whose ancestors were kidnapped to another.)

An hour's drive apart, Taharqa and I have communicated mainly through coded messages on temporary burner phones and obscure apps. Other than our careful spy-movie incursion at the Pardell Labs building (Chapter 4, remember?), the last time I got to be in a room with him recently, we were seven thousand miles from the campuses and fresh from a thrashing before our sister-in-fate Darisis when she was in full Queen Amanirenas mode.

"We stay quiet until the Avengers assemble." I toss my silliness at Archie in our last conversation, and he smiles. My friend is still my friend. I need to know that.

"So, buddy, how goes it?" he asks. "Still lonely?"

"As lonely as a camel turd ten kilometers from an oasis."

"You have such poetry," Archie jokes. "Must be all those art classes."

"I am such a find in the classroom, effendi. An Arab who does representational stick figures."

"We all must start somewhere."

Archie and I are outside. The moon has risen, and now a few Kushites have gathered beneath her beams. A wine merchant, his goods on a wheeled cart, offers us a goatskin to share, and we sit and drink, each man after the other. These are times when time stops, when even my slippery tongue is stilled by the spell of moon goddess Isis.

"We are, at best, on schedule," Taharqa says. "I wish things weren't so slow, and that we weren't so separated."

"You read my thoughts," I tell him. "But there is someone else you think of."

He has caught my meaning. "He is a good friend."

He's an even better lay, I want to say, but this isn't a time for joking. Instead it is time for this: "You need to tell him, son-prince."

"I don't want to get him involved."

"Too late, my brother. From what you say"—I'm still hiding the video surveillance from him—"he is very involved with you. And you him."

"And me him." He says it with sorrow. "But he cannot play a role. He is not of Kush."

"You two are sharing lab time, class time, homework time," (bed time). "You make him Kush with your presence."

"I miss him as profoundly as Isis missed Osiris." He sighs, shakes his head. "But will he be torn to pieces if our plan is discovered?"

"Isis gathered back Osiris's parts. She reassembled and revived him."

"I am no god like Isis."

"You are now a man, my brother, and a good one. You can do much and will do much more. But you must decide what you will do with this man you care for."

"You always taunt me with this talk of how I will do more. I don't know if that will ever be true." He sighs again. "These are the words to be said. I must deal with Brand. You are right. But must I do it right now?"

Intercepted missive 234:
Christmas break has come and gone.
Fuck yer mothah, life goes on.
Secrets creep while love is learned.
Sexy time till plot's returned.

CHAPTER 12
BRANDEN

COLLEGE CAMPUSES are a kind of bubble. A bubbly bubble for sure, with sports tourneys and national championships, touring theater companies and stand-up comics and pop bands, organization events and spontaneous protests. Add in classes and reading and long discussions into the night over very important subjects we can't change anyway (at least not now) and it's a champagne life.

Campuses in the Midwest are even more of a bubble. You don't want to step outside; the townies don't want you on their turf. And maybe it's the campus cops, maybe the locals fear of our numbers, maybe money, or maybe their own limited egos, but they don't invade the bubble.

Inside the bubble, we're mainly cool with each other. We're all studying for that test or writing that paper. We all eat in the dining halls, without the high school cliques or food fights. We all rush to get out of that winter wind or slowly stroll out on the quad in spring. There are exceptions—exclusions, really. The frats and sororities are a world of their own, as are the major sports jocks. I suppose at least a few of them wouldn't mind yelling "Faggot!" or tossing a raw egg at an immigrant. But they have their own sins to keep them busy.

I'm going on about this because Archie and I have our own place in the bubble. We are a committed gay couple. So many forms of gender identification are out and about, especially on campus, but he and I are unusual because so many gay men of our age are not partners. The "bois" may be in a temporary connection (cuffing season), may be monogamish until someone hotter comes along, may be lonely, may be in the grasp of Grindr. We committed gays are not much different than committed straight couples on campuses. All I know is that more than a few of the gay freelancers have asked why Archie and I are so goddamned together all the time.

Except for those times Archie slips off unnoticed. He can be gone for a couple hours, and when he comes back, his excuse is that he had to help a classmate at the lab. An unnamed classmate. *Hmph.*

Anywho, for some gay classmates we're a model, for others we're a challenge. But for each other, we are no more and no less than all we ever want.

Now it's early spring in central Indiana, which can be a time-lapse movie of climate change. One week there's a twenty-four-hour snowstorm piling drifts above the door handles; a few weeks later, tulips are popping up everywhere.

But spring is when the sap rises, someone's grandpa said. We are finished with midterms and anticipating summer break, which we will spend together at my place. And the magic elixirs of time, warm skies, and higher testosterone levels (plus the concern about how we'd hide our fucking from Mom) must have grown some wild hairs up my butt.

I ask The Question.

"Archie, do you… miss… other people?"

"Hmm?" He is proofreading my English comp essay on "Bugs Bunny and the Gay Aesthetic of Loony Tunes." I have already proofread his on "The Lies of Lawrence" (of Arabia). Neither of us is laughing.

So I ask again: "Do you miss… being with other people?"

"Other people?" He'd have pushed down his glasses if he had worn any. "You mean like my family? My mother?"

"No, I mean other… men. Of our age."

"I miss Ahmed."

"Uh, no, that's not what I meant. I mean, like, other men… for sex."

A sigh. "You are getting bored with me."

"Oh shit no! I didn't mean that—not that I… I-I am not bored with you!"

"And yet you ask? Why?"

Yeah, why do I ask? Because I've been invited into about a dozen no-strings-attached quickies, three ways, four ways, and orgies in the last week and a half. And I'm pretty sure he has been too.

"Because, well, people—"

"People? People who ask why we don't swim around in their human fluids?"

"Well, yeah."

"These gay fucks who want into your jockstrap? They tempt you?"

"No! No, but do they tempt you?"

"Branden Hickcock, I love you. In fact, I reject my family to love you. I reject my nation and my culture to love you. Only you get that."

"Aww, Arch, I meant no insult. Y'see what I'm sayin'? I mean, Archie, it's just that we've kept that dorm door closed from the first day we were together. And I wonder if you feel like you've... missed something."

"Do you feel that way?"

"N-no."

"There is a pause?"

"I don't miss anything with you. But everybody's got to ask once if there's something they haven't tried, something else, and what it might be like."

"That I do not ask."

"Fine, then let's forget it." And I really want him to as I start to turn away.

"Maybe not. Maybe...," and he sighs. "Maybe you want to see what that something is like. No, don't object, not quite yet, because I love you enough that, if you need to try—"

"But I don't!"

"But if you need to try, then go ahead. Only know I will not go with you, and I do not want to know about it, and I will be hurt thinking that you did it. But I love you, so go."

"I'm not going anywhere. I'm with you, for always, and I am totally happy with just us two."

"And you are not missing something?"

"That plot of grass looks pretty tasteless from over here."

"And yet you ask me what I miss?"

I have no answer for that, and so there is some silence, till Archie gives me a soft snort.

"You have disturbed me in my work, and for no reason. Now I shall have to show you what that displeasure does to me. And to you."

Well, here's a side of my always-controlled lover that he hasn't shown before.

"First I will finish your paper." He gives it a two-second look. "You still love the comma too much. But it is good. It is, how would your Bugs say it? Screwy, but good.

"And now—" He rises from the desk chair. "—stand up, you questioner."

"Yes, sir."

He holds one finger to his lips. "No talking. No questions. It is time to do as I say. And as I say, so shall it be."

Look, I'm a big lug used to getting my way with a muscle twitch or two. But this shit is turning me on.

"Flick the light off, then come back."

I step quickly and hit the switch. The light in the desk is still on, but he turns to get it. A sudden thought flies into my head, and I rush over and lock the door to the hallway, then do the same to the shared bathroom. Only the lights outside the dorm illuminate the place.

"I did not say to do that," Archie says.

"Sorry."

"But"—he smiles a bit—"it was an excellent idea."

"Thank y—"

His finger is on my lips. "Shh," he whispers, "you have said quite enough tonight. It is for me to say the words to be said."

His hand grabs my jaw; those black eyes bore into mine. He strokes my cheek, he smiles. He is not Archie now. He is Lord Taharqa, ruler, in control. He steps closer; his other hand touches my chest.

I'm the kind of guy who loves to be touched. Start me out and I am one big erogenous zone. My lord knows this, and that hand, pressing over my heart, has my chest on fire.

He is even closer, and I reach to pull him into a kiss, but he pushes back enough to let me know I am not to lead. He looks up at me sternly, shakes his head.

I feel awkward, nervous, like a boy caught cursing and in the principal's office. But I am excited too. Maybe the principal spanks. Maybe he does more.

The hand at my jaw releases now, spreads to a caress across my cheeks, coming together at the corners of my mouth. He lets one finger cross my trembling lips.

My eyes close. It is so gentle, so tempting. I force myself to look at him again, let him see how much I want him.

And then he pulls me into the kiss.

Now Archie and I have been at this for nine months, so there has been an oil-tanker boatload of kisses: soft kisses, sorry kisses, comfort kisses, raging hormone kisses, fun kisses, funny kisses, quick-for-luck kisses. But this is the Taharqa kiss, the surrender-and-be-captive kiss. I cannot let it go, my mouth slipping a bit up, a bit down so I can suck on one of his plump lips or the other. There is a spiciness to it. And then his head turns ever so slightly and just enough to let me know that it is he who is determining where the kiss comes from, where it is going, what it means.

I don't notice at first as one hand slips under my tight-fitting T-shirt, crosses my chest to my right nipple, which is ground zero for me. I moan in the kiss as he brushes over the hardened tip, then comes back and gives it a gentle tug. More moans. More rubbing, Another tug.

By now I'm nearly out of breath, and Lord Taharqa pulls closer. We are in a clench, each seeking new places to kiss—ears, necks, shoulders, chins, eyelids. His hands are behind me now, hefting up my tee, so I have to let go and lift my arms to get it over my head. I grab at his buttoned shirt now and gently tug, more a suggestion or a plea to let me see and touch and taste what's beneath.

He undoes the buttons too damn slowly, and he's wearing a tee under it, which I fear will take more time. But he does the crossed-arms pull that hikes his second shirt up and over his head in one motion. His nipples have hardened, pebbles under that dark skin. I smell his warmth, thrill at his passion.

He places that finger to my lips again, takes my arms, leads me to our mattresses and lowers me to sitting position on one. (Like it's been said before, dorm beds are not made for two, so whenever we are sure we will not be seen by outsiders, we pull the mattresses off the frames and go at it on the floor. I even stole king-size sheets and a blanket from Mom so we truly sleep together.)

Once I am down, he kneels and pulls at my belt and the waistband button underneath. I am quick to help, to pull off the pants and socks—I go commando at least half the time—so that I am sitting naked on the mattress. Lord Taharqa smiles an Archie smile, rubs his hands from my neck to shoulders to chest (nipple brush) to waist and then between my legs. I am ready, swollen member and all, and he kisses my penis head, licks around the crown, gently slides his mouth and tongue over the tip.

Now I'm already halfway to heaven, and he slowly, slowly inches his lips down my prick, sucking all the way to my crotch, then slips back to the very tip only to travel that path again. I want to touch his head, to scrub my hands over that crispy black hair, but he stops and pulls my arms away. I want to touch his shoulders, his back, but again he pulls me away.

I love him, and I hate this. I need to do something as he does this, and I begin to whine, really—to whine like some three-year-old who really wants that piece of candy. But my lord pulls off, touches my mouth, shakes his beautiful head no as his hands travel back down my chest (nipple brush). I am so aroused and excited and frustrated all at once. I fight myself to behave.

Then he does something he's done before. While fellating me, he doesn't suck or swallow, but after a few pumps, opens his lips so that his juices spill down me, soaking my balls and, eventually, my taint and my asshole. This he does a few times, sliding a hand between my thighs till he can use that saliva to wet my ass rim, press me open, and lubricate my chute.

Not quite lube, but you don't have to break contact to find the bottle. And it works. Oh, man, it works.

Once he has me nice and wet, and his fingers have loosened me up some (but never enough), he presses me onto my back, legs open and up, waiting for him. Usually he doesn't pause to knock at the door. But this time, he barely presses that mushroom head against the outer edge. And there it sits. For what feels like ages and ages and ages.

I can't wait any longer. "Taharqa," I whine. "Please. Please!"

He does not move, but I see his smile, devilish this time. "This is something you want, habibi?" he whispers. "Something else?"

"Please, Taharqa, please fuck me! Now!"

He smiles again. I see him move, but it's like super slo-mo. I feel the pressure grow on my dainty little hole. I feel it pressed open, and there is the pain and the fear and the want, so much want, as that cock widens me, opens me, spreads the little starfish and the back passage beyond, wider and deeper because he is so fucking long and thick, stalling and then pressing forward as I swear I feel every square millimeter of that penis, the veins and the growing bulge after the crown until it tapers gently, and then his crotch is up against my hips. And he pauses.

"I do this for you, my eternal love," he whispers. His words wash over me like an ocean wave. "For you and only you, I will do anything."

I can't pause. I gasp and press myself toward him, desperate to scratch that awful itch that a full dick puts inside me. I feel a throbbing ache that makes me serve and love him all the more.

The words come out of me, I don't know how, but I know from where.

"All I am is love for you," I say. "Every action, every day, everything I do is a way to love you and honor your love."

At this he smiles, and I bask in the glow from his gentle face.

"Then love me like this," he says, "and give me all that you are."

He grabs my thighs and pulls in tight. He stares down at me. I stare up at him. And only then does he start the slow work of in and out, thrust and retreat, fill and empty. I grasp at his muscled butt, pull him deeper, get lost in the sensation.

He has fucked me before, and I him, and always it is a joyride. But this is something so exceptional, so powerful and open and complete. I swear there are times this night that I come with no ejaculation, just intense, internal spasms of pleasure. He stops during these, leans down and takes my eager kisses.

We don't switch positions; we fuck missionary style. And I hope this doesn't sound racist, but this time I am the godless native and he is the missionary, and he gives me religion that night.

No. His name is a pharaoh's, and pharaohs were called gods. He is truly a god in this.

Finally, missing any sense of control, I beg him. "Please, oh lord, I need to come!"

"Then we must give you what you need."

He leans up a bit, takes my cock into his hand. He strokes it as his dick strokes inside me, each stroke taking me higher. Finally, with a grunt and a cry and I don't know what other sound effect, I shoot hot cum on both of us. I don't count the spasms; I let loose. And somewhere in there, Lord Taharqa comes too, his moonshots prolonging my missiles until both are spent.

With his last bit of strength, he pulls me into a kiss. He lingers as long as he can, then tilts left and topples onto the mattresses. We are both left panting, exposed, fulfilled. Minutes pass. He lifts his head to see me; I am looking at the man who did all this to me, and I am so grateful, so loving.

"Would you like to try someone different now?" he asks.

"No," I say. "I wouldn't try anything else with anyone else. Nothing compares to you."

Intercepted missive 285: Hey, what about that plot? Stay tuned for Red Army on the Air, part one of a series. They've gotta hide, but we make it run. Don't worry, our boys don't disappear. Yet.

CHAPTER 13

In other parts of the world

GOBI DESERT, China. Dr. Yang Bo-sin is worried. His rare-earth products (actually not his but purchased from that sneering middleman on that freakish island) are too good, too pure, too refined. Everyone is suspicious, especially the always suspicious Central Committee.

"Improvements in work processes," he lies in his digital reports. "More experienced labor force. Fortunate encounters with large deposits."

The only truth here is the last—except that no one in his labor pool has any idea where those large deposits came from.

His office, a small trailer cluttered with papers and tablet screens in an arid no man's land, is crunchy with windblown sand. His eyelids and mood are no less gritty.

"We believe the supply comes from the north," Dr. Yang's negotiator says on a Monday. He is a short man, and seated as he is, he is head-only visible above Dr. Yang's metal desk.

"From Mongolia?"

Dr. Yang wonders what force is braving the cold Mongol steppes. Are they somehow mining in the northern mountains, or stealing the People's Republic's thunder on their shared Gobi border? Or is the ore from farther north? Wouldn't it be like those cryptocapitalist Mongols to work a deal with Siberia? But no way Putin could get the oligarchs to invest way out east, and Vlad's US buddy is out of office for good.

What do the satellites say? Nothing! What the hell good are spy satellites if they can't tell you something?

"We are receiving the supply from the east," the negotiator says, back in the office on Wednesday.

East? Perhaps the Turks, still jealously trying to revive their Ottoman Empire? But where there? Wouldn't mountain excavation wash rare earths down into the Fertile Crescent? What are our relations with Iran right now? (What are anyone's?)

News gets scarce for a while, but by Friday a year later, the negotiator, a new one, shows up with his spy to say, "Australia is involved."

Of course, thinks Dr. Yang. *The PRC's greatest threat in Asia has a continent of its own.* He wonders if the Aussies are using aboriginal labor or are still stymied with attempts at racial equality. Better to be one people, like the Chinese (excluding, of course, the Uighurs).

"Something's strange," says the spy, who by now has replaced the latest ineffective negotiator. "Rare earth in Jeddah, under US private guard. Rare earth supplied through Ottawa Neither deals with the other. Or so they think."

"Too much world!" shouts Dr. Yang, shoving useless reports across his battered steel desk. How can something so limited in reality become magically diverse? Possession of this material is proliferating quicker than atomic weapons a half century ago. Soon enough will China even have a market? Or can it compete with the inhuman costs—in yuan and workers— his operation is running up without the secret purchase?

He casts his vision to the sand-spattered window. Rare-earth metals are out there somewhere, but there is entirely too much world.

"That may be the truth," the spy says. "We intercepted a message, a missive full of some form of word code. But we know others, beyond even the Americans and Australians, are involved."

And that brings up the current issue. Even after carefully—read, miserly—trickling in purchased metals to mix with the barely refined product Dr. Yang's desert operation is supplying, the pure stuff is running out. Which means that soon the actual useful amounts will drop. Despite extra efforts—and a few dozen deaths—there is no way his Gobi mining can make up the difference. The market is still hungry. And the Central Committee is watching.

The spy is replaced at Dr. Yang's request by another, who is replaced by the committee by a third. When a fourth shows up, sponsored by the nation's ultrawealthy, Dr. Yang is ready to volunteer for reeducation, or maybe a speedy trip through Hong Kong. And this fourth agent is swearing that rare-earth activity centers on a long-abandoned city in that bubbling pot of conflict, Sudan.

"Am I really supposed to believe this?" Dr. Yang tells his assistants. "Some coral-clogged port lost to the world since the Ming Dynasty? How can that be?"

Dr. Yang never gets his answer. Soon after, he is replaced by another, even three others if you include the scientist, a negotiator-spy, and a torturer-executioner.

Intercepted missive 302: What a world, what a world! *Rubaiyat*? Ruby slippers. They're eatin' crow with Yukon Gold fries. Lawdy, lawdy, Ms. Saudi, every ally is a competitor, except competitors form corporations. Corporations amalgamate (it's coming. It's coming). Business as usual in the dogfight pit. Our boys idle by the Big Water, and talk turns Black.

CHAPTER 14
TAHARQA

I LOVE Chicago. Or maybe I should say this differently. I love these people, the Hickcocks, who take me in and care for me and feed me, and they are in Chicago, so I love Chicago too.

Except for the haters.

In big cities everywhere, the force of change is rushing through like a sirocco. Chicago, New York, Berlin, Paris, Tokyo have changed the world and been changed by it. Even hard-line places like Baghdad, Moscow, Beijing, and Tunisia have their gay places and safe spots, though not safe in ways that any liberated human would accept or understand.

And yet in the most western of Western nations, there remain knots of bigotry, sexism, and homophobia. It is not really a surprise, merely a disappointment that the fundamentalist muscle, iron strong in the land where my people stay hidden, is still a force in a world opening to diversity.

When Ahmed and I were in grammar school, the darts came as "jokes," calling us "Pumbaa and Timon" (what tune-filled jungle films did that come from?) or screaming "terrorist" across the campus's open ellipse. Our apparently flagrant wealth shut some of them up, while others knew behind their smirks and self-righteousness that exclusion was the sharpest knife, cutting classmates like us out of their clubs and conversations. (Except when the "targets" didn't want in on their smarmy activities and events.)

Amun Ra never pulled back our bedclothes or cursed our skin color. The sun god wants love, and to love each other is worship.

Summer in Chicago is summer in the big city, and there are too many people who are different in too many ways for much microaggressive shit to have an effect. We are out and about, and not only in gay neighborhoods. We are as comfortable in the citywide Taste of Chicago as at Gay Pride parades, Fiesta del Sol events, and Koreatown diners.

It's a middle city, not old and cynical like New York or fresh and fictional like LA. It has its own sea of a freshwater Great Lake. There are many sections of sturdy brick bungalows, and there are high-rises along the lakeshore and decaying wooden ghettos south and west. People here are interested when they ask about you, and they are also willing to let you be unknown.

Illinois poet Carl Sandburg wrote it: "Love your neighbor as yourself; but don't take down the fence."

Here Branden and I are people, not suspects. And we are pulled to Lake Michigan like nearly every young person within three hundred miles.

For at least part of the summer we tow out Branden's father's sailboat and sweep up and down the beachfront areas. Black, Latin, indigenous, and White; gay and gayer; young people are jumping on beach volleyball courts, pedaling bikes along asphalt paths, and entering lakefront museums. We have to "dock" in not-so-legal places because the Hickcocks can no longer afford the fees for a marina berth, even if they could jump the considerable line of people applying for one. I am ready to make the payoff. No sweat off my budget's brow. But Brand stops me, saying the family really can't afford to keep the boat anymore.

So as often as we can, Brand and I trade places at the tiller as we float along the city's sparkling shore, north to Edgewater and south to Jackson Park. So peaceful and smooth and totally unlike my experiences along the Red Sea. A better modern name there would be "green" for the money traveling through it—trade that has made several national leaders rich and kept far too many nations' citizens poor.

The Hickcocks sold the boat before July was out. So it is goodbye, *Sharpshooter.* After that, I drive us over to the lakeside parks where we can walk, dip toes in fresh water, munch hot dogs, and dream. We hold hands or hug shoulders. If anyone else cares, we never see them.

My hosts made every effort to let me know I was not a burden in my sojourn here. That of course makes me feel even more of a burden, so I help out as best I can. Mr. Hickcock—stocky, brown-skinned, bald, and quick with a dad joke—lets me help him reorganize his library. So many books on so many subjects.

It's only later that I realize we are organizing his books for sale. His research sabbatical has become a layoff, and he is reducing expenses, cutting corners, taking what he can.

Damn. It's not like this world doesn't need history—not with the way it is repeating it, forever failing to follow love's ascent, instead chasing hate's tail of avarice.

"I'll be driving a school bus come fall," he says. "Otto von Notto, that's me. And the job will bring in some cash."

"The world owes you more. Such a job," I say, shaking my head.

"Nothing wrong with helping children, no matter what the role," he says. "I'll be happy seeing young faces. And texting while driving. Gotta keep up with the young'uns."

The kind of man Mr. Hickcock is, that's the kind of man I see in Branden. And the kind of man I am so happy to have love me.

Mrs. Hickcock—Frannie, she insists—is a different character completely. Light enough to pass for white, hair coifed in a french twist, she is regal with intelligence, not attitude. She relates her Black family history with more knowledge and pride than Henry Louis Gates can supply with DNA results. And that's where my lover gets his determination, his cockiness, his stubborn streak, and his unbridled brainpower.

Frannie has taken on a summer-school schedule this year, yet she insists on being cook, hostess, and homemaker. Less would be uncompetitive. And she has plenty of time to grill me about where I'm from, where we're all from, and where we all ought to be.

"I have taught several African students," she says one night after dinner. "Mainly from western or central nations: Ghana, Nigeria, the Congo. The same areas that many American enslaved prisoners were taken from."

"I am sure that in some ways we differ," I say, settling into an overstuffed easy chair near her couch, where she pulls her legs under her as if to sit above all.

"Each nationality differs from each," she says, "and they all differ from African Americans. I see Africa in all of us, but not all of us see Africa the same.

"I think, how much did slavery change us? How much did democracy do for us? How much of it all is the result of colonialism? How much or little passes down through the ages?

"Now I wonder how much is different, East Africa from West?"

I see Brand across the living room, his face intent. This conversation has become a learning experience, and he's eager to hear.

"So," I say, "what do each side of the continent share? Kingdoms, but long gone. Colonial pasts. Even the same Euro oppressors. The slave trade, yet so few Africans today take ownership of their historic responsibility in supplying those slaves. Pride that our nations are now our own, no matter how the world sees us. And yet each group sees itself as different: East Africa, West Africa, Southern Africa, and America."

"Interesting," she says. "In Western eyes, your nation has been ripped apart by ethnic histories and monotheistic war. Many in America see the Sudanese as either revolutionary Christians or radical Muslims. But as we have talked, I now see Taharqa as having no religion, except perhaps a faith created long before those two divided up the continent."

I see I must carefully correct my hostess and still not give away my truth.

"The Western world sees Sudan, which is a pseudo-nation manufactured for colonial exploitation. But there I see Kemet, the far more ancient land of Egypt and Nubia. We are many peoples," I say. "Some of us are as you describe, but there is far more variety than that. In truth, a few of us, born and reared in that quasi-country, are in our minds not Sudanese at all.

"I am Nubian and Hu, seed of the world's creation, a Kushite of the land once known as Kemet. Kush was descended from Kerma and Thebes, Napata and Meroë. The Kush empire spoke its own language, developed many beliefs now apparently forgotten by all others, established a prehistoric culture, and worshipped its gods in rites now archaic.

"If we now are Kushite, are we locked in that dusty culture, believing only what was believed then, professing a religion of asps and desert wolves and a solar disk?" I smiled "There are words to be said, but you'd have to ask each one of us for their own ways of expressing their truths."

I let that hang without further explication because my truthful answer would surprise the room.

"I have learned in my time here," I continue, "that what Westerners call Native Americans are not what Native Americans call themselves. They are Sioux, Apache, Navaho. As hard as your news media try to keep up with Hispanic, Latino or Latinx, those peoples are Cuban, Brazilian, Costa Rican, Chilean, Mexican. Thus there is no understanding that what others see as Sudanese, we know is Nuba, Nubian, Mapan, Angassana, Beja, Nilotic. Sixty-four ethnic groups jammed together and told they are the same. And that they are inferior.

"Westerners use the word 'tribe,' which they see as both accurate and an insult. Never do they refer to Irish Catholic, French Protestant, Russian Orthodox tribes. We, like they, are ethnic clans, each a collection of families with commonalities despite differences. You may call these clans of similarities religions, cultures, or nationalities. We call them identity."

To turn the pressure back to her, I ask the next question.

"But Frannie, what of you? I do not sense a particular faith about you."

"I was raised Methodist," she says with a sigh. "African Methodist Episcopal. But Methodist, Baptist, Presbyterian, Catholic, even Buddhist, Shia, and Sunni—they are all unitarian to me—units of the same lie, force-fed to conquered humans as a way to steal from those humans, using the false promise of a reward in the next world as compensation for their exploitation in this one."

"False promise?"

"Dead is dead." Quite a pause after she says that.

"Even that is a Western belief," Branden adds, earning a questioning look from his mother. I smile.

"Your son and I have had a few discussions."

"I certainly hope you two would *also* talk," she says, implications fully intended. So can Brand and I move into the same bedroom? I'll not ask that question tonight.

Frannie smiles. "I'm a historian. I study from a modern perspective. But I can also love the primal ways."

Primal ways. Like love and honor. Like me and Branden. Like life. Eternal.

Let's see if you can get the next couple of quiz questions all by yourselves. But don't worry: I won't be very far away. I promise.

Intercepted missive 364: Team sports—and spurts. Much ado about nothing new. His story, our story, your story told in heat and dust. And back home again in Plotsylvania, a team becomes A-team. One more man. One more target.

CHAPTER 15
AHMED

HEY! IT'S me again! I get another chapter heading! Are you happy to (not) see me?

Remember that chapter way up there that was a guide to the fabled land of Pardell? Well, it's time for another locator, this one seven thousand miles away. It's a place of pathos, but instead I feel abhorrence. You may call it my home.

While my best bud and his buddy enjoy the charms of the Second City, I'm here sweating away my summer just outside Lesser Sumer. By that I mean I'm in Sudan, which is somewhat beyond the Fertile Crescent's south end, and 3,300 miles from the birthplace of civilization in Iraq. Still, Sudan does encompass a chunk of that other cradle of civilization, the Nile Valley. This land is not all empty desert, though it's hard to tell with all the sand.

Being here brings up thoughts, memories, fears, and truths I rarely consider in the bland American Midwest. Those who remember the first section of their high school world history book know that this swath—from Egypt and along the eastern shore of the Mediterranean Sea, only to curve farther east into the land between the Tigris and Euphrates rivers—is the birthplace of civilization and (excluding the Hindus, Buddhists and less populous faiths) the hometown of big-time religion. That's why I mention Sumer: The world's first city grew in this crescent. Humans developed new ways of life here. People worshipped their own gods here. And they fought and died to force their own gods and their ways of life on each other here. Welcome home, mankind!

Let creation of society and creation of organized faith coalesce, and this area adjacent to the Horn of Africa is prime real estate for the result. The oldest skeleton of humanity's ancestors, from 4.4 million years ago, was found in what is now Ethiopia, southeast of Kush. Eons later, natural grains and an abundance of prey animals lured hunter-gatherers into settling down and setting up farms along the Nile and other stretches of the Fertile Crescent. True, the oldest human cities—from maybe 7,400 years ago—are to the north of Egypt near what is now Baghdad. That means the Egyptians and Nubians were late to the urbanization party by maybe 2,100 years. (But what's twenty-one centuries among friends?)

Part of human life developed in one spot, and the start of human society formed in another relatively nearby; what is now Sudan is stuck amidst it all. And in this fevered soil, rivalry and religious war, racial and ethnic hatred, envy and bitter violence have roots as deep as humanity. Is there any question that these are inherent traits of our one human race?

Every dynasty from Ramses II of the New Kingdom to the Ptolemy's Grecian Egypt to imperial Rome, from Ottoman Turks to the Mahdi's Muslim caliphate to British colonialists, have at one time ruled and schemed and warred in what was Nubia and what is now Sudan. It should be no surprise that today's ethnic groups and foreign puppet masters lust after and battle over its Red Sea ports and its politics. (Is it called the Red Sea for all the blood spilled there?) Recent wranglers include Putin's Russia, Qatar, Yemen, Turkey, Iran, Saudi Arabia, of course the US, and likely China. And that violence doesn't include the clannish, racist, homophobic, and religious anger that sparks strikes, insurgency, starvation tactics, and enough inhumanity to confirm that yes, man begins here.

Add in one of the occasional Sudanese governmental coups—the military grabbing control, and the populace revolting, and the promise of democratic change dangling until the next coup—and one could say this is not a place to sing "Home Sweet Sudan."

And the new nation of South Sudan, barely a decade old, is more than half Christian, where what seems like endless civil war keeps the populace near starvation.

As for the government sanctioned homophobia, it's just another example of ignoring the truths of the past. The oldest story in the world, *Gilgamesh,* tells the adventures of a Mesopotamian king and his "intimate" friend. When that wild-male friend, Enkidu, dies, King Gilgamesh cannot be consoled. Later, two male high officials were entombed together in Egypt; the wall paintings show them nose to nose. That's long before David and Jonathan. Or Taharqa and Branden. But probably not too far along in time from when that biblical crap about man love and abomination was being constructed.

Now don't get harshed by my downer thoughts. The truth is I think about all of this, and I laugh. The world is going to hell, has gone to hell, is hell itself. And yet it goes on, and all kinds of people live, love, build, create, and die here. Therefore, as the French, Looney Tunes, and Johnny Carson all so nobly said, it is to laugh.

And to plot the salvation of the world. I haven't forgotten our stratagem.

The previous time I was in Sudan was when Archie and I reported to Queen Amanirenas the progress of our American exploits. This time, the queen-sister and I meet on the southeast coast of Suakin port, among the ancient ruins: The port area is being revived, we have been told, thanks to international interest and global competition. We steer clear of any new construction and the (minimal) efforts at historic preservation, opting for a less traveled, more magical area. Pharaoh Ramses's white city, some have called it.

What she and I learn in that visit is that Suakin is too fucking hot to visit. This seems to be another part of Sudan's fate—a land of history back to before there was history is crumbling to dust because the weather could toast the tourist trade to a crispy black.

After the Suakin meeting (in nighttime hours), we adjourn and move my full debriefing and download into the cool semidark of Kush, concealed in the Nuba Mountains.

Yes, Kush is real. Kush is still here. Kush is secret. Kush is eternal. I should give you a quick tour, but I suspect that is coming in a few more chapters.

Queen Amanirenas is pleased with my software prowess, though not so taken with my report on Taharqa. I suspect that's because she wanted another report on Archie and Branden, and I wasn't forthcoming. I do believe our girl has a crush on our pharaoh-almighty-to-be. That's not strange: The gods and goddesses of this land bred with each other like prize cattle, and she is god-queen. Archie may soon be god-king. I will be, goddammit, left out.

And that's where my thoughts land me today, alone and lonely with my computer code and cock, neither of which are much use to me right now. Certainly I have internet access; certainly I live in an enlightened if secret society. But much of my work is connected to the efforts of Taharqa. Much of my private life too. All the way back to our childhood.

Being friend, fellow student, servant, spy, and psychic familiar to a Chosen One is all-consuming—and not nourishing for a love life. Archie and I have enjoyed each other, but never *enjoyed* each other. And when I discovered that that might be what I wanted, he had moved on. And I don't have many other options.

The Nubians of clandestine Kush are both committed to their cause and to their truly significant others. They traditionally pair off early. This may be because there are so few of us Kushites, being separate from northern Nubians of southern Egypt and southern Nubians of northern Sudan. This may also be because there is so much cultural mixture and conflict, you must grab someone near and HODL—hold on for dear life.

Add in the current stench stewed up by politics, religion, and race. Mainstream scholars reject the idea that Kemet (Nubia and Egypt) were Black or White, but try to argue *that* after a racist slave trade and colonial bigotry fogged the world's vision. Our modern mix of Muslim, Christian, and Coptic—and the arm-wrestling between democracy and dictatorship—foster more division. But one thing all groups here seem to agree on is that none accept same-sex romance. All of us in Sudan face national laws that punish homosexuality and anal sex with prison.

Yet there are some Nuba groups in which men presenting as women can be sold into marriage for the price of one goat. And in Sudanese work camps, the men spend much more time in the male-dominated camps than at home with their female-genitaled wives.

Does this clear up the questions about my romantic prospects?

Life can be so much worse outside our cavern home—so furtive, so disdained, so dangerous. Under Islam you can be hated for being gay. In the so-called secular West, you can be hated for being a Muslim. In many places, you can be hated for being either or both. Prison, beatings, execution (by some states), murder (by some families), all can be yours. Welcome to mankind, homie.

No more thoughts like that, okay?

Maybe someday soon, I will return to Naptown, where I will work diligently and impress my coworkers. And Grindr and websites will replace, but not equal, this night. Because this night I am alone. Unfucked. Fucking alone.

CHAPTER 16
BRANDEN

LIKE I said, a college campus is like a bubbly bubble. I mean, there are plenty of bubbles inside the bubble. We may all—or almost all—identify as whatever the school mascot is named. (Ours is Paulie Pipefitter, apparently because the football squad was accused long ago of recruiting a brawny plumbing crew from a local plant. And that name is perfectly fine with us gay boys.) There are the separate subgroup identities: computer nerds, sports jocks, frat packs, Black and Asian and Muslim student unions, LGBTQ+ organizations, theater crews, hard-core gamers. Like peoples in nations, not always getting along.

For the sophomore year, we all return to campus, hangouts, classrooms, study groups, and societies—all except the hard-core gamers, who flunked out second semester.

Archie and I decided during that glorious, love-filled summer to give the dorm another year rather than seek off-campus housing. I mean, apartment living is certainly in our future, but sharing a house with a few other guys opens a door I'm not sure we need exposure to. The mass of different backgrounds in a building of four hundred students means we all have to watch our behavior and our biases. When the residence is a house with maybe four other men, when is one dude gonna get drunk and go off on "sand rats" and much less repeatable insults? I don't want that for Archie in whatever home we share.

Otherwise, he and I returned to campus that August as tightly coordinated as a two-man army. We might as well be married, some suggest, and we certainly want to be. We are a duprass (read Kurt Vonnegut's *Cat's Cradle*) so united that we don't need a subgroup. We are our world. But we participate.

An example: the unofficial official Kerry Quad Winter Olympics.

Kerry Quadrangle, a mid-twentieth-century four-building monstrosity, has always been a set of men-only dorms arranged in a square around an open courtyard. It's dark brick with cement decorations and green-scalloped roofs resemble a castle, or a castle designed by an apathetic bricklayer.

Every winter after Christmas break, guys rooming there stage their Winter Olympics. Like no other modern Olympics, the "games" consist of one event, a footrace. And as was done in ancient Greece, the competitors run in the nude. Well, you can wear gym shoes.

The event is meant to be a private affair, dorm residents only as entrants and no outside-the-quad audience. As Bowen Hall residents, Archie and I would normally not be in attendance or entrants. But this year, one of our engineering pals suggests I enter as a ringer. I'd run for his building and floor, and he'd bring Archie in to watch.

Well, I have sympathy for the closeted, and this guy was so "nonchalant" about his desires, he only casually asks Archie if his cellphone has any nude pictures of us. And he teases me into running because I am the big guy from the Windy City. Hadn't I grown up with the Hawk, the wind referred to as the "giant razorblade comin' down the street" that cut through all your winter clothes?

Then again, Archie promises me a special warm-up after I compete. Never could turn down that man's offers.

So on the first Saturday in January, there I am in high-top red Chuck Taylors and the altogether, with about fifteen other very naked, very cold dudes at the starting line. There are no guns on campus, so someone shouts, "And they're off." And we start running.

Now, the object of this event is not to be first at the finish line. Really there is no finish line. Instead, runners run and run and run around the internal oval of the quad until they can't take the frost on their man parts anymore and they quit. The winner will be the one who does the most laps and lasts longest (and doesn't lose his man parts).

We are running, and I am with the pack. This is much less a sprint and more a spirited jog. We jog, our parts jog—well, the chill-shrunken versions of our parts jog. Out ahead we have two guys who have taken the challenge way too seriously. They are running top speed on the sidewalks that line the inner quad. Because there was snow before we left and while we were gone and when we got back from winter break, the dorm's maintenance crew has blown the courtyard snowfall into central mountains of white stuff, adding a crisscross X-path through the middle. Above these mounds we can only see the heads of our leaders bobbing up as they speed along.

I learned later from Archie about the first mishap. One of our leaders begins to lap the stragglers. Bad idea because one of the stragglers, a moving mountain himself, takes offense at the insult and body blocks the muthah into a snow hill. One man down.

Coming around the third turn, some of us discover the path betrayed by that plague of winter, black ice. A couple of runners slide into a couple of runners who grab at a couple of runners who trip… well, it's a pileup like on a fogbound highway.

After the first lap, I think we are down to eight bruhs. The rest of us tend to stay together, maybe to catch a bit of warmth from one another's breath. Oh, a couple more slide on the ice, but one saves himself. Another tries a smooth move and cuts across the X-path to lead us, but I catch up to him and toss him in the snow.

Soon enough we are down to four, and here my strategy comes in. If I win the race, it will soon be noted that I do not live in the dorm. Same if I come in second. Or third. Meanwhile, Archie and my Closet Charlie have had enough time to take all the naked pictures they want from a window in a second-floor stairwell, so what if I "lose"? Therefore with total abandon, I dive into the nearest drift.

Cold. *Brrrrrr*. I'm shivering so much I can barely stand, but I manage to run past the throng of four guys who had the guts to stand outside to watch the race.

I rush unseen to our dorm room, and Archie meets me with the warmest, softest, thickest robe ever. He towels my legs dry and brushes snow out of my hair. We laugh in honor of the "straight" guy, 'cause he won his bet by betting against me. Then Archie and I lock our doors.

You might be amazed at how quickly a body most recently ice cold can turn sweat-moist and heated with the right treatment.

It starts like this. Archie pushes the towel off my neck to lock his fingers behind it, pulling me into a kiss. The kiss lingers, moves as his caress slides forward to my barely scruffy cheeks. He brushes them softly, murmurs, "Spikey," a nickname that grew out of my stiff-growing facial hair. I pull away from the kiss because I have to smile.

"My poor frozen habibi," he says. "I bet you'd turn pale if you could."

"Now is this the pot calling the kettle color-enhanced?" I hit him with a factoid he taught me about what ancient Greeks called Nubians and all dark Africans: "Ain't we all Aethiopians—the people with the burnt faces?"

"Right," Archie says, "we are both the same over the skin."

Archie gently pulls open the robe and pushes it off my shoulders as he rubs across them from the neck out and back, then kneads the muscles just so. He spreads his hands again to knead the tops of my arms, then down to the biceps bulge.

We are trading off. He is kissing me at the base of my neck; then he backs off, and I kiss his hairline, his forehead, his nose; then he leans back in to kiss me some more.

"You are so damn handsome," he says. "I couldn't resist you even if I didn't love you."

"But you do," I say, "love me?"

"Come close," he says, "and let my body talk to yours."

The hands slide off my biceps and onto my pecs. His kisses land randomly, driving me nuts already. (I told you; I'm a body-sensitive maniac.) I am trying to catch him, hold his back, his waist, his arms, or his gentle hands. But he moves with my moves, so I am always a step behind.

By the time he's down to my abs, the robe is on the floor, and I'm naked—except for the red kicks melting snow over my frigid feet. He is fully clothed, so I slide a hand inside the back of his shirt as he is kneeling, holding my waist, lips tracing my treasure trail, dipping his tongue into my belly button. And I am starting that whine because I need to touch more, kiss more, love more, and his body is not close enough to me.

"Archie, don't run," I beg.

"Never from you," he says. "Only toward your pleasure."

These are things we do, things we have done in the fifteen months we have been together, and now we come to something very important. It is not exactly the same each time. Sometimes he kisses my dick head, sometimes his tongue traces the glans rim. Sometimes he takes that head in his mouth, sucks, pulls out with a soft but distinct pop. Sometimes he holds my balls, weighs them, or tilts his head to lick the hair and the heat there.

Despite all these variations, we both somehow know they mean the same thing. Archie is saying, in his way, "I want you inside me." And I am saying, out loud, "Archie. Archie."

He has to stand back then, and I kick off my wet Chucks. I pull him up and start snatching, pulling at belt and buttons and pants legs and every piece of his clothes I can get to. At points he helps, at others he lets me do it, and in all of this, he moves both of us to our floor-flat bed.

Before summer ended, we bought a king-size extra mattress to make our sleeping arrangements more comfortable—hell, make our fucking more pleasurable—and soon enough we are there, and I am on top, pulling him up to my chest with one arm, kissing and nuzzling and warming in his heat. I lay him down, position myself between his muscled thighs. Our cocks, rock hard, press flat across each other's bellies as the kisses continue.

"Archie, I love you. That's what my body says. It speaks my heart."

"Then let our hearts converse," he says. "And in the meantime, fuck the hell out of me."

Next to our bed is a box about the size of one for men's shoes but made of wood. Here is where we kept our condoms (until we were sure we would not be fucking anyone but each other). It also has a few sex toys, bought more for amusement than use. And there is always a good-sized bottle of lube, frequently replaced through mail order since the off-campus pharmacy seems to ignore it has a gay clientele to service.

Service? Oh yes, my service.

Bottle now in hand, I move down Archie's body, kisses along the way, occasional detours and backtracks to do a little worrying of his nipples, now pumped up on his chest. I "walk" the dividing center line of his softly defined abs to that tower of joy, his cock. I lift my head in tribute, then place my lips right at its tip.

This is the beginning of Archie's torment. As I ever so slowly widen my pout to get more and more of his dick in my mouth, I pop open the click top of the lube bottle and liberally wet my fingers. He knows I am doing this.

As my mouth is at the glans's corona, sensitive as fuck, I put one hand on an asscheek and push his legs up. He knows this.

I let one hand touch and moisten his ball sack; the other props up his ass. He knows this, and so he pulls his lower half up so I have more access.

Now I move my hand from the balls down his taint and to the tight circle of his asshole. Oh, does he know this, but I tap one finger, no entry; tap, no entry; and tap again. I can look up, mouth full of peen, and see him gasp, his head rocking side to side. He may be muttering something. It's in some other language, but I can understand it anyway.

He's saying, "This is fucking hot. Oh yeah!"

Now, sliding my mouth up and down his prick, I begin the invasion. One finger, nail trimmed and tip tilted to avoid scraping, is pushed inside him on a count of, say, ten. I stay there, twist my finger, press the ball of the digit into the soft sides as I wet him. I will pull my finger out—to his consternation—and rewet with lube, then use it to again lubricate him inside. Then two fingers. Then three.

Words are failing us. I've got him grunting now, and we are both slick with sweat. Archie is even pumping his legs a bit to get that sex-rock feeling going. And so I withdraw hands from hole, lips from dick; I kneel up and position myself between his legs. I put my cock right up against the opening to his chute.

And I look down at him and I say, "I love you, Archie." I always say this, because it is always important for him to know that I do love him. I love him before the elation of sex and during it and long after.

At this point the foreplay has caused a fever. I lean into the heat. I enter.

I try to take it slow, but my African prince is spirited, and he pulls me down and curls himself up toward my crotch to cut the entry time. Once I am fully in, I reposition, forearms along his sides, hands on shoulder blades, and I begin the loving movement of the stroke.

The long stroke makes our lovemaking sweeter, and I feel the sweat bead on my back. The quick, machine-gun stroke has him groaning, though it actually delays me from coming. So I hit him with a flurry of slam-bams, then slow stroke, repeating without uniformity. He moans his approval.

A few minutes in, I pull back and flip him over, pull his powerful ass up and fuck doggy style. I grab that night-stick dick, and it pulses with my fuck. This is where it gets super hot, because here Archie comes, whining and groaning, pumping himself back toward me as I hold on. He jerks through orgasm, soaking the sheets on that new mattress. Finally his head is pressed into a pillow, and his body seems exhausted. "Love you," he says. But I don't stop. Instead, I slowly pump again. And he says through a sigh, "Fuck me."

And Archie is up to the task again. After a few more strokes, I lean to my left side, taking us down to a spoons position. This tends to be my favorite—I'm not on my knees, I pull his back to my chest, I can reach down and pump his dick with my hand, and I can get all up in there. We fuck and moan and breathe and fuck for some time longer.

We can come down after coming, still holding each other, wet with each other, giddy with love reaffirmed, till exhaustion pulls me out of him and we fall into sleep.

Intercepted missive 394: Wee Willie Winkie's on the prowl, approaching my laddies' chamber. Who's that knockin'? Uh-oh, Richard, don't answer. Strange stirrings in the outskirts. All on our team will soon enter the game, but the other side's got reinforcements yet to be named. What do they think they know, and what can we replace it with? Time for diversion incursion, or do we sit tight like rare earth?

Holy schnikies! Ahmmy Boy needs to look into this.

CHAPTER 17
AHMED (AGAIN)

OH MECCA! The muck's hit the fan!

There is a prime rule of secrets: Keep the party list short. Too many people in the know means too little control, too much chance of leaks or betrayals. They can come from the accountant who has all the mob's shakedown records. Or the political aide who is in the room for the felonious phone calls. Or the secretary who is let go and takes the company laptop with her on a thumb drive. Or the one honest person who can't hide the lies anymore.

Added together, the probability grows for disclosure and disaster.

Yet keeping quiet is not part of my people's nature. Kush has adopted Mother Africa's historic societal rule, the consensus. We choose as our leaders those Nubians that all Nubians support. Those leaders meet in their consensus halls to debate, discuss, and delegate what must be done. They agree to agree, and they consider until agreement is unanimous. And the rest of us concede to follow the consensus.

A lot of this consensus shit ain't so hard to reach when you have an all-seeing god dropping edicts on you like spring rain. The priests, predictors, and hierophants are always eager to let the leaders and the laity know what the Sun Lord has decreed. And how do they always agree on what the messages mean? Who knows? (Though it may be what they're smoking.)

Even our stratagem is itself a consensus vote; it's just that only a few of us make up the consensus. Pharaoh-to-be and qore and me, plus a couple of high prelates to be named later. That's it. The Nubian masses only know that we have a goal, and that goal is saving life on Earth. That keeps them motivated and accepting without all the sticky vagaries, doubts, and questions.

What's the secret now in danger, and how did it get out? Blame it on the missives.

It seems our inside jokes weren't inside enough, or our confusing conversations somehow gave up some clues. Probably the mentions of love and sports, meant to be fun distractions, instead led our dupes toward the truth.

This is what I know.

After the usual chatter among the parties we are preying on, a message pops up in one spy group or another. Which one doesn't matter. What does matter is that a few words are scraped out of the thicket of their speculation. These words include "team," "couple," and "America."

Can you imagine the scene? Perhaps some window-walled room of an executive office. Weak morning light outlines hyper-modern furniture and a thick gray rug. It leaves a small square of shine on the resident executive's bald head. A minion (there are always minions) enters quietly, notes in hand. The executive, sharkskin suit tight and buttoned, glares across an acre of desk—a walnut cutting board for the nuts of those who do not please. The minion reads his report. The prime sentence is this:

"We believe there is a team, maybe a couple of agents, with these materials. They are somewhere in America."

Another group, perhaps not far from Beijing's Forbidden City, intercepted this convo like we did. They throw another log on the fire—the team is not currently in Africa and it is not part of the American government.

The pursuers' search has left Suakin and landed on Plymouth Rock. We may need the captive djinn of the coral city to break free and save us.

The next missive-made session may be in the basement of an old government building, all dark granite and chilled air. A dictator's prime henchman glowers at the scuttling informer who has spent days reanalyzing all the missives and bad guesses about missives that they could gather. Their glasses are fogging; sweat slides under their genderless uniform coat. They pronounce, "The Red Sea is a red herring. We do not believe we are dealing with any African government known to us."

"No surprise," the strongman sneers. "There's no African sophisticated enough to pull these deals off." There is no lack of bigotry against the motherland in this authoritarian crypt. "Is that all?"

"But there is a pair in America, somehow involved in a sport, and they have intimate knowledge of what we are seeking."

The strongman smiles. The gleaming teeth flash sparks on the slick wall and scare off the shadows.

The info of that info session spills out and circulates through spy discovery to spy discovery, and though our intercepted missives tried a flea-flicker maneuver to shake them off, two new words appear: middle and west.

Someone doesn't understand US regions, like the Midwest. Maybe they are searching in central Wyoming, sort of the middle of the West.

Columns (always columns) and whitewashed paneled doors are the face of a national leader's governmental residence. The public areas have shut down for the evening. The private rooms, historically furnished, have a gravity in themselves. Even in robe and PJs, the leader exudes respect and authority. A small group has gathered in his sitting room late this night to share their data.

"We don't know why our allies would keep this from us," a cabinet secretary says, her eyes flashing anger. "It could also be one of those corporate creeps with more billions than brains. But whoever it is, they have someone working on something in the US Midwest. Maybe a private lab. Maybe a small company."

Holy schnikes! Maybe a lab. Maybe a company. Maybe, just maybe, us.

I am composing my resignation letter to Burriers right now. I'm planning a quick call to Kush Central. And I'm dropping a message—a very secret, circuitous message—to my guy at Pardell.

Intercepted missive 355: Look to the east. Look to the west. We're not there so fuck the rest. Nanna-nanna boo-boo, can't catch me. And who says it's two? Maybe it's three. Or three hundred. You keep pursuing, we'll keep ahead. We'll light you up like Spielberg's Devils Tower. Close encounters? You think you got us? Wrong, said Fred.

CHAPTER 18
TAHARQA

IT DOESN'T take Ahmed or three wise men to tell me the time of great challenge has come. I've tried to avoid it, but it has to be. I have two overpowering concerns: Branden Hickcock, whom I love and would protect from all harm, and our stratagem, which I must complete no matter what harm we may face.

The time is here. There are words to be said. I have to deal. And as coincidences go, it is before I decode Ahmed's warning, even before I know Kush is creating a false trail in the West to deflect attention from us, that I realize what I must do.

The challenge of truth starts calmly enough with another lie. Brand and I are discussing our sophomore meteorology labs. Our lectures are scheduled at different times, but we can check into the lab building at any time it's open. He knows he can come with me, but I need to not arrive with him.

"My lab teaching assistant wants to be there when we come in," I prevaricate. "I think it's best that I do his early evening lab. Then I can come join your workout at the rec center."

It sounds good to me, but I'm being a bareassed liar. I am not meeting anyone at the lab; I am working silently without Ahmed in a darkened room to avoid detection. Meanwhile, with the college grappling season over—Branden took second place at the conference wrestling meet both freshman and sophomore years but didn't go to nationals—my man works out diligently, but he could do it at any other time with me. I even get on the mat with him sometimes. (How can I resist what that singlet is showing across his tight belly?)

"What's this TA's name?" Brand asks. I don't know why he should want to know.

"Pete Smith." It's the real name for that muscle-headed frat jock who acted all tough in our opening lab session.

"Obviously an alias," Brand tosses back.

"Why do you say that?" I respond too quickly. He stares at me. I feel suspected. I'm sure he wants to know what I'm hiding. I don't meet his eyes. Finally he speaks.

"It's an alias 'cause that name is too common." I am still well beneath the flight line of his logic. "There must be half a dozen Pete Smiths in this town alone, so I'm saying he gave that as a fake name to hide his criminal past." Blank stare from me. "You get it? It's a joke."

It's far too much like me to miss a joke and set off Branden's suspicions at the same time.

Why am I so shocked at his comment? Because I know there is no early evening lab, but does he? How would he?

Students finish by 5:00 p.m. on weekdays, noon on Saturday. I have made it a habit to hang back and make sure one of the building's back doors isn't locked. The stupid, trusting Midwestern staff don't check. So if I can get in when I want—and I can—I can get the class assignment out of the way and check out the lab equipment we need for our rare-earth testing. Some rooms even have prototypes directed toward reversing climate change, models that might be the next generation of ecology machines… unless my peoples' efforts at better technology make these advances obsolete before they can be deployed.

Only how do I do this secretive work with an untrained, at-risk, innocent American looking on? (And looking scrumptious.)

The next evening, which is the next chance I get, I make my move to sneak away. No point in delaying my ruse further, and if I make it a habit, maybe he'll get used to the game, accept it, and ignore it.

I don't excuse myself after dinner. Instead I act as the table's busboy by carrying our meal trays back to the cafeteria's collection area. Then I slip away quickly while Brand unwittingly waits for my return.

I am out the dorm door swift as a gazelle, and I make my way past the southeast arm of the X-shaped dorm (of course it's called SEX), avoiding the not-yet-melted snow piles, and plot my path to reach rear of the Neal Arnstrom Labs building. The alley is basically empty and quite dark in lingering dusk at this time of year. But after I cross the street, and as I pass through the alley toward the unlocked back door, I see someone is standing outside.

I first decide to wait him out. He decides to wait as well, apparently. He paces, keeps looking around like he might catch somebody. I sneak a closer view. Then I give up, since I now know the pacer is Branden. How did he know? And how long?

"So what's up with this?" he asks with hurt in his voice. "Why'd you ditch me?"

No way out of this one. "Something I need to do alone."

"And you don't want to tell me? We love each other. We share. Even if we can't be together, I like to be told."

I recognize that phrase. It's from a song Brand told me about from his childhood. A song for adults about children's needs, sung by the saintly Mr. Rogers, I can't argue with it.

"And there's no one here, no Pete Smith TA." He brings the hammer down. "Or did you two break it off when you saw me here?"

Now them's fightin' words.

"Branden, I would never cheat on you, and that is no lie." I take a deep breath before my swan dive off his respect for me. "The truth is, I have lied. Several times. But only to protect you."

"Protect me? From what?" It's as if he swells, muscles popping to show he's got defenses. "I got big-boy pants—I can take it. What are you protecting me from?"

"From who I am and what I must do." Next I ask the stupidest question. "Can we leave it at that?"

I see the rage flush his cheeks and fill his eyes with fire.

"You are always saying there are words to be said," he snarls, "so you had better say them now."

"I guess so," I say. "We should talk in here."

"I said there's no—" He's surprised when I jiggle a handle and the door pops opens.

"Here," I say, "let's get inside." Branden passes me and enters, keeping his anger aimed directly at my heart. What have I done? Okay, I know what I've done. But can I ever be forgiven for it?

The building's central hall is dark and quiet. The heat's been turned down, and the chill is invasive. Or is that the chill from Branden's stare? I sit on the cold tile floor, touch his arm to have him join me. He yanks the arm away, still staring, and squats down a few feet away.

Time to get this over with.

"I am Nubian, called Taharqa, named for the pharaoh, descendant of Kush."

"So you've said."

"Yes, but Kush is no dead legend. Kush is real and alive still."

The look on his face is clearly saying "Do you think I'm that fucking stupid?"

"Empires fell and invaders ravaged, but one advanced branch of the remaining Nubians of Kush moved to the Nuba Mountains. The aeries and the valleys are forgotten terrain, unpaved and unexplored. And what is underneath them is known only to us. There we relocated our libraries. There we hid our treasures. There, among many other peoples unaware of our presence, we keep a quiet watch on the world, learning what we can, teaching each other what we know."

"Man!" Branden's shout echoes down the hallway. "Don't be tellin' me you are from some imitation Wakanda!"

"Not Wakanda. Not imitation. Real people with an established history as old as man."

Brand's head is shaking like he's trying to toss the words out of his ears.

"I know it's unbelievable," I say. "Unbelievable and true. And here's something that sounds just as imaginary as those the marvelous movies and comic books. We have access, sole access, to a resource much needed in the outside world."

Brand's laugh is bitter. "Vibranium?"

"No such creation," I say. "Ours is something real but equally as valuable. Rare-earth metals. Remember freshman chemistry?"

This mention stops his knee-jerk rejection.

"Rare earths aren't rare," I say. The next we say together. "But getting a useful amount is rarely possible." Score one for our chem prof.

"Not impossible where I come from," I continue. "We have hills of pure scandium, valleys of dysprosium. They are, in the main, unadulterated and ready for use. And very, very valuable."

"For real?"

"For real. I can show you some."

"Where is it?"

"In our room."

Brand's face is now all confusion.

"Remember the trunk, the one Ahmed said has all my gold and precious gems."

He takes a breath. "You mean I've been tripping over rare-earth metals for nearly two years?" I nod an affirmative.

"But why? And how? And how come no one knows? Or who does know? Or—"

"Many questions, my man, but it takes time to answer them. Let me say it this way. We people of Kush understand the value of these resources, and we have seen the cost that rare resources put on native lands. We will not be raped. We will not be robbed. Not again. We will not be recolonized. We stay inaccessible to keep the vultures and jackals at bay. We must keep the materials secret until they become our strength to protect us.

"But we also know something is needed in the world. So in the name of Kush and its history and its culture, we are quietly testing our resources, looking not only at today's uses but also at future technology to feed the world like the Nile floods have fed humanity for centuries."

"Wow." My man is duly impressed. "Wow. Like… what?"

"Imagine a solar panel that converts not eleven to fifteen percent of the sun's energy, but sixty or eighty percent or more. Think of medical imaging devices that can detect cancer cells at the one- or two-cell level. Think of chemicals that reverse the effects of aging. Imagine electric cars with no mileage limits, and solar batteries that supply an entire continent's energy needs.

"Climate, computers, high technology. All use rare earths and want more than industries can get hold of currently. We can fill those needs, but only on Kushite terms and under Kushite control.

"We don't need oil barons, corrupt generals, or greedy politicians on our backs. The world has too many of them, and if we get this right, we might reduce their numbers while we improve life for everything on the planet."

"Bruh, you paint a pretty picture."

"I signed on for this. I was trained for it. You could say I was born into it."

"You're sharing this with me now, so I've got to be a part of it." Brand's face is eager; he's crossed the space that angry Brand had set between us. "So where do I fit in?"

I look into those deep, dark eyes. "You are my love, this is my life, and I can't live without you," I say. "We now work together to accomplish the mission and complete the stratagem."

"The others, your compatriots or your superiors, how are they gonna take that?"

"The only way they can: to let me do this my way. Now let's get down to the meteo lab. You remember this week's lab assignment?"

"Shit no," Brand says. "I could run back and get it."

"No. Never mind," I say. "We have enough to do here. Just a few tests." I pull out a small plastic bag holding a silvery white substance. "We'll have more to do tomorrow and maybe the next day. We can get meteorology homework one of those nights."

Brand rushes ahead, my earnest assistant. I was determined to do this stratagem work alone. Then I was so happy we could do it as a team. But with Ahmed's warning and the dangerous shadows that we know are chasing us, I am much less happy, much more concerned.

The words have been said. Threatened future, here we come.

Intercepted missive 399:
The team is complete
The word's not the street
The plot turns up hot.
Pursuers are s-not.

Coming up—money squawks. The opposition organizes, but it's plan stinks of old newspapers. So we all can check in on one dog chasing its tales.

CHAPTER 19

In other parts of the world

THE TECH near-trillionaire is smiling. Having almost unlimited wealth will do that. But he is not smiling happy.

Is it his aircraft-carrier-size yacht that displeases him? Is his control of several online services, supplying him with the toothpaste preferences and dismal sex-life details of any breathing homo sapiens, not delightful? Does his fake-friendly competition with other tech near-trillionaires disappoint? All those meganerds look silly to him, and they attract more news coverage than a tsunami swallowing Manhattan.

No. The problem is missives. These damn awful, stupid-confusing "intercepted missives" that his sources—always unnamed—have been supplying him in recent weeks, months, years. No one knows where they are coming from. No one knows who they are intended for. And most of all, no one really knows what all this gibberish, inside humor, and popular-jargon misquoting is supposed to mean.

They are worse than QAnon. And for the secret conglomerate of rare-earth-metal suitors forever to be known as Amalgamated, they are just as perniciously addictive.

Intercepted missive 401: One potato, two tomatoes, three caBezos, four. Whatcha see looking down from your space dick, huh? Zuck sucks and we hates the Gates. Gobi kinobi, the Force is failing. Aussies, dowse the barbie: You're only shrimps anyways, mate. It's still Istanbul, can't stand to topple. Saudis not sad, eh? Russian and pushin', Putin and lootin'. And what's that Musky smell? Call Oprah!

SEE! IT'S meaningless, mindless mush. Unless it isn't.

Everybody knows the tech near-trillionaire's phallic missile is active. But how does this pseudo-comic missive writer know that missile is searching the planet, looking for someplace pure rare earths are being secretly mined? How many pictures of central Wyoming has he trained its cameras on? How many Laramie labs have his forces infiltrated, with no results beyond the efficacy of bull sperm? His spies have followed every pair of Ethiopians, Eritreans, Egyptians, and Libyans anywhere near Devils Tower. You'd think that would be easy, except several have given his guys the runaround till his spies find they are following somebody else's spies. And he's zoomed in on the state's universities so often, they all should charge him for season tickets.

And then there's that dismissive comment alluding to fake-friendly competitors who are Amalgamated board members. And then there's a hint of another fake-friendly competitor about to join the fray? (Gotta get him as an Amalgamated board member, even if he can't program his electric cars to stop crashing into things. Maybe his satellite net is catching something.)

Gawd, this was so gawd-awful. The tech near-trillionaire is so frustrated, he may be ready to turn the search for the missive interceptor over to the US government. The FBI and the CIA are a lot better at this than most. The problem is they can't keep something like this a secret. By law they can't. That means it's tricky… but not impossible.

The tech near-trillionaire calls a board meeting, and somehow, dropping everything (like buying golf courses to cheat at or acquiring water rights to monopolize), all the Amalgamated leaders come. And they all talk and drink and slap backs and describe their trophy wives. It looks like a *Squid Game* reunion.

"Which wise guy likes the motion on the table?" the tech near-trillionaire asks.

"What motion, sir?" asks another, putting down his Cointreau and soda.

"Come on, the motion to have something done about this missive bastard."

"Something must be done!" shouts a third, waking up.

"Yeah. So do something!" The group is finally moving away from the canape table.

"Yeah. But who's gonna pay for it?"

Now who let that spoilsport in here? Silence falls like a hatchet. Everyone looks around the board room. Seconds tick by, yet no one speaks. Then…

"Get the government to pay for it." This is echoed quite bravely around the table.

"We *have* the government paying for it," the tech near-trillionaire says. "I mean, really, the governments are us." That sets off a lot of mumbled assents and congrats around the room.

"Anyway," says the tech near-trillionaire, "let's have the voters endorse our strategy in this situation."

"Hey," asks a board member, "what is our strategy?"

"To make someone else responsible for what we should be doing."

Intercepted missive 432: How they spent their summer vacation—an essay ecstatic. An old mistake becomes a new direction. So a fable of firm foibles grows into a glassy glow of glory. But alphabetacomically, only you know the whole story.

CHAPTER 20
BRANDEN

THIS SUMMER, between sophomore and junior years, Archie and I are in the suburbs of Chicago working as interns at separate small ecology-directed firms. Archie's employer concentrates on battery recycling—which means he's popping the caps on the Energizer bunny's waste products. Me, I'm working in the solar-panel business, but you won't find me on any roofs like Brad Pitt with bare chest and a power tool in my hand.

My job sounds a lot sexier than Archie's, but my main activity is categorizing, numbering, scanning, and storing years' worth of schematics for the products and tools the firm has made in years past. The industry is growing rapidly, but this little firm was never good at recordkeeping.

Like I've said, I grew up with history, and some of these plans go so far back they tell a story of technical development. But there are so many, and some are merely faded photocopies or crude hand-drawn memories of copies. I need to blow the chaff off this wheat, not only for history but because current designers, engineers, and the manufacturing plant connected to them need to access this shit, like, yesterday.

Our plant and office complex are in one of those faceless megabuildings you see from the interstate—gray metal, gray cement, gray parking lot, gray roof, gray outlook. We have windows, but just barely. No problem—ain't nothin' t'see. And who knows what's jammed into all the other cubbies slotted into this giant doughnut box.

Slotted into my half-walled cubicle, I am left for hours at a time, half buried in paper and struggling to stay awake. And at times an engineer, a boss, or a secretary breezes in needing "This design, not that one," and "This is one we got rid of years ago," and they're plowing through my carefully arranged piles and categories and leaving me to clean up the mess.

The life of an intern.

And then there's Albert. Albert is (at this point in my story) a salesman, and a pretty lousy one. Paunchy, with a hook nose, in his forties, and cheaply dressed, he looks like a recently fired Walmart stocker, not someone I'd buy anything from. He usually ignores me, the lowly intern, but when he doesn't, he'll wheeze out a smile and call me "OJ." Not good. Not at all good.

Oh, Albert brings in customers—by lying. "You're seeking energy savings? You need a piece of glass panel and this kind of tool to attach it?" he tells them. "Well, we can get that tool to you in a week. Sign up with us for all your tool and glass needs."

When the customers call after a week, they find that not only do we not have a tool or panel like that, no one does. And to develop ones that work and fit in tight spots and don't break on first use and yet supply the required tension takes weeks if we have no other projects in development, months because we do.

So who is the tool, then?

I can't really complain, but our boss does. A second-generation manufacturer, he hates the backtracking he has to do with these reasonably irate clients. Still, some of the duped customers appreciate our other products and stay. And I get the chance to do actual work on product development and testing because the firm is so strapped for qualified help.

"I did torque tests for a left-handed solar-panel power wrench today," I tell Archie one night.

"Great," he said, "can you test my torque for me?"

Archie has many such tests, which I always ace. Yes, that's pronounced with a long *a*.

One day, each of three secretaries asks me about a very particular solar panel once used in a particular experiment some years in the past. For some reason, Albert is very eager to get several of these panels. There is a part number, but it isn't among the items I've already logged into the computer. It isn't in the schematics on my desk either, or lost in some old file cabinets.

Finally I go down the corridor to ask the plant workers, who are always the employees who know the most about what's been built and rarely get the respect they deserve for that knowledge. And they are unquestionably the people almost no executive ever talks to.

Entering a space of machine smells and fluorescent light, I find a small group of guys near a glass-cutting machine and give them the description I got from the secretaries. One old hand named Richard stops me. He takes me over to a dusty stack on a back shelf in the warehouse area. A sticker on the top of the stack provides a stern warning: Discontinued. Recycle. Do Not Use.

Richard slides out one of the panels, not black glass like your usual solar receptor. This one was about one foot by two and mottled gray with tan sparkles. "This what ya lookin' for?" he asks. He's got a tobacco-stained smirk that says he knows I don't know shit about this panel.

I hold it in my hand. This is it; I am sure. And I am about to take the piece up front when that warning smacks me in the forehead.

"Thanks, Richard. I think I'll leave it here."

Back I trot to the secretaries, and I tell them all the same thing. Such a panel exists, but it was ordered discontinued and unusable. It's supposed to be recycled.

I guess word got to Albert. Word, that is, that didn't include the full meaning of Do Not Use, because Albert goes into the plant himself. He gets Richard to show him the warehouse shelf. And he decides to take the panels, every last one of them, and haul them to his car. They have some weight, and it takes him three trips, and that's after Richard warns him and gets cursed out for his trouble. Richard goes back to work, a grim smile on his face, and the rest of the assembly guys do too. All of them shake their heads, hoping that this time that a-hole Albert will get his.

That was a Thursday, and come Monday, after a gorgeous sunny weekend for two gay dudes on the shores of a twinkling blue Lake Michigan, I glance up see to Mark, the VP of production, storming toward my desk with a face as dark and angry as a Saharan sandstorm. Under his arm are a couple of those mysterious panels. He tosses them near—but nearly at—me.

"What do you know about these!" he demands.

"That they are discontinued, supposed to be recycled." I wear my most sincere I-didn't-do-it demeanor. Well, I didn't do it, did I?

"Recycled? And how did boxes of them get delivered to some of our newest US customers?" Maybe my demeanor isn't innocent enough?

"I-I don't know," I stutter. "I told Vera and Laura and Maggie all the same thing. It was on a shelf, stickered and marked Do Not Use."

He doesn't wait to clear my desk before he shouts, "Vera? Laura? What's going on?" And his gale of outrage blows off in that direction.

Well, it's not like I try to eavesdrop, but the conversation (if aggressive shouting can be called conversing) is all over our small business office. The VP is demanding. Vera, who looks like Gwen Verdon and takes less guff than Charlize Theron, yells back. The story evolves to include that all the women relayed my info and warnings to Albert, but—by this time Richard was up front—Albert took the can of worms despite the entire plant's objections.

Albert drags in at about ten thirty this morning—salesmen can always claim they have morning sales visits with potential customers keeping them out of the office—and is immediately engulfed by the VP's rage.

"Hey, hey, hey," Albert says, hands up like he's blocking blows. "I was looking out for this firm. Do you understand how much business I got by giving them a hot sample?"

Mark, already in Albert's face, pushes past the hands, grabs the sloppy 250-pound sack of man, and rattles him like a cocktail shaker.

"Hot sample? Do you understand?" he shouts "Can you possibly understand how many people you may have killed with this hot sample? It's deadly!"

The ladies have to pull him off Albert, who is quickly directed to hide in the boss's office. Meanwhile, the boss, who is the founder's son, has witnessed the assault. Because Mark took physical action against another employee, he is summarily fired.

Mark takes it well, says he understands, and apologizes to the entire office. But before he leaves, the former VP says this: "Make sure that son of a bitch tells you who got these panels."

Immediately on Mark's departure, the boss turns back to Albert, who is pacing behind the office's glass window like a metal duck in a shooting gallery. Voices are heard, and then shouts. (This office is no more soundproof than the cubicles.) Why did Albert go after this panel? Who told him about it? Didn't he know about the panel's failure? Didn't anyone tell him?

Under one of the last projects of his late father, the boss says, this company had tried to build a super panel that could collect the most solar energy in the quickest manner, but it has a fatal flaw. Fatal in that the energy cannot be controlled. Fatal in that, attached to a roof, within minutes, the roof is on fire. Fatal in that, even installed on the ground, its energy cracks the glass and scorches the earth around it. And no installer would know that fact, not until the sun shines and the heat rises, and the panel blazes, and a whole plant or retail store or housing subdivision goes up in an instant inferno. The panel is so dangerous, the boss shouts, his father stopped production, took retirement, and lived, heartbroken, by himself and with his failure until he died.

Albert doesn't know this. Or so he says. And Richard, ambling by the window, shouts, "I told him so!" His ambling carries him back through the plant door and out of this tale.

So how many customers got this "gift" from Albert? Well, Albert doesn't know that either. Not offhand. He knows he sneaked into the firm's delivery office over the weekend, got into the address lists, and used the company shipping account to send out every one of the failed prototypes he had pulled off the shelf.

The boss doesn't wait for Albert to finish his narrative about how long it took to do this and how his hand hurt from sticking on all the preglued address labels. The boss fires him right then. He doesn't let Albert clean out his desk or say goodbye, just "Get the fuck out!"

Albert is too stupid to be hurt, only angry. On his way to the door, he looks at me as a part of his betrayal.

"OJ, I thought we had each other's back!" he shouts.

I look up from my work and smile. "But I'm on good paper. I don't need anyone to have my back, *Alvin*."

He snarls and storms out.

Mark, on his way back to clean out his own desk, sees Albert in the parking lot and breaks the ex-salesman's hooked nose. Since they are no longer company employees, there is no further job action.

In fact, Mark joins us, including all the hands outside the plant, in calling every business on the customer list and begging them to destroy the panels Albert sent them.

Archie listens attentively, smiling as I relate my day, and he laughs out loud at the on-the-beak ending. But when I have finished, he's still pondering something about my tale.

"I wonder," he says, "how we could get a hand on one of those panels."

"Why? You think there's something useful there?"

"It could very well be," he says. "Perhaps they came up with that most sacred quest."

"Unlimited energy," I chime in. I have been learning my lessons working with my tech master Taharqa. We've found some highly reactive compounds of rare-earth metals. Along with Ahmed, who has relocated to someplace we can reach only by satellite phone, we're researching ways to collect that energy without burning up. We are close, but even with us sneaking into each other's company for testing and info gathering, we aren't there yet.

"Yeah, those panels might have held the secret," I say. "However, the phone calls got to everybody who received a panel. We even listened over the phone on speaker to hear the panels break. I don't think any business will try to use its panel, so we are spared a human disaster or even a lawsuit."

"But left with a mystery in broken glass," Archie muses.

"Maybe," I say, "maybe not. You let me drive the car today, so there's one panel, one of those that Mark tossed at me, locked in your trunk."

Archie beams. "Well, fu-uck me!"

"Sure," I say. "It's my turn tonight." And I grin.

Archie can smile so sweetly before he does excitingly nasty things.

"You think Mom is asleep?" I ask.

"I think she won't hear," he says, moving in for a kiss. "Or mind if she does. Let's do it."

Intercepted Missive 499: A-tinkle a-turkle, evil at work-el. Boys, rest up and rest well. Anger is bubbling like radiation soup. Tests turn testy. Some tricks are upcoming, and mistakes must follow.

CHAPTER 21

In a scary part of the world

"WE HAVE had enough of this Western nonsense: maligning missives, missing missions! We are too important to be minimized!

"For months we have gathered information, pored over coded documents, stood as the butt of jokes we don't even comprehend. All in search of rare earths and our right to them.

"It is our right as the real heirs to the former empire of the East to have and produce and sell and hoard these earths. We have more right than all the others who want them.

"I mean, these earths are all over, so why can't we have some, some we can use?"

This the strongman in the charcoal suit says, passing before his fine leather chair. His hands sweep the granite room set secretly beneath ancient relics of an even more ancient city; his voice booms in the corners. His audience is all silent attention.

"The feeler put out by Amalgamated is an insult. Why should our government cooperate with them? And why do we need our government to do what our network of the faithful can do alone? What do those corporate crooks and corrupt countries have that we don't? Okay, they got a chunk of that pure stuff, but that was three years ago. What have they done for themselves lately, much less for anyone else?

"And the rocket man and the EV technocrat? They must be sniffing lithium to think current forms of current-making are the future. Better chemicals are the future. More reuse is the future. Infinite power collection through rare-earth metals is the future.

"We are the future. We just have to find the right neck to squeeze." His black eyes burn with fervor.

The metaphor, if that's what it is, is not lost on this crowd. There are smiles and nods. Hands touch weapons as if they are tokens of ultimate triumph.

"We have knowledge of a new power in this game, and a new power source. Broken bits of glass painted in a fine dust we have recovered near solar businesses all over the States, but they were acquired too late to piece the whole event together.

"Yet someone does have the whole of it. A concoction prepared from one or two of the dread products can become lightning in a bottle. Someone out there has that bottle. They sold a drop of elixir to China, a dribble to the Aussies and the Canucks and the Arabs-slash-Americans. Now they sell none of it to no one. Why?"

The strongman's question sits chilled above the heads of the attendees. They wait for him to continue. His stare dares them to move.

"Why? Because they already have new uses for it! They are initiating the betas, rushing through the tests, amassing the research, refining the products. They will choose those who will get these products. And our name is *not* on that list!"

The strongman's long, spindly hands again sweep the room like a scythe. The heads do not turn, but the eyes follow fearfully.

"We must be on that list! We must own that list!"

The strongman pauses, letting the echo of his words die in the corners, reverberate in the ears that hear them.

"We must find the source. We must find the originator of these secret missives. We must locate all the areas of pure rare earths, and we *must* secure them under our control. If we must spy, we spy. If must we betray, we betray. And if must we kill, well, so much the better."

"Send out the spies; infiltrate the groups; interrogate, terrorize, and torture all who might know what or when or how," he shouts. "And know this—the location is not in America. It is in Africa, somewhere near the Red Sea. Go, search, find, and return with what we need!"

In the granite room sit the surveillance experts, the spies, the double agents. There are the corruptors, tempters, deal makers. There are also the negotiators, ransom payers, appeasers. Add in the torturers and assassins, with their reputations in flesh burning, pain enhancement, fear mongering, serial dismemberment, suffocation, and various forms of slow death. And one very large grinning man reaching behind a shoulder bag to stroke the huge knife it covers.

Heavy or thin, sneering or blank, all of them sit silent in the room, and all understand: Do this or die.

Don't get antsy; I'm still here. The missives may be clearer now, like little lights in a shining cave. As we move on, the cavern opens, so the next passages are paths through secrecy and into danger.

Intercepted missive 504: Skies darken along the coasts. Hurricane Terror meets the Aussie sou'easter. Soil hunger hits the billions, and only we collect the coins. Down a lazy river, but who can find the queen, Monty? Who can find the queen?

CHAPTER 22
TAHARQA

I TRIED all kinds of excuses not to return to East Africa this rising-senior summer break. The Covid lockdown has made travel dangerous since February; we should not endanger all Kush with disease this May. Anyway, the school-year work we have done for the stratagem should be enough, I wheedle. We are showing success. We have new assets, new ideas, new paths to follow. Leave us here to keep up with our stratagem; don't pull us back at this important time. (What I don't tell the Kushites is I want another summer in the American city, walks along the lakefront, visits to the festivals, tickets to the concerts, love with my man.)

What finally brings me around is a promise of a shortened stay, my mother's unusual plea to see her child, and my queen's vows of reprisal if I don't fly home this month.

That and the promise that Branden can come with me.

So masked against the virus and enduring two changes of airplanes and an entire morning-to-evening in the air, we arrive at Khartoum's new international airport and its old governmental troubles. We are at the confluence of the White and Blue Niles, in a city of fabled wars and bloody street battles, militia against militia and the local people take the hindmost. It is fair to say I do not feel we are safe in this town.

And not a Covid mask in sight.

Add that we are met, after enduring petty customs inspectors' queries, by a man unknown to me, a security type (but you couldn't exactly say he is a royal bodyguard). He's a huge man with a huge, toothy smile. He is tall in height and big in belly, beard, and manner. He wears a light tan correspondent's jacket and matching pants, a thick brown belt, and a leather bag hanging from a shoulder strap at his side. And for someone I have never met before, he is oh so happy to see us.

"Young prince!" he shouts, "Welcome! Welcome home! I am Rashid bin Harun. You are Taharqa. And this is your friend Brando?"

"Branden, friend and roommate," Branden says. We had agreed on those designations to spare us what horrors could easily come to gay men in Islamagulch: Arrest. Prison. Canings. Executions. Murder.

"We shall see about that," Rashid laughs. And before I can respond to the implied threat, he shouts, "Let us go!"

And like that we are platooned into a group of six uniformed men and marched swiftly through crowded corridors and into dark, quiet halls in a private area of the airport.

And here is where the first crisis strikes. Brand and I had decided to take one suitcase each, Sudan's desert weather being better suited to native dress we'd acquire here than the shorts and tees we could bring with us. Rashid points to each bag. "Yours?" he asks, and I nod. "Yours?" he says, and Brand nods.

And suddenly Brand and bag are whisked away.

"What… where… where are you taking him?" I ask in near panic.

"To the five-star hotel," Rashid tosses these words behind him as he and two minions herd my lover off toward a waiting limo. "Very nice. Very comfortable. Western meals. Brando will like." The remainder of the group prods me (without touching) toward an aged Land Rover.

So my lover, called out of his name, is being taken to a tourist resort— not likely a bad place, but well away from where I know I will be. Or where I can see him, be with him, protect him.

Rashid returns, and my group takes off. I am alone, not sure how to combat this affront. I suffer silently rather than insist on my demands, needing my man's support. I am sped away, lost and distraught. As the Rover's driver, scared-shitless eyes under his skullcap, tries to navigate what Khartoum calls nighttime traffic, I can't think of anything except that I must correct this offense. The high priests must change this; Queen Amanirenas must reverse this order. I will demand—

Minutes later, we suddenly turn onto a small dock in the dark at the outskirts of the city. It leads to the legend, the great White Nile. Why are we here?

"Wait! We're on the river?"

I am completely confused. While I thought we'd be heading to some Sudanese suburb, Rashid is all business, hustling me off to the riverbank. My bag and one of my escorts are soon on a waiting motorboat. How did that get here?

"Yes, boat. Very fast. Very nice. And the best way, I am told, to get you home where you should be."

"We are meeting south?" I am moving as slowly as I can, trying to stall and gain information while supplying little in return. I am hoping to delay a separation that will put Brand and me four hundred miles farther apart.

"Qore's orders. Very hush-hush. Prince Taharqa comes. Brando not welcome."

I'm about to object, both to the disinvite and the corruption of my man's name, when my phone rings.

It's Brand, risking roaming charges and I don't know what pressures. "It's me. I'm in a hotel room in the Corinthia. Are you here?"

I know that place, very modern, built like a lopsided egg. A gift from one dictator (in Libya) to another.

"No. No. They're taking me to, well, to a headquarters." Though I've shared lots of information with Branden since our first lab foray, including all the work we've done on the rare-earths stratagem, I've been holding back some important details, specifically the location of Kush—not just in the Nuba Mountains, but under them.

It's important to keep this from him. The less he knows, the less he can be forced to tell if he's ever taken captive. And may Amun protect him from ever facing that challenge.

"It's a place no one knows is there," I say.

"But when will I see you?"

And suddenly I hear Rashid's booming "Hah!" and he grabs my cellphone. "There will be enough time for that, Brando. You must settle in." Rashid tosses my cell into the boat, where it bounces off a padded seat and splashes heavily into the waters of antiquity.

"So sorry," he shrugs. "Not needed anyway. Amun Ra's high priestess has much for you to do."

And I am pushed bodily onto the boat, barely larger than a weekender's fishing dinghy but outfitted with a makeshift roof and an inboard motor. My escort stays with me. Rashid and the others stand, gladly grinning, to see us off, then turn toward their car.

River travel here traditionally involves feluccas, small boats with white linen sails billowing to catch south winds blowing toward South Sudan and Uganda as the White Nile current flows north, eventually joined by the Blue Nile as they rush to Cairo and the delta of civilization. Blessed be all the holies, this tub is modern and well-kept, probably doing more than twenty miles per hour while skimming the current. So it only takes us more than eighteen droning hours, including stops for well-concealed gas supplies and an occasionally offered snack of millet and vegetables, to get near the border of the new nation of South Sudan.

The truth dawns on me that I'm headed toward the home base of Kush. But that is at considerable distance from the White Nile, so why are we taking it? Could it be that Rashid and his cohort are hired guns with no idea of where I am to meet the qore? My silent boatmate seems quite interested in the surroundings, not as a tourist, but more like a scout collecting data.

As if there's much detail to collect. The fertile banks support farm villages all along the river's length, but since we are not near any town, there's not much to differentiate them. Outside of checking the time between Al This and Al That, he can't be gaining much.

Yet I could be losing. I am at the tiller. If I take him to Kush, I could be betraying my people. There is a rendezvous point where I must find other transportation, but I don't want this thug with me. I decide that I must insist that my escort leave.

Noticing a private dock, I pull over and stop. I then invite him to step off, but when he's out, I turn and restart the motor.

"But how do I get back?" he shouts with none of his commandeering bluster. He is visibly uncomfortable. In truth he is shaking in his Sudanese military uniform, which is a target in this resistance-held area. Whose security is he?

"*You* have a cellphone," I say, dismissing him as I pull away. I rev the engine and lift a sail to the prevailing wind. "Give Rashid a call."

I slide away, but minutes later I kill the outboard again. My little boat, which I have dubbed the *SS Pudrucker*, is tacking quietly along until a collection of cone-roofed huts rises on the western shore. Here, like it has been forever, people make their living and try to survive. My people are among them, and I must work my way to them.

I know there are rendezvous points along the White Nile, places where allies can help me reach home. But I must find one without being noticed. Therefore the silence. Populated spaces are not so good for unobserved approaches by a noisy, very unusual watercraft.

Nubia is prehistoric cattle country, and the land at this point nearest the river is alive with a small herd and a few herdsmen. One of those men is very alive himself; he is waving frantically.

I pull the boat over to the riverbank, sliding it sideways so it might push up partially on soil. I grab my bag and jump off even as my greeter is rushing toward me.

"Hu," he says, touching his chest and identifying himself as old Nubian.

"Hu," I respond, then, with a nod I say, "Kush."

His head nods vigorously as he takes my hand in a powerful grip. We shake, only he doesn't let go. He pulls me forward as we pass along the moist grass and the cow turds, getting only lazy stares from the cattle. My new friend finally pulls me into a shoulder hug and steers me around the nearest hut.

Behind it is an aged but well-kept European truck.

Someone has cared greatly for this precious old beater—the white paint, many times renewed, is pristine. My host propels me toward the driver's side door, then pats the truck's roof like he's petting his prize heifer. He lets my hand go and backs off, allowing me to climb behind the wheel. With no words to say, he waves goodbye, and I crank 'er up and steer off to the west.

It is far too short a drive to get off the green parkway provided by the nurturing White Nile and enter the sands of southern Sudan. And then there is the trip to the scrub-green mountains of Nuba.

The Nuba Mountains look old, hill-like, barely two-thirds the height of the Appalachians. And old they are. In the middle of a near-desert country, this environment has vegetation and domesticated flocks. One can even scratch out a crop during the rainy season. So why were nearly a million people starving there only a few years ago? Blame a jealous government in Khartoum that tried to drive out the Nuba peoples, poisoning their crops and murdering their farmers while the peoples took up arms and the world (and George Clooney) took notice.

At the foothills of this place, I see a mother and child play a hand game among the rocks. I pull up to a rock outcropping, get out, and retrieve my bag, and by the time I round the front end, the two, smiling and nodding, get to the truck's other door. Mother plants daughter in the flatbed, slides across the bench seat from the passenger side, and takes the wheel. In seconds they are gone.

"Farewell, Old Susie," I whisper as a goodbye to my disappearing ride. "And godspeed, SS Pudrucker, wherever they took you after my departure."

I climb an embankment between two green hills, hauling a modern suitcase into a land of goat tracks. It is nearing an end to daylight, but there is enough sun to have me sweating under the effort with this wheeled device in a pathless stretch of low bushes and sparse grass. Viewed from space, I would make a sorry picture, strange and stupid. Until....

The next hill to the right boasts a massive stone outcropping with a low opening at its foot, barely big enough to slip a bag in, and then a man.

The cavern inside takes up all of the interior of the mountain, so much so that I wonder if any foolish lamb would dare to munch ivy on the topside without fear of falling through. Nature and Nubian skill have dug a cathedral out of rock and soil. The walls glitter with their own light as if candles had been carved into them. The floor is cold and smooth as glass.

As for walking in this cave, why do that when electric scooters sit waiting? I snap my bag onto the back rack using bungee cords left there for such purposes. I have nowhere to go but one way. I settle onto my seat and turn a key. Presently I speed into a curving, narrow tunnel, strangely lit without torches or electricity.

These hills are not all honeycombed passageways, but enough are. It is amazing what a few thousand years of human habitation, expertise in rock carving, and a bit of pluck can create.

My path is winding but not treacherous. Along the way there are widenings and narrowings; side caverns used to store secrets or vast libraries of papyrus, paper, and stone tablets; temples to hold worship rites for multiple gods; laboratories performing experiments; entrances and exits. Our priests and viziers maintain our historic knowledge, our high priests add the past to the present, and viziers debate truths as the world ages. They, like Ahmed and I, learn from advanced institutions all over the globe and bring that expertise for use by our people.

No Hu lives totally underground. No one is to be seen going or coming into its caverns. And yet no place outside this interred kingdom is more human, more necessary, or more dedicated as in here.

I slow my machine as I approach another huge cavern, lit up to resemble a cathedral, all of it done with tiny ever-glowing lights. I park the scooter, disembark, and head, suitcase in hand, toward what may be a passage not so brightly lit.

Once I pass through to the other side, I am met by security. They are two tall men in snow-white jellabiyas, linen pants, and skullcaps. They could be any robed men in Sudan.

A third person, a woman in a school uniform, approaches. I go through the motions, play out the smile or solemn nod, say the words to be said, pay respects, be what is expected. In all this time, I have had no thought about how coordinated the legs of my trip have been. We of Kush know our needs and fulfill them routinely, yet as cautiously as a spy network.

I am all rote, not myself, not at this moment. Not as I consciously grow my anger for having Branden taken from me.

I am ushered into the inner chamber, the throne room of our queen, high priestess and worship wife of Amun, qore of eternal Kush. (Like the Brits, our peoples have a special love for our female leaders. Therefore the special names qore, or royal, and *kandake*, or queen-mother.)

Amanirenas is, as always, resplendent. Her visage mirrors Nefertari, Ramses's queen. Her gowns conceal their age in colors rich and dazzling. I'd like to sneak in one morning and find her in PJs.

"Brother Taharqa, greetings."

I'm not having any of that. I barely salute her as queen. I'm attacking my equal with righteous rage.

"Darisis, why has my friend been separated from me?"

"Already with this? Have you no kind words for your qore or your sister-in-fate?"

I meet her eyes, glare for glare. Two powers meant to join forces face off instead. I snarl.

"I want Branden!"

CHAPTER 23
TAHARQA

THE CHILL in this underground African chamber is now cold enough to freeze the Sahara.

"You are named qore, but I am named to be pharaoh, and there will be no difference in rank between us," I remind her. "And yet your prince was greeted by the message that his best friend is uninvited."

"You are telling me he knows of this place?" Her lips barely move; her words echo from the stone walls.

"No, but you and I need not to have met here, four hundred miles from nowhere. Khartoum, Port Sudan, even Suakin could be used."

"Those places are not home. They could not do. Kerma, Napata, Meroë could be home. Instead they are dust." Her eyes turn soft. "Only here, in our only remaining homeland, can you do what must be done. It is your place, brother-in-fate who will be Arensnuphis." For the first time she calls me this, the name of the Kush god, son of Ra, creator of all. "We hired protectors to entertain your friend because he cannot be here at the time of your labors."

"Labors? What—" But then I remember: my ennead, my time of nine. At last? And already?

Across Ancient Egypt and Nubia, temples were built honoring each of nine major deities, Amun and his progeny: Shu and Tefnut, parents of Geb and Nut, parents of Isis, Osiris, Set, and Nephthys. Not all areas dedicated themselves to all in the ennead, but our particular Kushite clan, through its research and cultural belief, came to celebrate an ennead of tasks, nine labors the ultimate leaders of Kush must each complete to earn our position among our Nubian people.

I have always known of the ennead. I was told Darisis completed hers while I was away at school, where she gained the name Amanirenas. I often tried to convince myself I had completed my nine once Taharqa became my name. I would count my achievements: Three times washed in the Nile, was it three times three that they held my head under the sacred waters? (It seems like much more.) Nine times challenged to physical feats by my adopters? (No, that was ten.) Three circuits through underground

Kush in each of three circuits through the Nuba Mountains? (No, those were errands.) Surely meeting mother Abar must count as one task. How about the questions I answered before the hierophants let me out into the modern world? (But why did they always stop at seven?) I could never come up with a proper total. Recruiting Brand was only number eight, or maybe seven, on my most recent task list.

Despite years of training and correction, memorization and holy rites, only one lesson stays with me, and it is the phrase that begins so many magical acts, the phrase I use so freely: The words to be said, or in ancient Egyptian, *djed medu*.

"You are named for a pharaoh of the Nile," Darisis reminds me, "ruler from the confluence to the delta, as your namesake was. Your ennead must be glorious and unbearable. And our priests must watch, judge, and determine if you get a new name or lose the one you have.

"Whatever you have done," and she pauses. "Whatever you and your roommate have done is but part of the stratagem. You must face your ennead and return as Arensnuphis. Either that or be found lacking."

To be lacking is the real threat to all our hopes. We Kushites still on the Earth are few in number but proud of our membership and dependent on each to do their best. To be lacking is to be outcast. Bad enough that I'm a bastard; if I am found lacking, the whole stratagem is a failure.

"The priests will meet with you now." No time to freshen up? "Your vestal mother has advice for you after that. Your ennead begins tomorrow, and once begun must carry on until its end. Only then might you meet with your… friend."

Her majesty doesn't sound like she believes that we are just friends.

"But tell me," she continues, "how goes the stratagem at your school?"

Outraged as I am about the separation from my love, I am eager to debrief her about our progress.

"I'm not sure what Ahmed has told you, but Brand and I are far along in our efforts. We have an extensive algorithm for proportions of solar energy collection, and we constructed a storage device that we believe can power a city for a year." I am smiling despite myself, and she joins me. "Brand cut out various sizes of our collection panel, and with the right rare-earth mixture, we can burn through marble, rival a hydrogen bomb's energy, or heat tea."

"Father Amun's gift waits where he left it for us," she says, offering praise to those above.

"Yes, the gift awaits." And god only knows what that means.

Whether you believe in gods, magic, or pure science, you must know our planet's survival and humanity's destruction both exist within the universe that holds us. In this one example—collection of the sun's energy, "his" energy—there is enough power to burn us all to cinders if we greedily grab for it. A fact that demonstrates that danger: In space the difference in temperature between the white, reflective surface of a space suit turned toward the sun and the surface of that same suit turned to darkness is 275 degrees Fahrenheit. No wonder Branden's employers' solar plate was marked for destruction. But collect a small percentage of that power and you have today's solar cells. Collect too much, you have inferno. Only our learning and care may help us benefit and protect our world.

Amanirenas and I share a salutation to the Creator. Amun has left this world, bequeathing it to us as our home to maintain, improve, or destroy. That is what Kush believes (and I know better than to dispute that belief).

"Brand and I will continue to test various devices under varied conditions," I say, "while Ahmed codes programs and transmits results."

"That is his art." We smile again, as art school was his cover role.

A certain bustle in the entryway interrupts our debriefing. I turn and hear them arriving, high priests and hierophants, here to test me before my trials. Many of these people I know. I grew up under their care and discipline until I became Taharqa. Their names, like mine, were cast forth from antiquity. There is Amenemhat the tutor; fair Ankhaf and Ankmare, who played with me; Khamhor, eternally young and goateed; Ankhnesneferibre, who foster mothered me; Djedkare, who teased; Nitocris, my comforter; Bakenranef, who shamed me, and old Haremakhet, who taught me to think, dream, and fight for the truth. Nine names from imperial Egypt or Nubia, all meant to have meaning for the gods.

Khamhor places a cane-woven chair behind me, and as I sit, the preliminaries begin.

"Prince Taharqa," says Nitocris in her sweet tone, "you are named for conqueror and conquered, the pharaoh who lost and who held forth. Are you ready to face failure and forge success?"

"My path has tested me." As I begin I look into each stoic face, some black, some brown, some fair as a movie Cleopatra. "My teachers have strengthened me. Thy gods await to see that I am worthy."

"What must you do to approach your ennead?" asks Amenemhat.

"I must face truth, flourish strength, value faith."

"And whose faith do you hold?" asks Haremakhet, a frown on his grim wrinkled face. He above all has put this question to me again and again and has dragged the answer out. For a long while, the answers I gave were not what he said the answer must be. My knuckles remember his cane-administered corrections.

"My faith," I start, thinking about what I believe, if I believe in anything at all. I have learned of fascinating things, seen some near miracles, pulled off a few, but is there anything beyond what merely comes out of me? Is there anything that can't be explained with a physics book and a logical mind? What are any of the world's faiths to me? Yet the elders ask about faith, and I must answer truthfully or fail before I start.

What do I believe?

I believe in Branden. I believe in our love and the rightness of it. I believe in that with all that makes up my being. And that is faith—not just the uniting of two humans, but a divine gift in this world.

"My faith," I begin again, "placed within me through whatever the gods wish it to be, holds firm. And they, who know all, will be bathed in the river of my worship in return." Not so explicable a statement, but, thank Amun, it works.

The questioning goes on for maybe an hour. Tactics, learning, expectations. Finally the nine file out, and I am taken to a new room, dark with darker shadows, to sit on a woven bed. I wait, knowing not what is going to happen. I hear soft footsteps, the swish of long fabrics on the stone floor. Soon enough she appears.

"Welcome, Mother Abar."

"Welcome, child of my womb." It's as if she can't stand the concept of my being her son. I accept that now. "It is time for your ennead?"

"Yes, the day breaks tomorrow."

"Then you must rest," she says. "Tonight I deliver to you three gifts."

As she has never given me more than my birth, this is interesting.

"First, I give you your paternity." How is this possible? "Your father drew you through me, just as Ra drew the world through him. I am vestal, so your father must be god. Now you are to be pharaoh, god and son of gods."

Hell, I'm another virgin birth. Jesus, what a discovery!

"Second, as you shall meet our father-gods, I shall give you your purpose through them, which is to rule and to share rule wisely. All power may flow through you. Let it fill those around you and around them and around the rest."

Stranger still. Who will be around me? Branden? Definitely or I won't live. Ahmed? Amanirenas? The nine gods? The countless other deities? All of Kush? I guess I'll learn soon enough.

"Finally, through fathers and mother, purpose and life, we deliver your power. As of now it lies within and will awaken in time after time. It will use you as you use it, so take care to use it well."

"Thank you, Mother."

"Give thanks to the gods, my son." She says it! Son! I smile to myself, finally I'm a man with a family. And when I look up, she is gone, like smoke.

In this room on this plaited bed, I know I must be ready for the next day. In the gloom, I see my suitcase, so I pull it to me, open it, and hear a furious singing in a frenzied scale.

The satellite phone! Brand and I each packed a sat phone, anticipating the now-certain situation that smartphones would not be enough to maintain contact. Branden must have been calling for nearly twenty-four hours straight. I sit back, take a deep breath, and speak.

"Hullo?"

"Archie? Man! Where have you been? I mean, where are you? I mean, where were you all this time?"

"I'm in a special hidden place, a home for lost Kush. And I didn't answer because I didn't hear the sat phone through the suitcase. I was on a long boat ride, then in, well, meetings, and I only opened the case just now." Hearing his voice finally hits my heart. "Oh, *eashiq*, my lover, I miss you."

"I miss you too. I keep asking Rashid about where you are, when I'll see you. All he says is, 'Soon enough.'"

I wonder more about this Rashid; he is not one of us. But I hear footsteps approaching.

"Habibi, I must go. They can't know I can contact you." I pause. How much can I tell the man with whom I share all? "I have something going on, very intense, for tomorrow, maybe two more days."

"I can't see you, then?" He's both worried and sad.

"What is going on here is very important, but I will get through it as soon as I can. And I'll call as soon after. Okay?" Though I know it's not at all okay.

"I guess I can't change that," he says. "Be careful and come get me when you can."

"I will be with you soon."

I don't say Amun willing. I don't care if he is. Branden and I must be so.

Intercepted missive 599: Inhale a long, sweet breath of the past this modern day. The Wayback Machine wafts up… the Future? It takes Time. Prepare for history and mystery. See y'all on the flip-flop.

I'm putting on my myth-spinner hat. I'll tell the tale; then you get to live it. And after that I disappear for a few chapters. Hope you enjoy the ennead.

CHAPTER 24
AHMED

THESE ARE the words to be said: The time has come, O brother-in-fate. If you are to be king, the day to be tested dawns. You must find the strength to overcome. Fail and you fail us all.

I say this knowing Taharqa can't hear me. I say this for those following his story and those rooting for his success.

Here I relate the rites of ancient Egypt and the rites of ancient Kush that we melded into the eternal ennead facing Prince Taharqa (i.e., some heavy shit that goes down for my bruh is coming up). By providing some contact with antiquity, the mystery and magic history, and the imagination of methods lost in time, I hope you all may experience the celestial awe our son-pharaoh-to-be will inspire as he not only transcends the arduous labors of the nine but also conquers the unknown astral adversities of the future.

That happens, or we are a world on the hellfire highway to perdition plaza.

To start to learn about this ceremony, disabuse yourself of images of an age-corrected Tom Cruise, the hunk version of Brenden Fraser, or a moldy old Boris Karloff. (And give no thought at all to that split-personality geek from Marvel comics.) So much Hollywood is in the modern mind that shiny film scenes cloud the mystic visions of Kemet/Egypt/Kerma/Kush. What I will now show you is beyond death masks of gold, basalt scarabs, and alabaster vials.

Instead let your mind go outside. See a vale between low mountains, hillsides of grass where cows were grazing yesterday and goats were on the inclines. The sun is so bright, it chimes in the ears. The winds stay high. The rest is empty silence.

Until...

The clamor of hands clapping in a swaying rhythm, the sounds of small drums and the rabab fiddle and the kissar lyre, the shouts and responses. These break the calm as the Nubians of the eternal empire of Kush arrive. Here is the song of the Nubian kingdoms; with independent spirit its citizens stride out from their secret city carved from cold rock into the blazing sunlight of the Nuba Mountains. And their message is clear: Kush lives, and its future shall renew its past.

We see fine clothes of sacred linen dyed in indigos and reds and blacks, our own mined gold displayed in rings and on ringlets, ceramic necklaces of faience beads, sandals and caps and kilts that seem pulled from hieroglyphic walls.

There among leaders, teachers, holy guides, and magicians walks the initiate, our chosen one designated to be our pharaoh, watched by all as he comes to face the gods' challenges and claim the leonine title of Arensnuphis.

The celebrants form a wide circle in which Taharqa stands center, facing judgment from all the gods of the present and the past. The people stand, sit, lean, kneel—their presence delineates the limits of the ennead arena. They wait unprepared for what may happen in this most rare of ceremonies, and therefore they are prepared for anything.

The ennead itself is anything and everything and nothing like any other rite.

Our Kush ennead represents a fully opposite direction from the best-known translated artifact of Egypt, the *Book of the Dead*. As descendants of Kush, we had to write our own *Book for the Living* to bring about our kingdom's earthly resurrection.

At this point I cannot tell all that will happen to Taharqa. Even I have been kept in the dark. You will see for yourself, should you decide to read on. And if you do, know these nine things, lasting from prehistory to now:

One: That gods change names with addresses: Atun here is Amun there and is Amun Ra or Re further on.

Two: That magic is in the Nubian soul, good and bad, used against enemies and to benefit friends.

Three: That our linen is holy, made from the sacred plant flax. And knotted cloth is *heka,* meaning magic. As are amulets. And blessed staffs.

Four: That black cats and ravens are good luck; owls are destroyers.

Five: That women are royal leaders of our society. And our most revered gods wear cow horns: the magical healer Isis and goddess of the sky Hathor.

Six: That all true knowledge was hidden by the god Thoth, yet Nubia has saved and stored much.

Seven: That the gods have left the Earth and left it for us to maintain unless we petition for their intercession.

Eight: That *ma'at* is the gods' infinite blueprint for the world, and yet sometimes we can draw a new line on the plat.

Nine: That watching all of this are our Nubian gods, including Apedemak, lion-headed warrior god of victory; Sebiumeker, god of fertility and agriculture; Anhur-Shu, son of the god Shu; and Arensnuphis, who is Sebiumeker's partner, son of Re, and the companion of most holy goddess Isis.

Believe this as you must.

TOO LITTLE is known about our ancestral culture because Western historians would not see that Black African societies had importance. To too many of them Nubia was merely a captive of Egypt, though Egypt was once the captive of Assyria until Kush came to free it. Much history has been ignored, forgotten, and lost, and our Kush priests lack knowledge that could have been handed down. Some of that lore lies under the Sahara sand or sunk beneath the waters behind the Aswan Dam. Some of it lies in stories told or even assumptions made.

It is fair to assume that what I relate here is gods' truth, total fabrication, and *bamiya*: stewed facts and lies cooked up to create a digestible dish for readers. Are you smelling what I'm cooking?

To end my dissertation, I paraphrase (meaning "steal") a translated inscription from Jebel Barkal, the most holy place in all of Kemet and home of the sun god Amun: I knew when you were in your mother's womb that you were to be ruler. I knew you in the semen, while you were in the egg, that you were to be lord.... As a father makes his son excellent, it is I who decreed kingship to you.... It is I, the Lord of Heaven, who gives you the royal charter. None other can decree who is king.

Let us hope, and even pray, that Lord Taharqa, the choice of the sun god, grabs hold of that royal charter and fulfills the predictions written in his conception. Our Archie must add the god's name of Arensnuphis, representing the gods' approval and support. Together with Amanirenas these two will be like Isis and her brother-husband Osiris.

What about Brendan? I have to say the priests and magicians teaching me didn't predict that possibility. But I believe love will find a way, effendi, for even in mythology, Arensnuphis had his Sebiumeker, a god for a god.

If I could I would be there for this ultimate transition and epochal rite. I would stand at Taharqa's side, whisper the bits of secrets I have learned about impending ordeals, their witchery, and their reversal. I would team with Taharqa till he achieves his new name and his eternal glory. Even in the sunlight of what our then-pharaoh knows as eternal love, I would love him too and serve as loyally as Branden, as selflessly as a supplicant, and as close as his own shadow.

I am down with you, bruh.

But I am not granted such a role. Instead as I have learned what I could from my father and the other priests, checked the ancient scrolls for the rites, had dreams and had those dreams interpreted, all I can do is try to sense what is ahead of him, in some psychic way to feel what he will soon feel, yet never be near to his challenges, never be able to calm his assailed mind.

The words are to be said: The time has come. If you are to join the gods, may you have the strength of kings.

Missive never sent: Magic time….

CHAPTER 25
TAHARQA

The ennead, the beginning

VIZIERS AND hierophants, high priests and protectors come to feed me, bathe me, and oil me (once I have hidden the sat phone in my bag). I am like Hercules being prepared for his labors. Well, maybe baby Hercules since he had twelve tasks, and I will suffer only nine. Naked, I lie back on the not-so-uncomfortable bed and try counting tasks instead of sheep. I count too many and sleep too little.

And the next day starts too early. Roused from my bed by a singing chorus, I am oiled again (in a woodsy scent of myrrh), dressed, and then escorted outside to a glen between three mountains. A fierce sun has found an open pass to blaze through, and before my eyes can adjust, a throng of clapping, chanting, singing Nubians leads me like a wave, and I can only ride it out.

Every Kushite in the Nuba must be here, and their celebration noise spills into the open area. Strings twang and calfskin drums throb. The clothes and robes flow in a crayon box of colors. Jewelry and sacred stones, runes and relics adorn necks and hands and waists.

This stately promenade is like the processions held throughout my youth to honor holy days and ancient victories. The thing is, for many of those processions, I was not there. While all of Kush met for those rites, I, like Cinderella, stayed home to sweep cavern floors and restack books of incantations. Only shards of music and echoes of brief shouts were audible enough for me to know what was being celebrated without me. I therefore turned my sense of rejection to one of internal power. Out there they were spending time with myths and ghost stories, while I knew there were no such things. I reveled in my agnostic reality. Who's afraid of the big bad gods?

But now I am in the midst of the march. The crowd carries me along without touching, without comforting. I am led into something that I know little about. Maybe none of us know much at all, but I'm the one who must face it, whatever it may be. Maybe I should be the one afraid of the gods.

Outside, the parade enters an oval space where the marchers form a wide ring with me and two keening escorts in the center. The crowd grows silent, watching. The scrub grass is so green, it gleams. I hear wind but feel not a breeze. And the sunlight moistens my skin. Is it a sweat of heat or of fear?

I am dressed as an ancient pharaoh king in a white *shendyt*, or kilt, with a ruby-red apron and a red-striped *neme*, my headcloth. My crown bears the paired symbols of upper and lower Egypt, the cobra and the vulture, because at one time they ruled Nubia and at one time were by Nubia ruled. White for upper, closest to Kerma; red for lower, down to the Mediterranean Sea. Around my waist is a thin strip of linen folded lengthwise twice, forming a sort of loose-fitting belt. At my neck a leather cord holds a rough cube of brittle metal. It is, I am sure, a rare-earth element.

My closest escorts join the ring of attendees. I am alone when Haremakhet, bent at the shoulder and leaning on his cane, takes one step forward and intones the words as one wrinkled arm reaches skyward: "Djed medu! Heka!" "The words to be said: The magic!"

And my ennead begins.

Standing stock-still, I am presented with a wide dish. I guess breakfast in these parts is no picnic. I see bread, boiled millet, sorghum porridge, and a dollop of red beans. Looking into this mess, I don't notice saintly Nitocris on my right until she whispers a clue: "Reassemble the puzzle."

Puzzled am I. What could this puzzle be? How do I reassemble the thing when I don't know what it was? I pick up the small loaf of bread to bite into it, but I stop. Yes!

I replace the loaf dead center on the dish. I divide the millet mash and the porridge each into two, running a line of millet from each bottom corner of the bread, and a line of sorghum from each top shoulder. My spoonful of beans serves as the head.

It is one of the best-known Nile myths: An angry, jealous Set kills his brother Osiris and cuts him into pieces, spreading them across the land. Their sister and Osiris's queen, the goddess Isis, seeks out and reassembles the body. She has life breathed into it, reviving Osiris.

"Osiris returns to rule the dead," I say. "His wife is god of magic, and their son Horus rules the earth." Nitocris steps lightly before me and takes the plate. A copper bell *bongs*. End round one.

Djedkare next steps up to me, a basket held before him. He stops, tilts the basket until it spills out a large number of twigs. He looks into my eyes.

"Restore the cycle."

I kneel carefully (this is not a simple accomplishment when you're going commando in a knee-length skirt) to better view this challenge. The twigs are thin and willowy, easy to bend.

By Amun's breath, are they translating Nubian challenges into English? Ma'at is the god-blessed cycle of life. So I quickly arrange a large portion of twigs horizontally, then slide twigs in vertically, weaving them in. I am creating a mat.

"Ma'at is the order of life," I say. "It is unity. It is peace."

Djedkare sweeps the twig mat up with his hand, steps back, and nods. A copper bell *bongs* twice. And, I guess as a reward, someone hands me a filled bronze cup. I take a taste. A beer!

Ankhaf and Ankmare, the lovely twins, step forward. Each has a staff in her right hand. They stop, pose like images on a tomb wall, the staffs outstretched and clashing. In unison, they chant, "Settle the war of the two brothers."

The brothers in my first thought are Set and Osiris, they of the dismemberment and reanimation. But for the Egyptians, godhood is all in the family, and among the eternal, incest is best. Set's nephew, Horus, is at times called his brother. These two battled eighty years over who should rule the living once Osiris, Horus's father and Set's brother, took over the afterlife. But that is not the fun part.

Old Haremakhet told me the story again and again and again. At one point, Set comes on strong (as Brand would say) to his brother-nephew, who is willing to take a little up the ass for some of his uncle-brother's strength. They do the deed, with Set believing that spilling his semen into his kin would give Set an edge in their power struggle, but Horus's mom clued her son in on it, and he caught the godly splooge "in his hands."

"How does one catch another's seed in one's hand, father priest?" I often ask as a child.

"Just listen to the story," Haremakhet says, always testily.

End result: Isis put the splooge on some lettuce and fed it to Uncle-Brother Set, who broke out in a golden disk on his head. Worse than acne, I guess. And Horus wins.

I can say this story left me confused as a child, and further confused as a man. But now I'm up for full pharaoh, so here goes.

Reaching under my shendyt, I begin to massage my penis. Having an audience doesn't help, but I keep my mind on my prick—and on my lover. I actually whisper "Branden" as I ejaculate into my spare hand. And this I eat. (Not for the first time, either.)

"A god swallows his own life force, forming gold out of his sperm. I am marked forever by my ancestral self-love, and I can no longer fight my brother."

Ding-ding-ding goes the copper bell, and they give me a cloth for my sticky hands and another beer to wash away the evidence.

I'm a bit light-headed with this beer and no breakfast, and the next challenge is already upon me. A sad-faced Khamhor faces me. "Free the enslaved," he intones. "Free the enslaved."

If there is an immortal evil and a universal sin, it is slavery. Egyptians enslaved Nubians, and Nubians Egyptians. All Africa was raped in the slave trade: west, north, south, and east. Slaves to commerce. Slaves to religion. Slaves to conquerors, family, ideology, politics. How do you free any? How can you free us all?

I need a symbol. I look down. I pull the wrapping of linen from my waist, wave it over my head.

"I recognize no right of one person to own another," I shout. "No slave serves in my presence or can be treated as any but a free human. I decry the slave masters and deny their claims.

"The order of life is ours to make. I free all slaves in my world and dare all others to do the same. And any who enslave themselves may break their yoke and be welcomed among all."

I let the linen lie loosely about my neck.

Quite a speech, and I could say it is the beer talking, but there is silence after. Then four bells. Then more beer.

Tasty beer, yes, but it's not cooling or refreshing; it's hazing my gaze.

"Ankhnesneferibre, foster mother to me, this is not beer alone you give me."

She waits to answer. She waits until I drink more.

"It is intoxicant, my child. It opens heka to you." She calls me child, but do you drug children?

"Thank you, fair mother, for invoking magic in my cause. Still, what intoxicant do I drink?"

She pauses, speaks low. "Beer of wheat, bulb of poppy."

Brewski and opiates. Surely that will help me think. Not. I'd shake my head to loosen the cobwebs, but I fear that will call out the drug spider inside my skull to eat my brain.

I heard four bells. Didn't I hear four bells? Don't I get a potty break now?

"You do well," Amenemhat declares, stepping forward with a half bow. Easy for him to say; he's not lost in this drug fog. "It is time for your historiola."

I don't like the sound of that. Histor-what? Is that why I'm naked under a kilt?

"A historiola is an incantation in a short mythic tale," Amenemhat says. "The gods love stories, and we tell stories about the gods. Now you must invent a story to please the gods."

Oh man, what do I do? I'm more lost in Wonderland than Alice, high on all her cakes and tea. The brilliant sun is knocking on my head bone like a cop on a SWAT call. I need a story to please gods? Do I even believe in them? Gods? Or stories?

Hell, I only have one tale to tell. I wipe sweat from my eyebrows with my linen cloth, and a silly smile rises on my face.

"I have a story. It is about humans. Maybe the gods would like something other than a god-centered narrative. I sure hope so, 'cause here it goes."

CHAPTER 26
TAHARQA

My historiola: The legend of Stevie

ONCE UPON this time in our junior year of college, Prince-to-be Taharqa Nimiery, descendant of Kush in his twenty-first year, and his consort, young Branden of the Hickcocks and of similar maturation, established their newest citadel in a place a few leagues from the holy campus of Pardell the Universe City.

(Really, it's the Country Day Apartments, one mile from the Pipefitter Basketball Arena. It's a first-floor one bedroom with industrial-quality putty-gray carpeting. An AC unit juts from the living room wall. There's a kitchen divided from the living space by a yellow Formica counter. The mini-dinette set with three chairs, the love seat sofa and the one overstuffed easy chair are all college-rental cheap. Walls are decorated with posters hung via globs of wall putty.)

There they live lavishly on an imperial income, reigning benevolently, loving each other so fully that comfort spills out to their courtiers, counselors, and subjects.

(That means teachers, pals, and classmates.)

(Wait! Who is telling this story?) I am (and I am too). I think we need another beer, dear.

Anyway, here they live happily while learning great engineering magic: fluid flux and fluid flow, ohms and siemens, the chemical contents of dirt.

And they entertain visitors.

One of whom is a great college wrestler and Branden's teammate. This man, call him Manley, is not a friend of Branden or Taharqa, but is a team idol that other wrestlers look up to. (I mean, he is six foot five.) But he rarely looks down. So it is a surprise when, one evening, Manley comes knocking at the citadel door.

Taharqa answers and bids him enter. (Can we stop the fairy-tale language? It's making my head spin.) Okay.

Manley thrusts his way in, saying, "Hickcock here?" And before I can answer, he bulls right past me.

Brand and I had recently finished dinner, so I ask Manley if he wants a beer, which he seems desperate to gulp down, and we direct him to the couch. Brand and I sit together on the overstuffed chair, waiting for him to state his purpose.

And he blurts out, "Hickcock, you're a homo, right?"

I guess we both looked shocked at this, because he says to me, "No offense. I mean, really, you two… do it, right?"

We won't deny that. He goes on.

"So can a guy," Manley asks sweatily, "can a straight guy… uh… butt fuck and still be straight?"

The eternal question, usually coming right before "Then will you do me?"

I was really interested in Branden's answer. And considering the possibilities of rape, coercion, a bad bet, or a drunken stupor, Brand asks, "Did the straight guy like it?"

Manley's face contorts in self-disgust and embarrassment, but he finally says, "Yeah."

And as Brand is about to respond benevolently, there is another knock at the door. It's Skylar, a gay friend at the LGBTQ+ student union. He seems about as flustered as Manley, nods to everyone, but heads straight for the beer, then takes to the floor between where Brand and I sit and where Manley broods.

"I need to ask you something," Skylar says. "It's personal." He looks at Manley; he looks at us. And he says, "It's about Stevie."

"Stevie!" Manley shouts. "My question is about Stevie too!"

And at that point, unannounced, the guys from across the hall walk in. They are Bob and Brad, seniors and celibates, or so we thought. Bob in buttoned shirt and bow tie, Brad in a Physics RULES!!! T-shirt—both stand room center like they were invited in.

"Hi, guys," says Brad, the studious one, "Having a party? Can we join?"

Joking, I ask, "Is this visit about Stevie?"

"How did you know?" asks Bob, the even more studious one. "Have you met Stevie?"

"No, but—" I'm stopped by another knock at the door. I answer, and there is our freshman English composition teacher, Jack Spillane.

"I'm sorry to barge in," Spillane says. "I need advice, and you two are the only ones I could think of."

"Sure," I say, "and have a beer. It's a Stevie party."

"Stevie!" Spillane shouts, freezing near the front door.

Suddenly, a village campfire is the perfect model for this amazing event of fable gathering. We have a room full of frightened souls ready to confess their dreadful sins—or get off professing their fun. I get Professor Spillane a beer, guide him to a dinette chair that we add to the conversation circle, and I say this:

"So we are all here about one thing, yet we all have different stories, yes? Let's handle this in the old ways, as told in the legends and ghost tales of time immemorial."

I take a seat on the overstuffed's arm. Brand is in the chair's seat. We are two regal potentates on a Greek-key-patterned green-fabric throne.

"Like a royal court, Brand and I shall listen to your stories as each of you in turn tells it, and when all are finished, he and I shall determine answers for all. Or else let the ghoulies and ghosties take off your heads."

There actually is a bit of pause as our guests look around, almost expecting some ethereal giant with a scimitar to burst through the floor. I then say, "As is the custom, the last shall go first. So, Prof. Spillane, tell us your tale of Stevie."

"He's, well, just another freshman in my comp class," the professor says, adjusting his horn rims. "Not exceptionally notable. Kind of a skinny late-teenager. Thick-rimmed glasses. Not all that good a writer, even.

"So this week I gave his oleaginous essay a D-plus and wrote 'See me' on the top. Papers were handed back to students, the next assignment was discussed, the bell rang, and without thinking, I headed to my office.

"Well, the little red-headed rat must have followed me without a sound because I was opening the office door when I noticed him behind me. I mean, he wasn't directly behind me, not threatening or anything. And it took me a minute to think why he was there.

"'Oh yes, you've come to see me about the paper,' I said, 'Come in.' And he did."

The professor takes a long, sad look at his beer, takes a swig. More sad look.

I say, "And?"

"And…. And… I don't know why I did it. No, I do know. It was something about him—something about him near me—and a heat washed over me. He stood inside my office and closed the door. He was ballet thin with tousled hair, barely a smile. And a… a sense. I sensed him, not just saw him. All my senses registered him. But most of all, I smelled him. He had a scent of youth and male and… and sex! Before I knew it, we kissed."

"He kissed you?" I ask.

"Yes. No! I kissed *him*," Spillane says. "And more than that, kissed and licked and grabbed. I pulled his shirt off, pulled mine off, pulled his red, hairy chest close to me, and that smell intensified. And I couldn't stop. I pulled down my pants. I pulled down his. And then I saw it."

We all pause for him to continue.

"His… junk, his prick, his angel-awesome penis! It was perfect, like a pink marble statue, veiny and bobbing and just the right size. And we did it! Right there on my desk! Me, who has never ever slept with a student, gave up my ass to this sexy little twerp. And I loved it."

Our guests, in unison, go "Ooooooh."

The prof pauses again, and we all wait. He swigs his beer. We wait more.

"So what do I do?" he asks. "Do I flunk him so he has to take my course again? I already changed the grade on his paper to A-plus. Do I quit my job because of my ethics violations? How do I face him in the next class period without tearing his clothes off again? What do I do about Stevie?"

"That's what we want to know," says Brad, interrupting with a shrug. "Bob and me."

"We are at a loss," says Bob, touching his bow tie. "We always were, even when we first found him."

"Stevie," they both say. Each moves differently, but at the same time, like a Bob Fosse dance routine.

"We were coming back from Chester's," Brad says, naming the only grocery store near campus since Walmart sucked all the retail out of town. "We had stocked up for a busy weekend of reading eighteenth-century German philosophers, with breaks for CSPAN, so our load of groceries was substantial. And as we reached the main door, we met Stevie."

"He held the door for us," Bob says, clearly disconcerted. "He even followed and helped us open the apartment door."

"It was my fault," Brad says. "I thought we should reward him. I asked him in."

"Some reward," Bob says, brushing back his thinning dark hair.

The rest of the story gets rotational as the two men interrupt each other to give details. But the gist totals one tale with hand gestures: A strange heat (wavy fingers), a sexy odor off the stranger (hands fan). Desires suddenly erupting, exploding (eyes popping). Clothes gone (one arm thrusts). Inhibitions gone (the other arm thrusts). Cherries gone (all arms pump) as each roommate plays the meat in a sex sandwich. Before they're done, that infernal penis has had its way with them with such magic, things didn't end until they had their ways with each other.

Our guests, in unison, sigh "Ahhhhhh."

"Now what do we do?" Bob pouts, "Wait around for Stevie to come back? Or keep doing each other?"

"Well, at least you have an other," Skylar says with a whine. "What about me?"

Skylar is no virgin, certainly, but Stevie took him for a ride anyway. And right there in a reading room of the student union.

"Hell, I'm not even into PDA!" he shouts. "So what am I doing ass-over-shoulders as he plows me with that prick? And I came! In public! Three times!"

Our guests, in unison, whisper "Hmmmm."

"And no one saw you?" I ask.

"Saw me? The fucking crowd applauded! My fuck is trending on TikTok!" He gulps his beer, then cries: "Oh, Stevie, I turned porn star for you!"

"Man!" says Manley. "Man, man, man! But you're all gay anyway. What about me?

"I was in the gym late after the last home wrestling meet. Y'know, Hickcock, you had left, but I was still working some moves, something I could use at the conference championships, maybe even Olympic trials.

"I'm speedin' around on the mat, and, bent over, I see him to one side. This guy. Like you all said, kinda skinny, glasses, crayon-orange hair. Just a little smile on his thin mug.

"I figure he's gay. I mean, I've had gay guys look at me—even you, Hickcock. I learned looks aren't touches, and it's kinda nice to know somebody appreciates you, appreciates," and he literally pumps his upper torso into a biceps crab pose, "the work, y'know?

"The guy comes up to me and says, real soft like, 'So everybody's gone?' and I say 'Yeah,' and then he says, 'Well, I'm Stevie, and you'll do.'

"He walks right up on me, and I figure this kid wants me to kill him, and I up and stand my ground and—whew, there it is! Heat, smell, sex; horny, heavin' bodies. Snatchin' off my singlet and his sweatpants. And hot damn, there is that dick. That dick. So tempting. I want it. And I got it. Right up the bunghole. I came like a five-alarm fire engine."

Our guests, restraining their laughter, chuckle "Hahahaha."

"So am I gay?"

Back to that ultimate question. But Brand and me, we don't go in for the hammer blow quite yet.

"So this Stevie," I say, "is the cock of the walk? The preeminent prick? The penis that's meanest?" And they all nod sadly.

"And you come to us? Why?"

"Well, I came first," Manley interjects. "And I told you why. I need to know if I'm queer."

"And would you do it again if this Stevie appeared again?"

"You betcha," he admits.

"Then you got your answer," Brand says.

Winning score for my jock boyfriend. And we gain a sex-orientation teammate.

"As for the rest of you, since Stevie is making the rounds, you can wait for your turn again." (I nod to Manley.) "Or take care of your own business." (This to Bob and Brad.) "Skylar, I hear Just For Fans is the new porn-business way to go. And as for you, Professor, keep your office door closed and sin no more.

"But know that Stevie is a magic spell, an incantation toward sexual fulfillment. You should call on him whenever you make love, because he makes physical love magical.

"These are the words to be said, and so it shall be."

"But what about you?" the prof asks Branden and me. "What about you two?"

"Yeah, you," says Skylar. "You are the magnificent monogamists. What if Stevie comes knocking at your door?"

"Yeah, you?" they all ask as an accusation. "What will you do?"

Well, we won't know until he does.

And he does. Not that night, but one time he does. And what happens then? Well, that, my friends, is another story.

CHAPTER 27
TAHARQA

The ennead, Part II

DO THEY like my story? Hell if I know. Ale and opiates, silly story and stern challenge have me all mixed up. But I notice one thing—the crowd is thinning. Mightily.

I watch my teachers, my tormentors, my people rise from stone seating areas or stroll from where they stood leaning against valley walls. In twos and threes, they move out and back into the underground city, and I am afraid. I am afraid to be left alone here. I am afraid they did not like my historiola. I am afraid I've failed in my quest.

My eyes close, my head droops. A world of dark and wind fills my mind. And then I hear it: Five long tones peal out.

I wake, more alert and alive than I have been this day. My lungs feel refreshed, my heartbeat is strong. I look around the empty space, and it is not so empty.

Staring back at me is a figure—something far too giant to be a man—all in gold. His golden shendyt stops above the knee, a black-and-gold apron at its front. Gold gleams from his neme, the headcloth spreading out like a lion's mane. And the precious metal contrasts fully with his ebony skin. He smells—no other word for it—fantastic.

A name comes to me from my Nubian education: Dedun, Kush god of incense and of prosperity, protector of Nubian leaders who have passed on. Awed, I kneel, and his smile gleams. With his arms, he indicates that I should rise.

"Son of Nubia, it is time for you, named for one I hold close in my heart, Taharqa, pharaoh of empire, to stand and face the enemy of all. Confront the chaos."

Suddenly there is wetness licking at my toes. Water rises around me ankle high, then to my knees, then at my waist. They are the waters from before the world began, sloshing and swirling without discernable pattern or flow. I am in the middle of them as if in a river; I can see the banks before me and at my back. But I only sway as the waters buffet me. I cannot move.

Circling me in the water, I see a dark shape, long and sinuous, thick as a man's chest. It spins faster and faster, blunt head featureless until…

It breaches. Black eyes, black head, scaly and sinister, Apopis, the serpent of chaos, stares me in the face.

Chaos is existence before Ra. Its toxic bite kills order, and its endless belly may swallow the people, the world, the universe. But Ra who is Amun who becomes Amun Ra pulled all from chaos, and if he wishes, he can drown us all in its vastness if he should return.

The lessons swirl in my head like the serpent's river, but I find no answers there. A human does not confront an ur-god empty handed, and a pharaoh is a human after all.

The answer is magic; I know it, but what little heka I've tried in the past resulted in coincidence if not failure. The spells of the ancients have traveled far but not so successfully in a scientific age. And everything scientific about this situation says, "Archie, you lose."

I pull the linen strip from my shoulders. What good is cloth when facing a mythic monster. But one thing comes to mind from hieroglyphs I have seen growing up. I begin to tie knots in the cloth, and before each knot, I say the heka words. "Djed medu," and I tie a knot. "Dejd medu." Another knot. "Djed medu."

The snake's gotten tired of our staring contest. It strikes out with open mouth and comes within inches of my head, then pulls back its feint with mouth closed. I swing my linen weapon above my head, then slam it forward. And before it can fully retreat, the beast's jaws are clamped shut. My makeshift rope has lassoed it.

Not happy, the sinuous fiend swings and splashes, but my linen holds firm. Isn't it true that the crocodile's jaw muscles are much weaker in opening than in biting down? I'm using school biology and a waist decoration to fight eternity.

Still, one of us is going to drown in this water wrestle. The churning stirs up waves that wash over me, changing my breath, shaking my stance. I wish I could get away. I wish.

I remember wishing as a child one night I could fly at the speed of thought. And I did. For a second I was somewhere else, and then I was home in my bed.

Holding tight to my would-be destructor, praying that heka comes during an opium hangover, I wish us both to be away, far away from this spot.

And we are. And in the full second that I spend in this new place, I let the serpent go. And before it can strike again, I flash back to the Nuba

Mountains glen where I had stood a moment before. I am still waist deep in the flood. But now I am safe. Now I am alone.

Only not quite.

"Like Anhur-Shu," Dedun says, invoking the warrior name of a child of Ra, "yet you reverse the message of his title: One who leads back the distant one. You take Apopis to the distance."

He lifts one hand holding a golden bell; the other holds a golden mallet. He strikes the bell to a crystal ring, six times. On the last echo, he approaches me, smiling.

"Heka follows you like a black cat at your sandals," he says, placing one pan-sized palm on my shoulder, his fingers brushing my chest. "Let us see if she follows in your search for knowledge."

His giant hand presses down and shoves me under the water. I barely have time to gasp, and I think, *I am of a desert people. How do I stay alive under a river?*

Close your mouth; open your eyes, I think. *Get hold of your fear; own the moment.*

Strange. I am floating not far below the water's surface, stock-still in a calm space. It is a thick atmosphere I dare not breathe. I look down where the depth swallows the sunlight. I do not see the bottom, not at first, but slowly I make out a spot of sparkle on the thick mud floor.

Trying my version of a frog kick (another lesson from prep-school gym class), I drive myself down for a closer look. It doesn't take long until I see my sparkle is a thin line, a crack emitting its own yellow light. I reach for it, and anticipating my touch, it moves, widens, exposes gold. Blocks of gold. Spirals of gold. Books and papers and scrolls of gold.

What I see is knowledge—all the legendary knowledge collected by Thoth, Egyptian god of learning. It's like the legendary Library of Alexandria redeemed, further stocked with all the truth collected ever since. Take that, Julius Caesar! Take that, Google!

I reach my hand down, and one parchment—one page in the world data pool of truth—rises into my palm. I pull it close, a treasure unassailable, and the motion propels me upward as the crease of gold below closes, to be lost until the people, the right people, find the way to discover it again.

Gasping, I burst out of the water like a porpoise, and when I come down, my feet touch solid ground. The water is below my knee, and the river is draining like an emptying bathtub. My clothes, a bit disheveled, are dry to the touch. Above my head gleams a solar disk, intricately etched with a cartouche. I know that cartouche names me Taharqa, emperor of Kush and handsome man. And then the etching melts, fades, and evolves. I cannot read the symbols.

I still clutch the knowledge taken in my seventh task.

The sun is at its zenith. In Sudan, this is no time to sunbathe. Who knows what this is doing to my brain? Flashing back through much of what has happened, I see it's possible that my experiences are explainable as drug-and-alcohol-fueled heatstroke. Has this all occurred, and so much of it without witnesses? I feel made anew and still unsteady in my changed identity.

Yet the sun seems cooler. No, I seem taller. I am rising as the water shrinks, then rising above the ground itself. I hear around me distant booms, like thunder in a clear sky. They surround me, and only as I ascend, past the crest of the surrounding hills, do I count them in memory. There were seven. Yes, seven.

So is this the start of the eighth task? Still I rise, unstoppable. The gold disk of my self-knowledge floats above my scalp, and it flashes wildly, reflecting back the sun's glory. They seem to speak some gleaming code from sky to disk, disk to sky. What and why?

"I deliver your paternity," my vestal mother had said. "I deliver your purpose, your power."

I open myself to this continuing elevation, stretching my chest toward the benevolent fireball. I rise, and the heat caresses me, calms me like a babe in a parent's arms. I must speak, though I don't know where the words come from.

"Father Ra, your son to be named Arensnuphis exalts you. He seeks your benediction, and begs your favor in his people's cause."

There is no sound, not even a rushing wind, and I reach an outstretched hand into light that is gilding the world. From a sky uniformly bright, a separate beam strikes that hand, paints my arm up to and across my shoulder with warm comfort. I feel its heat on my face as it moves up, up to that solar disk over me. The disk itself glows brighter, then flashes an arc of light to my other hand, the one holding the golden truth. I am aglow like a candle, and the shining parchment curls, shrinks, folds into my palm. But it is not gone—I sense it slide inside my body, coat my heart, and send a gleam back up to the disk above my head.

My rise stops. I dare not look down but feel the whole of Earth's joys and sorrows rising to me, surrounding me. And as that moment ends, there is a mad tinkling of bells, strung bells like a belly dancer's skirts. Are there eight? Who can tell? But when the last echo fades, I am released. I am falling, gently falling…

Until I land in a shady spot on grassy earth. I lay there for little more than a few deep breaths before I hear a great crowd entering the glen with pounding drums, tinkling bells, and twanging instruments. My people dance or march in time, and I am greeted with touches and handshakes, song and praise.

"What's this? Is it over?" I ask, but I get only smiles. I reach up, but the cartouche disk is gone. Have I failed or succeeded?

"The ninth challenge? Did anyone hear the bells?"

But all I hear is chatter, friendly comments, welcoming hugs as they lead me back inside our hidden community and into the damnedest jubilation I have ever seen. Looks like they even killed the fatted calf for me—make that a fatted pig for pork roast. Add a goat or two. High times with beer (without opium). As they say back on campus—Par-tay!

Even as I sate my day of hunger, there is one thing on my mind, and it takes a while in the glittering dark for me to work my way around to the ever-revered Queen Amanirenas. She nods beatifically at my approach, gold flashing from her raiment, her jewels, her smile, and before I say anything, she speaks:

"You may now contact your friend," she says.

How pleasant, and certainly different from our previous conversation about Brand. But how did she know I could contact him. That's not important right now.

"Reaching him will bring great joy. May I bring him here, queen-sister?"

"I would not think that we are ready to do that." A strange way for her to put it, knowing how much I need him in my life. "Perhaps you meet at Rabak. It is far enough from here. He may take the train and meet you. But I warn: Trains bring rats. Their lines are forever prowled and infested by the underhanded. Better to reach Khartoum in a traditional way."

Tradition means by boat. With sail and river current, we're talking another twelve to fourteen hours. All that time with my love, sailing the longest river on earth—not all that bad a prospect. And I can think of a way that might cut that commute down a bit.

Out of politeness, I sample some more dishes and share a few dance steps before I make my way back to my sleeping quarters and the satellite phone. It is late evening. Would Branden be asleep? At least we are in the same time zone, though in cultures separated by millennia.

I am still in my ceremonial clothes. I believe it's time to see if my magic, what my mother called my power, has matured in me. So I will wish.

But though I wished and took away the serpent, I may not be able to wish myself to Branden. If I fall back into the cavern of Kush alone, what does that mean? Is there still a ninth ennead to face?

How did my mother say it? My power will awaken time after time. If that time is not yet, I will try later, and again later still. Meanwhile, I must be prepared to fall back on a more realistic tactic.

Intercepted missive 610: The end is the beginning: Ain't it always so? But while we begin again at the end, there is mystery in the middle. Two as one now split. What happens to your other half? Temptation rears its sexy head.

CHAPTER 28
BRANDEN

I THINK I hate Rashid.

His men plop me into a hotel room: "Rashid has ordered. You will like." The place is nice enough but empty without Archie.

My brief conversation with my love, cut off so abruptly, leaves me lonelier and more worried.

According to the glowing room clock, it's after 7:00 p.m. here in Sudan, which makes it about 11:00 a.m. back home, and I'm feeling jet lag. I slept as much as I could on the planes in, but when you're seated next to the Lord Taharqa, it's hard not to be excited all the time.

I kick off my shoes and lie down on top of the covers, which are a very pale pink, while the room walls are very blue. If I turn my head from the rather firm pillows, I can see through the floor-to-ceiling windows the banks of the Nile. Actually, the Niles. As Archie told me, Khartoum is at the juncture of the Blue and White Niles. Romantic it would be, but I don't have my romancer with me.

Instead about forty minutes into my nap, Rashid bursts in (despite my electronic lock) to shout, "Brando must eat!"

He hustles me down to one of the hotel dining rooms, and even tries to order my meal.

"Thanks, but I'll make my own choices," I say. The menu sports, of course, fresh fish, but I go for a steak, local vegetables, and mini potatoes. I've been warned that in some places steak means horse, not cow, but at these prices, I expect a fresh slab of Osiris himself.

Rashid excuses himself, then returns from the bar with a mixed drink, which he places before me.

"That's okay," I say. "I'm fine with water."

"Oh no. Water is not fine here," he says. "Trust me, you do not want the stomach trials this water can bring. The drink will protect you."

I take a sip, and it's a sweet-and-sour mix that has a taste of alcohol to it. What's to worry about that?

The meal continues—the steak is fantastic and the right state of medium rare—and Rashid regales me with tales about Khartoum. I'm also enjoying my drink, except now I taste a bit of bitterness in all the sweet. Oh well.

SOMEWHERE WITHIN this time, the conversation subject changes to me and what I do and what I study, and what I know about what I am studying.

When Archie and I became partner-scientist-engineer spies, he warned me about letting anyone else know about our lab work and its success. I know to be careful. But there is something too fuzzy about this Rashid and this evening. I feel my tongue wanting to tell wonderful anecdotes about rare earths and their qualities and locations. It's an urge hard to resist.

So I bite my tongue. No, really. I bite it. For real.

"Ow-ow-ow!" I shout. "Ooh, that hurtsh."

Rashid plays concerned, but when I say I want to return to my room, he's not so agreeable.

"No. Gotta go," I slur. "I musht be too tired."

Rashid accompanies me to the room, even offers to tuck me in, but I fend that off. I kick off the shoes again, hit the bathroom, and splash my face, but I'm still feeling loopy and talkative. I have to convince myself that, since no one is here, I don't have to say anything. I manage to get pants and shirt off. I flop on the bed, and I… am… out cold.

That bright room clock says it's 7:00 a.m. (11:00 p.m. Chicago time) when Rashid bursts in again.

"Brando must shower and dress! The airplane awaits!"

What airplane? Going where? My mind is still fogged, but I stumble into a shower and walk out feeling better, if not best. I brush my teeth using bottled water from the room fridge. (Oh, how much will this trip set Archie back?) Rashid looks out the window while I dress. I appreciate the approximation of privacy. While being ignored, I fill a backpack with more bottled water and, more discreetly, with the addition of my satellite phone.

Then it's off to the races (I mean back to the airport), where we take a puddle-jumper to what I learn is Port Sudan. From that industrial city, we transfer to a car that rushes us south to a place I have heard of—Suakin.

This place is fucked up. I am swamped by its history, the facts Archie has told me. I sense in the decay trapped spirits. I feel the pleading, ghostly fingers of the enslaved. My ancestors may have been dragged from East Africa, not west, but their fate was no different. There is a smell of antiquity here. It contains mystery, sorrow, threat, and death. Who-knows-what can do whatever it wishes, and we spiritless humans have no way of telling where it may come from.

In real life, the sea breeze cannot cut through the burning heat, and I'm soaked with sweat before we can round a corner of tumbledown rubble.

I also don't know where I am going. And strangely enough, neither does Rashid, though his assistant from the flight seems to be taking notes.

"You would go this way," Rashid says. Not exactly a question, and I'm sure my response won't help.

"I would go anywhere there is shade, dude." But I do have a mission. "Is Taharqa here?"

"Perhaps. This is where you met before?"

"I have never been here," I say. "Never been out of the States before this trip."

"Oh," he says. "Then perhaps he has told you about this place?"

"Only Scheherazade stories about ghostly powers and the horrors of the slave market. Spooky for a place so damn bright."

"Lord Taharqa has not been here?"

"Not that I know of. He's from Sudan, but he hasn't been everywhere. It's a big country."

And it seems jolly Rashid has turned dark. Though I am already lost in this maze of relics and debris, he swiftly leads us back to our waiting car and then the airport. He moves so effortlessly for such a big man—smooth and, in his way, menacing. I am sticking to my seat in the plane, wetter than a spaniel in a springtime duck pond, gulping water from my backpack stash. He looks at me with a mix of superiority and disgust.

"Brando is not dressed for this weather. We will stop at the market when we get back."

The rest of the flight is in silence, though he does briefly mention that we are passing over the ruins of ancient Meroë, once the Kush capital. And because my interest is piqued, he has the pilot circle so I can get a good look. (The assistant takes notes.) I see Nubian pyramids, many of them with missing tops (and looted contents) poking out of the sand. The land here shows sharp, broken teeth.

And as he moves, I see Rashid has a tooth of his own, a very long and most likely sharp knife behind his man-purse. He hides it when he leans forward to talk to the pilot. I find it better not to ask about its purpose.

Upon landing in early afternoon, Rashid and his buddy, joined now by a driver, take me to the Souq al Arabi, the largest market in Khartoum. It covers several blocks near the city's Grand Mosque. Filled with noise and smells and crammed with stands, it looks as it would on a PBS show, and just as strange as you might imagine.

With Rashid's assistance in bargaining (better known as arguing), I walk out with a skullcap and a jellabiya, an ensemble made up of a jibba, or long, open coat; a kaftan, a shirt nearly as long as the jibba; and a sirwal, an Arab version of pants. We wander a bit as I go for street food, something with rice and some meat I don't ask about, but it is delicious. And I am ready to head back to my room as a return of jet lag has me in its grip.

However, the day hasn't been enough punishment in Rashid's mind, so he takes me to a tourist-trap corral for my first experience with a camel ride. The less about that the better.

Finally off by myself (and with the door chain in my room secured), I take the time to try to reach Archie again. That's when we have another stress-shortened conversation. I miss him so much, and to be cut off is agonizing. At least he promises to come back to me in a day or two.

Rather than subject myself to another one of Rashid's cocktails, I order dinner in my room. Rashid tries to drop by, but I stop him at the chained door.

"Too tired for company," I say, and I ain't lying. I almost fall asleep over my spiced broiled agashe. (Nile fish have a flavor different from freshwater lake varieties at home.) Having undressed and showered, I am off to bed.

The next day becomes a whirlwind of stops and starts. Breakfast here, shopping there, quick trips to galleries and museums without purpose. It's like Rashid is trying to make up for his personal control of my trip by showing me every damn thing a tourist would want to see.

I get questioned about many things: What I know of what I see, where my knowledge comes from, who I discuss these things with. I fall back on my parents for most of this, even stuff I learned from Archie or, rarely, phone contact with Ahmed. Having African history in the home provides a lot of ways to not disclose confidences.

There is one spot I was glad to visit, and I took my time there. The National Museum of Sudan holds a wealth of Nubian artifacts going back to prehistory. And standing guard at the main entrance is a statue of my love's ancestor-namesake. Taharqa's image seems to have transferred down the millennia, and I recognize my Archie in the granite form. I learn the Horus name of this pharaoh is "exalted of appearances." Yes, he is my pretty, pretty man.

"The great Taharqa," Rashid sneers. "Ruler of upper and lower Egypt. He lost half his empire to the Assyrian horde in the end."

Ends are just new beginnings, my mind counters. I stay silent, and Rashid nudges his assistant to take note of me. I wonder about that, but I am too inspired to care.

Our day continues into evening, including a return to the market, where I find another version of the street-food stew for dinner. Spice dishes for a spicy man, and I am full of the meal and the day. Time to depart.

But if there is no rest for the wicked, I must be a warlock of the west, because Rashid has one more plan for me, and if it includes going to bed, it isn't an empty one.

"Brando is a young man, and a young man has needs!" he exhorts. "We must show Brando our nightlife!"

Off I am whisked to a Khartoum club—more a hole in the wall on a dark street with recorded music blaring on bad speakers. I should say an illegal hole in the wall because, as Rashid proudly tells me, bars and nightclubs are banned here by Sharia law.

"A true adventure, eh, Brando? Come! Dance! Drink! Enjoy!"

Dragged into a mass of happy, churning Sudanese, I am pushed, pulled, and directed to a corner where, somehow, a small table appears. Rashid has me sit, then leaves, only to come back with a drink. But this time he doesn't stay to question me. A few minutes after he melts into the crowd, a young woman appears.

She is quite the looker, a body sleek and slender, a sparkling red dress not meant to cover much of what a man wants to see. Her hair is pulled back into such an intricate set of braids, I could get more lost trying to unravel it than I was in Suakin.

She sits and leans in, and I can hear her husky voice despite the crowd. I can also smell her musk perfume, and I know that it is rising from her exposed cleavage.

"Hello," she says, "my handsome American man."

I am a modern dude, and I have had my experiences with women as with men. Some were a lot of fun; as some comedian before my time said, even bad sex is great. The imp on my left shoulder is whispering nasty thoughts. There is temptation causing a rise in the sirwal I'm wearing.

I have made my life choice, and it's Archie. No doubt about that. But Archie's not here. I have been away from him the longest since Christmas break freshman year. My body misses his.

"Don't be shy, young man," she smiles, teeth gleaming in the dark room. "I have a warm spot for you."

I bet she has. I got a little something here too.

"You buy me a drink?"

I hand her the Rashid Special. "Have mine, I'm not drinking."

She pushes my hand aside. Her hand is delicate and slightly damp. Maybe it's the oil she has used to make her body even more gleaming. I put the glass back on the table.

The DJ seems to have paused between sets. There is only a murmur in the crowd, and I can hear her dulcet tones like a siren's song.

"You me go back to hotel?"

That's my cue. "No." I say it flatly and finally. "Is there a bathroom here?"

I rise and very quickly move away from the table. But I'm confused. How did I get in here? Where's the door? Slip-sliding across the dance floor, I head for the light coming through a partially open door.

And I'm in the bathroom. Damn. I look around. It's big enough for a couple of urinals and a grody sink but no back door. Only a small open window, which does nothing for the smell of male liquids. I am not going to get my wrestler shoulders through that mousehole. I turn to leave, when…

Directly in front of me is the hottest Arabic man I have ever seen. Dark hair, large dark eyes, athletic build, beautiful face. He is exactly my height, and he wears a shirt that must be painted on, only the paint isn't enough to hide the top of a thicket of chest hair below.

"Hello, stranger," he says in accented English. "I saw you come in."

I'm facing another perfect smile, this time beneath a glistening black mustache. Perfect and very seductive.

This isn't fair! I love men with hair, body and facial hair especially. Archie, my sweet love, is all-over smooth as a baby's bottom. Even his pubes and pit hair are limited, tightly curled and short.

"I have to leave." I croak.

"Oh, don't be unfriendly," he purrs. "Let us show our visitor a good time."

And his hand falls firmly on my groin. Worst yet, he likes what he feels, and he gives my jimmy a squeeze. Then he steps forward, moving me back.

Should I take up this bold offer? What about Archie? My left imp hisses. Archie was in Sudan for weeks without me. Who says he was faithful at the time? And if I never asked, how would I know?

I smile back.

As I smile, I turn, bringing his movement into a slow half circle. We stop; I nod my head and look down as if I'm shy. Considering everything, but shy.

I shove his hand away and make a quick exit.

As luck would have it, there are a couple of dudes outside the door waiting, and from the looks of them, what they are waiting for is what my accoster had in mind for me. I slip around them, and their presence slows the sheikh from pursuing me. The crowd outside is back to boogying, so I disappear as best I can.

It takes much longer than I hoped, and I fake a few dance steps in the process, but I finally find the front door. And as I exit, there is a new couple (male/female) getting out of a cab, so I grab it. I'm not sure I can trust the driver, and since I know he's taking people to an illegal, multisexual bacchanal, why should he trust me? Still, I have no idea how we got here. Desperate, I use the Yankee tourist get-out-of-jail card—I let him know I have American dollars, and he is very helpful in getting me back to the Corinthia.

I take about three good breaths in my hotel room before Rashid comes banging on the door. That isn't a problem. Before I went upstairs, I told the desk man I had lost my key, so he made another and changed the computer code on it. My too constant escort-companion can't shove his way in anymore.

"Brando! Brando, are you there?"

I put on my best sleepy voice. "I'm really tired. I've gone to bed."

"Did you not enjoy your evening?"

"Great fun. Whoopie-doopie." I don't know where that came from. "I need to sleep."

"Okay," he says. "Get your rest. We have more fun tomorrow."

I'm not sure I need any more of Rashid's brand of fun.

Nervous as I am from all that has happened, I feel weariness overtaking me. Days can seem to go on forever when you don't get enough sleep. I am lost in the land of Morpheus when the sat phone rings. I have it in bed next to me so I can answer before others (Rashid) might notice.

"Hello? Oh, baby! Hi!" My heart is pumping and jumping with joy.

"Hello, habibi. Are you alone?"

"Yeah, finally. Rashid is keeping me on a short leash. He barges into my room, he takes me places I don't know, and he tries to be with me constantly. I only get private time when I order in dinner or go to sleep. And he asks lots of questions. Did your people send this guy?"

"I don't think so," Archie says. "He does not seem Hu. Likely some outside hire, but strange even for that." I hear concern in his voice.

"He tries to act like an okay dude," I say, "but he calls me Brando. He took me shopping, so I don't have to worry about clothes. He jokes a lot, translates for us, has his own set of assistants. He did get me a camel ride. I get on, I fall off. After that, he called me yuya. He says it means 'master of the horse.' Big joke.

"I never challenge him. He's too hefty, and who wants to be on the wrong side of a big bruh with that knife in his belt?"

"He's armed with a knife?"

"I saw it during a plane ride from Suakin. More like a short sword. Brutal."

"Yes, steer clear of that. You were in Suakin?"

"Sadly, he took us there. I have no idea why. It's more haunted than the phantom's opera. But he asked if you were there, or if you had been. I told him no."

There is silence on the other end of the line. Archie is thinking something.

"By the way," I say, "you guys must have a whole lot of heritage sites and ruins and ancient temples, and it looks like I may have to visit all of them."

"But they are not in Khartoum," he says. "And travel to these sites is not easy."

I know this. While the Muslims and the Brits afterward placed their capital at the confluence of the two Niles, the ancient Nubian capitals of Kerma, Napata, and Meroë, many miles away along the Nile, were left to sink into grit. No one goes there anymore.

"You ain't jokin'," I say. "Rashid talked about a twelve-day camel caravan. Then he laughed and said 'or for yuya, maybe the horse. The iron horse.'"

"It would take a mix of trains and boats and maybe desert buggies to get to the sites at Kerma, Napata, and Meroë," Archie says. "There are cataracts in the way. And those aren't Western trains. It's a lot of shoulder-to-shoulder riding with no seats and only the food you bring with you."

"Then maybe I'll opt to stay here by the pool."

"And maybe not," he says. "I think it is time we must shake off this Rashid." He pauses a bit. "Let me try something. Hold still."

"Okay, but why?"

"Just a minute."

I sit in the silence. "Can I move yet?"

"Not yet, habibi."

More silence. I sigh.

"Give me one more second," he says. And for a moment, the room lights dim. Electricity crackles in the air, and over there, in the room's large mirror, I see a man's shape. But it all fades too soon.

Archie finally breaks the silence. "Brand, do you know how to get to the open market of Khartoum?"

"I can take a cab. Rashid showed me where it is."

"Good. I want you to get out early tomorrow, as early as you can. Bring your passport, your plane ticket, and your keys. Take a cab to the market and stay till the shops open. I want you to find a couple of electric fans—old black-metal bodies with steel cages around the vanes. And a roll of black electrical tape."

"Is this gonna be easy to find?" With the variety of shops I saw there, I'm dubious. Archie is not. He gives me multiple instructions: How to leave the hotel, how to get from the market to the minibus to the train station, and how to buy a ticket to El Obeid. He tells me where to get off before El Obeid, at the town where we will meet. These details are etched in my mind, and I will not let him down.

Come tomorrow, we will be together. Come tomorrow, all will be well with the world.

Intercepted missive 700: The gods know the story. Man fakes it, makes it false. Fate takes the K train, the River God lifts its brother-son. Look out for the lookers. Set a scientific speed. But there is time for one dance when love is in the air.

And we're back. The next morning before the cock's crow, Taharqa (or is he now Pharaoh-god Arensnuphis?) has made his way to the Nile, acquiring a traditional felucca. He dresses Western, carries a metal briefcase filled with a rare-earth mixture and sealed tight with tar. On his neck he wears his leather cord with the rare-earth-metal cube. It will require some serious haste to reach the meeting place before Branden arrives. May this boat sail easily, taking them both toward home.

CHAPTER 29
BRANDEN

MAN, IT'S like being Denzel in some thriller! I get to move the plot!

So as far as Rashid knows, my lazy Yankee ass is still asleep, while I'm already out and about. I walk two buildings down from the Corinthia, catch a cab that for ten piastres drops me off at the first corner of the Souq al Arabi market.

Even as early as this, some shops are open, and as I stroll, I see a middle-aged man throw the heavy cloth cover for his business over its tent roof. Surprise: He sells used electric appliances. Right up top, two black fans hang from a pole, and with some fumbling in English and an Arabic word Archie had me repeat, I get them and the electrical tape too. With the fans tied together and the tape ring around my wrist, I catch a minibus to the train station and get my ticket to El Obeid, easy as shit through, well, a shitter.

There is a bit of a wait for the train south, and as more and more people arrive, I realize I have more reason to fear being discovered. I mean, I dressed local in the clothes Rashid bought for me, but I still move Western, talk American, look not quite African. And who knows who might be working for Rashid or whoever Rashid is working for?

The train arrives and I hop on. First-come seats only, so I'm a bit crammed on the floor next to a Sudanese man whose rather rambunctious twin boys are climbing all over him. All are laughing. Facing us is the mother with a beautiful daughter of maybe eight years and a baby whose mom will at one point suckle behind layers of linen abaya, hijab, and chador.

Our iron horse rattles along, and I cannot tell if I'm drawing attention or just strange. Nearly every space is taken. Nearly everyone is talking—Arabic, English, indigenous language, and sometimes all three. Nearly everyone is smiling. Those who aren't are so sunk into their own thoughts, I wonder if they know they are on earth.

As we near Sinjah—and I know this because a conductor came through announcing it—I prepare for my next ruse. Excusing myself—and getting hugs from my two little friends and a handshake from Dad—I edge my way to the train door. At Sinjah, the track splits, one line going further south to

El Damazin, the other east toward the White Nile and El Obeid beyond. As my transport stops, I get off, even wander a bit as if waiting for the south train. Then, just as it starts again, I rush over and hop back on, with a couple of men there helping me with my fans.

Train takes off slowly, and I'm not sure, but I think I see someone pushing through the crowd make his own quick jump aboard. Have I seen him before?

The trip to the next "stop" is only a few minutes. I put quotes around stop because the train doesn't really stop at Rabak, just slows a bit. At any rate, I hop off. A few others do too. Who are they? I don't have time to wonder.

Rabak is one of the few locations for bridges across the Nile, and I head to the pedestrian part of the span. But before I would step off onto the bridge, I turn and slip down the embankment to the riverfront. And to a small boat being held at the shore by grinning, beautiful, regal Archie.

As much as I love the man, seeing him now is enough to make me lust for him all over again. There is a glow to him that wasn't there before, a spark in his smile, and a confidence that tells me everything will always turn out right. Damn, I missed him.

I clamber aboard. Archie joins me. We share a great but awkward hug with the fans on my shoulder, and as out boat floats to the other side of the bridge, I look up and see a scowling man staring daggers at us.

"Look," I shout, pointing back. "I think he followed me." Some secret agent Denzel I am.

"It's all right," Archie says. "We are ahead of him and will be beyond his grasp in moments. Fans?"

I hand him the fans, and we sit together, letting the current carry us northward. Archie pulls out a multi-tool (sort of a Swiss Army knife with pliers), unscrews the fan bodies, then pulls the power cords off the electric motors. Following his lead, I cut off the plugs and a portion of the wire and reconnect the cords to the motors, wrapping each cord in electrical tape until they are, I learn, waterproof. We push the other ends of the cords into small holes on Archie's suitcase.

Archie asks for the power source. "Your keychain."

I reach under my jellabiya (flashing Archie with my lack of underwear under the kaftan and sirwal) and pull a money belt from around my waist. I pull out my keys and disconnect the small grayish square on the key ring, handing it to him. It is about an inch on a side and an eighth of an inch thick, covered in painted glass.

When we arrived in Sudan, a customs officer didn't want to let us in. "What is this?" he kept asking, shaking the square. "What is this thing?"

"It's decoration," I kept saying. "Just decoration."

It took half an hour and a Sudanese pound note in bribes to get us outta there.

Archie takes the square, quickly scrapes the paint off, tapes the ends of the saved pieces of cord on it, and dangles the fans into the river at the stern of the boat.

Within seconds we have an electrically powered sailboat. Seconds more and we are cruising, easily passing the other feluccas and on our way north.

Our trip takes a sudden turn into a waterfront area, and Archie pulls us to midstream.

"So how do we get out of here?" I say. "We can't take the Nile all the way to Cairo, much less Chicago."

"No, we stop at Khartoum," he says. "We'll need to slip back in, change our tickets at the airport, and fly out. I hope we can lose anyone tailing us, then get home to your parents' house."

"The flight from Khartoum. Sounds like a movie title. A desert romance."

"Sorry, young lover, but a daring new camel ride is off the agenda. And we'd have problems getting around the cataracts farther north. No, it's Sudan Air, at least to start."

"What about the hotel bill? I'm sure Rashid and I ran up a hellacious tab."

"I'll pay it by phone." Archie leans back on his seat, looking me over like he's reconstructing that sight of my... money belt. "You are so handsome, habibi, so excited by our adventure. My hero, here at last. I have something for you."

Reaching around his neck, he pulls a cord up and over his head, then drops it over my head so it settles on my chest. It's long enough that I can see the cord has a decoration, a small dull metal cube, attached.

"Does this mean we're engaged?" I joke.

"We are bound forever." He leans forward, touches the cube and my fingers. "This is *sa*. It is an amulet, our connection, and your protector. You must never take it off."

"But at wrestling meets?"

"Place it under your singlet. They will never know it is there, I promise. But you must swear to wear it always."

"It's from you, so of course I will."

I feel the heat of his gaze. He is so casual in his college T-shirt and loose jeans, yet so elevated. Everything about him is changed, lifted, even more royal African.

"And you are so heavenly cool, Archie. What did they do to you while you were gone?"

"Come sit next to me. Let me regale you. I have a new name."

And regale he does, with one hand on my knee, the other on the tiller. He begins explaining for the first time the gathering place of the last Kushites—without disclosing precise locations, which is all right with me. He talks about the queen who is his sister-in-fate, his birth mother, the high priests and viziers. And when he gets to his ennead, his descriptions are so clear and concise and astonishing I could swear I was there—acting, fighting, swimming, rising with him.

"Taharqa, you are a god!" I am fully awed.

"Some might say that. The god Arensnuphis in fact."

"But everything you did, every task you took carried you into the realm of the heavens."

"Not at first. The first four only called upon my training, my memory, and my morals."

"And after that?"

"And after that, who knows? Who knows what dreams one might believe on an opiated high." I look at him, incredulous. He starts to quote, "In Xanadu did Kubla Khan a stately pleasure-dome decree."

"You really believe this was all like Coleridge's opium dream?"

"How can I tell? All the witnesses were gone, except the gods, who may have been the images I was taught to accept by the priests." He pauses and frowns. "I may speak of Amun, his children, and their ways, but I'm still a man of this century and this reality. I do not yet feel I am Arensnuphis. And in truth, science or magic, gods or drug visions, I believe only in what gets me through the next challenge."

"Your ninth challenge." I say. "Do you have any idea?"

"Not really," he responds. "I have inklings. Something to do with what my vestal mother said about my power. I know I am changed in a way, but I don't know how that change will manifest or how soon. Power can be so many things."

I have to sit up. "This is scary. I knew I was in love with the descendant of a pharaoh, but now he truly is a god and son of gods." I look into Archie's dark eyes, eternal in their depth. "I don't know if I measure up."

"This is what *I* fear, being taken for some nonhuman," Archie says. He takes my chin in his hand. "Branden Hickcock, *eashiq*, love of my life, I am still Archie. I am a man, and I want only to be your man."

I have to smile. "You will always be my man," and I lean in to kiss him. "I will always be your man." We kiss again. "But I gotta wonder what it would be like to fuck a god."

He laughs. "Maybe I can arrange that." We kiss again, hold it for a while this time. Then he leans back.

"This is your ride to paradise," he says at last. "There's no cabin for sleeping, and the boat is too narrow for a rocking good time. But I have a cooler with some food and some beer up front, and we can glide past history for a few hours. Make that several hours. We likely won't see much traffic other than the occasional fisherman, the farmers on shore. And once we get on our plane...."

"Yes?"

"I have heard of this thing, the Mile High Club."

I join him in a lascivious smile.

Our cruise is relaxing, even though we know we are not really secure. I have told Archie all the details I could remember about my time with Rashid. Archie does not appear at all happy, but he says the Nubians will deal with it.

While we have daylight, our scenery is so compelling: land tilled for eight thousand years, often in ways little changed in all that time. The strips of fertility hemmed in by desert. Life itself is hemmed in. The Sudanese people—with lives hemmed in by government corruption, fear, war, and hunger—choose life here, and they find that life worth living no matter what the price. Mourn or celebrate them, the peoples of earth will always choose to live.

Now it is late. Despite a full moon and all the stars, the riverbanks are hard to see, the current finds it easy to rock us, and we are weary.

We have eaten. Archie made cold sandwiches from the contents of our cooler: smoked meat (I don't ask what animal), vegetables, and cold cooked beans as a condiment. He also produced (that rascal) a split of Champagne, which capped our celebration. But strain and effort can overpower the blood rush of excitement. So now the elation of escape is over, replaced by the unsettling task at hand.

Archie is on the foredeck with a kerosene lantern in his hand, peering forward to help me steer. It's like he's George Washington's boatsman at the Delaware or some High Renaissance painting of Orpheus crossing the River

Styx. I don't know if he sees more than I do. There is a bright moon above us, no other earthbound light around us.

Only suddenly not so "no other." A bit north of us I think I see a glowing.

"Archie, put out the lantern and look right."

He sees it too, and as we get closer in, the gentle glow illuminates a dark form.

"A town," he starts, "I think it is Ed Dueim. Yes, I think so."

"Friend or foe?" I ask. That constitutes all the distinctions we need right now.

"It's a university town," he says. "The college there trains teachers. They draw students from all over Africa."

"And nary a cow in sight, I bet." I pause. "But I hear something? Is it music?"

Our electric outboards are so quiet, we can pick up the strains of a song. What we hear is a jazz instrumental, slow and dreamy. I remember the words, sung by Nat King Cole, my father told me. The song is "Nature Boy."

Next to me, I see Taharqa Nimiery, my very strange, enchanted boy, listening and still. I reach out and pull him to me. We gaze into each other's eyes. And there in the moonlight, we slowly dance in place. We are both so tired, so relieved, so in need of comfort. We kiss.

We have never been talkative lovers. We're more into the gasp, the whine, the moan. But not tonight.

"Oh, bae," I whisper. "Oh, bae, you are my heart, yes."

"Eashiq, my love, I am yours. Always yours."

"I will never let you go. We die together."

"Yes," and he smiles, "but let's live together first."

Tomorrow we will make our getaway, trade our seats to the US for tickets to Riyadh, Saudi Arabia, only to double back elsewhere until we can get to O'Hare International and home. So don't dwell on two men clinging in a modified canoe. There's love in the air too.

Chapter 30
Taharqa

"You are American?" the Saudia flight attendant asks, nodding her little capped-and-curtained head and wearing a matching cloth Covid mask, one that's made to protect no one. "You fly to Almanya?"

"Yes," I lie behind my Fauci-approved mask as I place our one suitcase, bought in the King Khalid International Airport, in an overhead bin in the back. "We have some business to handle in Frankfurt before we head home to the States."

This is partly true. Now that I know someone (or some*thing*?) has put evil Rashid on our trail, we must take precautions not to lead them to the center of our stratagem. Our Saudi side trip is allowing two trustworthy Kushites to become pseudo-Branden and Taharqa, who will travel multiple circuitous routes to nowhere.

Have fun smelling our false scents, you dogs.

"By the way," I say, "might we have a couple of your blankets and pillows? It's already been quite a trip."

The real truth is we picked the quiet of a red-eye flight, step one on the way to membership in the Mile High Club. The overnight to Germany seems ideal. Step two is establishing our need for privacy, and step three means obtaining some cover in case privacy is impossible.

"Certainly," she says. "Thank you." That's the universal phrase for those unsure of or unable to speak English.

"And thank you," I reply. Our first three steps are accomplished.

In a miracle of the Middle East, this flight is not filled with passengers. By the time the plane pulls out from its gate, we have three empty rows directly in front of us. I see no eyes looking back, and our fellow passengers seem oblivious to our presence. So it's masks-off time. Our path home may be spy free.

Or not.

This jet is not a wide-body, so there's only one aisle; across it is a possible problem. It's a businessman, suited up like he will be stepping off the plane straight into tomorrow morning's meeting. He is in a last seat, a briefcase at his feet.

"Witness next door," Brand says. "Looks like he's got work to do."

"We'll wait him out," I say, "till after dinner."

"Bet he stays up late," Brand counters. "Looks like a hard worker."

"I bet on early," I reply. "Winner gets to bottom?" We shake on it.

Some long-distance flights from oil-rich airports still serve something approximating a meal. And as we are leaving in the late evening, the flight crew barely waits for cruising altitude to roll out the beverage carts. You can't sell overpriced liquor to sleeping clientele.

Brand and I request water, but Mr. Businessman buys vodka. Not looking good for Brand's end of the bet, but there will be no losers here.

Next into the aisle are the dinner carts. Their movement forward empties the kitchen cabin near us. Time to strike.

I hit the left-hand lavatory, and I wait. Unfortunately Brand makes his move later than he should—there's always a couple of people out to "wash their hands" before they eat, so he must stay seated as they use the right-hand lav. But soon enough I hear Brand knock twice, then once, and I grant him entry.

Airplane toilets are the Fantasy Island of Mile High, but you have to wonder why. There is barely enough room for an average man; how you fit two bodies inside seems unimaginable.

I have my feet on the stool seat and my back against the bulkhead by the time Brand joins me. He starts to laugh, but then I pull him into a kiss. It is easier to touch heads and necks than much else, but I manage to pull open his newly bought buttoned shirt—we are dressing Western now, his robes and skull cap are in that new suitcase—to run my hands across his pecs.

"Love of my life," I say. "How much joy you bring me."

Not that he couldn't give an approximation, considering the pleasure we had last night in our Saudi hotel room. Instead he says, "I love you more than anything, Archie."

We both dressed commando, so soon enough our cocks are out and being stroked. Branden grabs the side of my waist, pushing me harder against the bulkhead as he leans over to taste my hot flesh. It is a weird calisthenic exercise for him to move his mouth up and down my prick in that tight space, but he's up for it. I breathe heavily but manage to keep my noise to a minimum.

I use my hands to urge him to back up. I slide down the bulkhead to sit on the plastic cover of the toilet seat, my ass on something that has been spilled with fluids we don't want to know about. My pants are at my ankles.

I can't move much, and the best he can do is adjust his height as I stretch over to blow him.

Envision this: He is pretzeled like a frog; I am arched over sucking his dick. Okay, don't try to picture it, but know this. If airborne ejaculation equals Mile High, we filled out the membership form.

I am sure there was thumping and gasping, but once I pull up my pants and slip out the door, there is no one waiting outside. I go back to our seats, where Brand sits grinning.

We had skipped the meal, so there are only our water cups to collect the next time a flight attendant goes by. I take a quick glance over to Mr. Businessman, and he is packing up his laptop, quite happily into his fourth vodka. He smiles and nods, and I wave back.

Safely seated, we have pushed up the armrest between us to be as close as possible. I look in Branden's eyes, and I can see some troubling thought is bubbling up inside him.

"What worries you, habibi?"

"About our boat ride," he begins, "Something is preying on my mind. When we reached a safe place to dock outside Khartoum, we disembarked, but then the boat slipped off into the current, fan motors still humming, heading north. What if someone finds it?"

I can only smile at his concern. "It might make for some interesting conversations."

"You think there is no way to link it to us? I mean, we did wipe down the area and ditch the cooler, but were we really careful?"

"Where have you left fingerprints to be recorded and examined, my bad man?"

"Okay. Okay. I guess they can't get DNA from my butt prints either."

"DNA," I ponder. "I wonder what my Ancestry profile would show."

"So would the felucca sail on for miles or maybe strike another boat or maybe sink on its own? Could somebody catch it, maybe at the sixth cataract, and find its strange power source?"

"So many maybes," I say. "Do not worry. The boat will take care of itself."

"But how?"

"Remember the briefcase I left on board? There is enough material in there to fry our dear felucca into charcoal bricks. That's all they will find, and I wonder what the latest Sudanese dictator will do with that."

"Oh," he says. Then with a big smile, "Oh. Cool."

"And as for our bet, I win." We can both see our hardworking middle manager is asleep and breathing heavily.

Our big adventure in the air has us relaxed and joyous. I wish I could write down all the silly, sweet things we say to each other, futures we plan, and pasts we relive. For now, our time together looks endless and bright. We will have all kinds of tasks to manage once we land—getting back into the US, contacting Branden's family, making sure we really are safe, and returning to campus to try a few more rare-earth tests.

Our conversations eventually show signs of how tired we are and how late it is. We pull out the blankets and pillows for some well-earned rest.

Only not that much sleep.

A message to frequent fliers who hate fellow passengers who take off their shoes on a plane: Fuck you. After our nap and well into late hours, we take off our shoes—and our pants. Spooning under a blanket, eyes closed in reverie but not sleep, each in his turn swelling in the heat and contact of the other's body. I press back, eagerly sliding my butt crack up and down his girthy cock's length. I feel his strong thighs against me. His arms are around me in a possessing hug.

Before we left for the airport, we cleaned ourselves inside and out in our hotel room, but there's also a little container we created by emptying a travel shampoo bottle and refilling it with something more lubricating that we found in the duty-free drugstore. (Amazing what they sell in a hyperconservative nation's airport.) He soaks a finger, presses it into me. I let out a sigh; then we both shush me. In a little while, he soaks another finger, then another. I am his for the taking, ready to shout, plead, groan. Instead I gruffly clear my throat, and he presses forward toward my pressure.

And it begins—him entering me slowly, him breathing out, relaxing into the pleasure. We take our time. Mile High requires discretion. He has me, all of me, to the hilt. I grind a bit so that he feels me all around him.

"Branden, my sweet man," I whisper. "You are my home, my heaven, my forever. Every second with you is beyond magic. It is love."

This begins the slowest motion of slow-motion fucks, and I actually bite my pillow as I feels every bit of Branden, how much his penis slides up past my prostate, then back, then up. His chest is against my back. His thrust comes from his waist curving in, curving out. His left arm, under me, presses against my chest. His right hand strokes my pulsing phallus.

All of it says love. I am in ecstasy.

It does not take long, though it feels like it lasts forever. His thrusts speed up, become uncontrolled. He pounds into me as nature's demands take over. My climax is not just penile. It is all over me, and I am hugged tight, pulled closer. He buries his curly head into my shoulder, and I hear and feel his moan. We let our breathing go, and it slowly returns to normal. Only then do I realize he has already come.

That's when we take in our surroundings. Most of the cabin is dark. Our air-conditioner tubes, open full blast, must have provided some cover for any noise we made. I hear busy voices in the kitchen cabin, where a couple of flight-crew members gossip. Across the way, the businessman dreams of laptops full of future.

We skulk about, rearranging clothes and folding the blanket so any fluids are hidden. (My apologies to the next user.) We sit up a while, nod off a while to the endless hum of jet engines, and then we do it again. My turn inside.

Mile High Club, multiple memberships. This trip we will not forget.

Intercepted missive 802: What happens in airplane seats stays in airplane seats. (Nasty!) But look ahead to stratagem work—and weddings! Who is that handsome man on the rooftop? In the alley? At the gym? All the pursuers want to know.

CHAPTER 31
TAHARQA

THE REST of the summer goes by quickly. Perhaps too quickly for us to stop the tidal wave of woe from catching us even as we prepare for it.

Frannie Hickcock is glad to have us home, and I am so glad to be with her this Independence Day. We cook together, the three of us. Mr. H. mans the grill and taste tests the burgers. For Branden and me, our sex life has settled into regular and loving evenings, occasionally erupting into passionate impromptu performances. (Mother Hickcock is not perturbed. "It has been too long since the sounds of young loving have been heard in this house," she says.)

In our free time, we take bikes to the lakefront, sometimes touring the city's length of neighboring parks, sometimes wading in fresh water—crystal clear near the shore, sparkling blue as we look out across the lake. We watch summer theater. We join a weekend sailboat crew, practicing some of our skills, loving the silence that swallows us when we are far from shore.

We stand and cheer the Pride Parade in the queer neighborhood of Northalsted. That's at the end of June, and Chicago has become a resort town. Tight bike shorts and flowery, flowing summer dresses are on display. Sunglasses and slow strolls down Michigan Avenue ensue.

Late July rushes in, and we stop at the art booths during Northalsted Market Days. The neighborhood turns into a street fair of dubious art, socially conscious appeals, meaningless junk, and one superhot guy in a lifeguard chair spraying the crowd with a water pistol. The water is most welcome because the street is asphalt and the sun is killer and the crowd is gloriously half clad in tank tops and shorts; or no tops, tight shorts, and leather vests; or full-on carnival drag. The bars set up outdoor tables and offer their cocktails poured into pineapple shells. Top it all off with the effervescent, hell-bent-for-joy attendees set free from restraint, and you have a street beat only Rio can rival.

The summer heat peaks in August, but we are back on campus by midmonth, hiding out in our apartment's AC as the nearby farms harvest corn and soybeans. But a new Covid scare shuts down Pardell briefly in the fall, and we return to Chicago in time for Halloween celebrations in Northalsted. No one parties like queer folk on our holiday of All Hallow's Eve.

Brand and I stop by late in the afternoon and make it from Addison south to Belmont, sipping drinks and gawking at the human scenery. It is coming on evening when we get to the block containing Hellstorm, the BDSM club. It's a place I had read of, a busy bar with an even busier bondage-and-domination back room. Not my cup of tea, but Brand seems compelled to at least take a look at the outside.

In the purple twilight, one black-and-blue-striped bondage flag flies above the open door of a very nondescript brick structure. Outside, a line of fifteen people shuffles and sways to a rhythm not exactly heard, but felt. At the door stands a narrow, very pale White man with a ball cap and a powerfully built Black giant—six foot six at least—with bare chest muscles straining the black leather harness he is wearing.

My irrepressible lover jumps in front of the line, shouting, "Aren't you Joe Stone?"

"So I am. So I am." His voice is warm as the closing day, but something tells me this guy can beat the joy out of you—or the ecstasy into you. "Do I know you?"

"I doubt it," Brand says while White guy lets a group of four into the door after checking IDs. "But I wrestle at Pardell like you did."

"Well, hello, fellow traveler," Stone says, offering a huge hand for a shake. "I hope you do it better than I did."

"Oh no! You still have such a reputation down there." Branden is now a total fanboy. "It's really a tough break what happened to your hamstring. And right before the Olympic trials."

"I guess it was fate," Stone says. "At least I didn't have to face that Russian who dropped people on their heads. How'd the team do at nationals?"

Another bunch of revelers makes it into the door, and I notice a similar number is exiting at the other end of the building.

"Really well. I came in strong, first place," Branden says. "I'm going up a weight class, but I think I can make the Olympic team this year."

There's the sound of a ruckus coming from inside, and we all look. A White person in full makeup, stilettos, capri pants, and a half-open blouse showing chest hair is using claw-length fingernails to hold someone by the ear. I see above the room-length bar a huge bondage flag painted on the brick; a red neon heart is in the upper left corner. The person in heels leads their victim out of our view.

"There may be something I need to pay attention to in there," Stone says.

"Sure," Brand says, "sure. It was great to meet you. They still have your tapes in the coach's office. I watch 'em all the time."

Stone's smile is genuine and a bit embarrassed. "It's good to know I still have fans. You all interested in coming in, having a drink with me?"

Brand looks at me. I look at him. Suddenly he says, "Thanks, but we need to be traveling on." He leans in for another handshake. "Really great. Thanks."

"Y'all be careful tonight," Stone says. There is an unmistakable seriousness in his tone.

As we move to the street, I have to ask. "Why did you turn him down? It was a chance to drink with your hero."

"I only have one hero," Branden says. "And meeting Joe Stone was enough."

We turn back to retrace our path, but at the first corner Brand stops me, runs up the alley behind Hellstorm, then comes back.

"You needed something?" I ask.

"I had to mark my territory," he says. "Let's go."

We head north again through a crowd that is thinning yet revving into a fever of frolic. There is giddiness, lots of happy noise, and the edge of something dangerous hovering. We both sense it pulling at us; temptation wafts through the atmosphere. We escape home before we can be caught up in that fever.

Back at school we return to surreptitious science, but Brand and I know we have a much more imminent task—keeping me in the States. Being an engineer is usually a good way to get a US work visa, so I apply.

"Maybe we should go the next step and get married," Brand says. But something in me says not yet.

"I want our marriage not to be rushed, habibi. I need the statement to be open and public," I say, "and then there is the stratagem. Those at home are expecting us to complete the tasks, not take a break so near the finish line."

Branden, bless his loving heart, does not argue. Then we get word that Ahmed, my old bruh, is coming to the campus. We meet him at the miniscule Pardell bus station, and the first thing from his smiling lips is, "Aren't you two married yet?"

"I thought—" He cuts me off.

"A pharaoh wedding is all we talk about back home," he asserts. "Where is your marriage license office? Is it on the way?"

And like that, it is the autumn of our wedding. Ahmed stays over as we wait for a county judge to become available. And at 1:30 p.m. on a mid-November Wednesday, we stand before the judge and our witnesses—the Hickcocks, including Brand's brother, wife number three, and their kids, Ahmed, and some clerk's office staffer Ahmed cajoled into evening out the number—and we are exchanging vows.

"Now is when the couple may speak words of their choosing," Judge Sherrod says. "Do you have things to say?" Brand and I stare at each other, but then he speaks.

"This is all so sudden," and everybody laughs. He holds his amulet, the one I placed around his neck months ago, as he continues. "Taharqa, I have loved you since the day we met, and I have wanted you and me to share our lives together. So this is the day all the days count for. This is the day we are one couple forever." He gulps, then says, "Forevah evah."

More laughter. My turn.

"I think the want came for us a little before the love." More laughter, mainly dirty. "But my soul has waited to say these words for centuries, for millennia, yearning until it was you I stood before to say them. We are one. Together. As our spirits have intended for thousands of lives before. My Asim, habibi, eashiq, bomani, and Sebiumeker, forever yuya." We both laugh at that one, though no one else does. "One love eternal. Forevah and evah."

"Are there rings?" the judge asks. We look blank; we hadn't thought of that. But Ahmed jumps up, pulls something from his pants pocket, and hands one ring to each of us.

"There's a tracker in them that syncs to a cellphone," he whispers. "Uses GPS. Covers a city, maybe more." And he winks.

The judge has us speak in unison. (She probably had more couples waiting.)

"With this ring, I thee wed," we repeat. "With this vow, we plight our troth: to love one another and forsake all others," and blah-fucking-blah, the end.

The wedding party cheers, insisting the newlyweds kiss, which we do with shyness. Till it becomes thirsty, then hungry; then Brand's brother shouts, "Jeezus, guys, give it a break!"

We have an off-campus motel wedding reception filled with a familial joy I am totally unaccustomed to. Brand's brother has one scotch too many and tries to make a piss-poor joke about "homo wedding nights." Branden pushes him into the motel pool. Even the third wife laughs.

"Those names you called him," Ahmed says to Brand and me, "Quite a collection of praise."

"You mean it wasn't Egyptian for shithead and smartass?" Brand jokes.

I say, "You know habibi means my beloved, and eashiq is lover. Asim is the Arabic male name for protector; bomani is old Egyptian for warrior; and the Nubian god Sebiumeker is Arensnuphis's partner and eternal love."

"And you," Ahmed says to me, "are Arensnuphis, Kush companion to Mother Isis."

"That's a lot better than shithead and smartass," Brand says. "I wish I had even more names for you."

"There are several more," Ahmed begins, "like—"

I interrupt. "I am not yet all these things. But call me love and all I need hear will be said."

The rest of the fall semester, our time is filled with sneaking into various labs, modifying equipment, doling out portions of ytterbuim and gadolinium, testing and retesting, getting our coursework done, and fucking like we're married, each time a little different, a little more loving.

There's only three weeks between Thanksgiving's long weekend and Christmas break, so we fill that with projects for the stratagem. Such as…

For those who don't know, gas-powered automobiles have something called a catalytic converter. Simplified, it converts toxic pollutants from burning gasoline into less toxic substances. Materials used include expensive items like platinum, rhodium, and palladium. So what if more catalytic (and suddenly less expensive) materials get used? Might there be a drop in air pollution levels in big cities? Too bad only a few campus rats left their cars parked where they were available for conversion, but we did test them successfully ourselves.

Some guy in Missouri got his solar house damaged. Or was it damaged? He learned the multiple solar panels on his roof got disconnected while one six-inch square near his chimney invaded the circuits. He not only heated and lit his big suburban house, but he was also paid his salary equivalent for the electricity he sent back to the power company. Too good to be true? It is. He had to sue the greedy company managers to get his fair payment. And they keep coming back to look at that little six-inch plate.

Permanent magnets have major roles in electric car motors, and lithium plays a big role in making them. Rare-earth metals could play a bigger role if they were easier to mine. Lithium mining can be damaging to the environment, and the mining is drawing protests. But the Pardell experimental solar car team lost its last national competition to another college competitor with strange new magnets, and the winners didn't even get the improved solar collectors we have on hand. Wow.

Branden got to the wrestling nationals in the light-heavyweight class. (Guess we fed him too well.) Anyway, the championships were held in Detroit the first week of December, and he took second—yay, team. But after all the hoopla and sweaty events, when they came to clean up and close down, there was this one little LED light on the wall of the men's dressing room that never went off. They couldn't switch it off because it wasn't attached to a switch. To any switch. They couldn't turn it off when they took it from the wall. And better than any LED known to city and college experts, its soft yet powerful luminosity provided light to an entire room. Which is what it is doing now... when local electrical experts aren't probing it like alien technology in a science-fiction flick.

A Sunday newspaper in December provided a deep but questioning analysis of a Northalsted incident. Remember Halloween, when the street was electric with happy bodies and wanton desire? A former wrestler was doorman and bouncer at what the news story said was his "gay-oriented" nightclub. I recall how he looked so serious when he told us, "Y'all be careful tonight." And Brand slipped into the alley behind the place to "mark his territory." Come to find out, Brand left one of our test lights outside the club's back door. It served its purpose to protect that club and its clientele. It protected that manager too, according to the article, and it played a major role in foiling a murderous attack. It helped catch a serial killer. But the reporter could find no one who knew how the light got there or how it worked.

You may remember Ahmed's description of the Pardell University campus? Maybe you recall the conclusion where he mentions that giant smokestack we call John Pardell's last erection? Well, the furnace was still being used in heating some older buildings, so it did put out air pollutants. But not anymore. Not after we fixed it.

WE HAVE all our coursework done to earn graduation by December, half a year early, and we fill the last semester of the school year with elective class hours, more rare-earth tests, and reports to Ahmed and beyond. We stretch our time on campus for happy reasons: Branden has qualified for the Summer Olympics, and we're marking time before the trip to Rome.

One humid May evening, we walk out across an open field to the campus airport. (Pardell has an aviation school.) It's a shared time for us of excitement and apprehension for the changes we know are coming. The blue lights of the short runway there both dazzle and calm us. A campus cop car comes by, but it's obvious we have nothing on our minds but our love, and he drives off. Lovely end to a lovely school career.

Mr. and Mrs. Hickcock drive down the next day for graduation, and Frannie is so pleased to see Brand and I have letters declaring we graduated "with high honors."

In Chicago, we visit our old friend Lake Michigan till Brand heads to Olympics training camp. The Hickcocks have been saving up, and we'll all head to Italy to cheer on our hero.

That night before his event, I have a dream.

Intercepted missive 925: Pay attention to dreams. What happens when what happened secretly becomes what is known? Threats are plotted tightly, chapter and verse. There is truth in dreams.

CHAPTER 32

Taharqa's Dream

IT IS a sultry night with nil but sighs of an ocean breeze, and I am walking on sand. Or is it feathers?

I know I am in a dream; my people of the Nile take dreams to our hearts. The first interpretations of dreams live in hieroglyphs on the most ancient walls and papyri, and this, like all dreams, is a message. I only hope that in the proper time I can read it.

I have left ancient Suakin's beach, wandering south and west along a Red Sea coast wrapped in mythic tales. Here, storytellers say, virgins on their way to meet the Queen of Sheba were impregnated by ghostly spirits. The air has the heavy feel of pleas from humanity betrayed. The sky is a glitter bomb of stars, and yet the night is as quiet as a fairy's wings. I am alone.

Suddenly, above the sea's whisper—no, barreling out of the sea—horse's hooves come galloping. I look up to see the silhouette, horse and tall rider, black against the dark, thundering forward directly at me.

I turn to run, but I am sinking in the sand. It sucks at my feet, making each step more arduous. Above me I hear the horse whinny, and the hooves rush up.

The dark rider grabs me, lifts me effortlessly, and I am held, feet dangling, pressed against the steed's heaving side as we rush onward. I look into my captor's face in the moonlight.

Of course it is Branden. Who else but my yuya would be my champion?

But we seem to be rising, climbing ever higher. Are we off the ground? Are we in the sky? The stars seem closer, the wind fresher, his arm holding me strong and caressing.

This must be heaven, magic, or some lovely dream. Clouds pass us by, we are shrouded in mist, and we break free into the night air above, below, and before us.

Ahead I see… what? A tent? An Arab tent like no Arab has seen outside of the silent movies. How is this? I have fallen into a dream of a movie I've never watched, and despite its colonial bias and sexual aggression, being taken by *The Sheik* is rather sexy.

Suddenly we halt, the horse stirring sparks rather than sand. Valentino—no, Branden—leaps down, at the same time swinging me further up into his arms. He steps forward, and with a sweep of his turbaned head, walks us into the tent.

Turbaned? Have I slipped into a Sikh space in India?

Whatever. He tosses me upon a pile of pillows, and I land like a silver-screen goddess, seated with my legs stretched out, my arms behind me. I guess, since I'm the kidnap victim of this picture, I am so positioned as to expose my cleavage and my crotch. My silk pajama shirt is mostly unbuttoned and open. My pajama pants are outlining what's beneath them.

I breathe a timorous sigh.

Branden looks down at me. Or I think it's Branden. Of course he has the face, but his boyish looseness is now all haughty control. His dark eyes flash diamonds, and the smile he flourishes is hungry, wolfen. My loving boy has become domineering man, asserting his right to me as he paces before me. I am going to be taken.

He dives down to his knees before me, pulls my head to him, and kisses me. It is a hard kiss, not loving but demanding, insistent. I am hurt, shocked, confused by it, and when I open my mouth to object, it is his tongue that is there, while mine is taken, stilled.

I am about to be ravished!

Let me say this right now: I do not condone sexual assault or any form of sexual aggression without consent. But this is a goddamned silent-movie wet dream, and a fling at role-play-forced pleasure can be extra hot, as long as it stays consensual and inside the mind.

His sinewed hands snatch me up. I cannot bring my arms from behind me, so he is free to ravage my open chest with kisses, licks, bites. He nips my ears, exposes my shoulders to press his teeth along them. He licks and sucks at my neck.

I am at a loss. This is not what I asked for; I agreed to nothing. But the passion in his attack has me stunned, almost paralyzed. It is only the passion that my body responds to.

He releases me. I drop, no, float back onto a softness like a dream of clouds. I am flat on my back. He looks me up and down, all sneering fire in those coal-black eyes. My breath is gasping, uncontrolled, begging. Begging to be wanted, begging to be taken.

"You are mine," he says. "Now I will make it so."

A few decades ago, writer Erica Jong came up with this phrase: the zipless fuck.

With a wave of his arm, Brand's clothes fall away. Somehow I am already naked, and he grabs my ankles roughly, pulls my legs up. My knees bend. My hips rise. I am as open and exposed as a patient on a stirrup table.

He is there between my legs, radiating his power down onto my trembling form. And his eyes soften, well up. He will make me his lover, and I have no way to deny it. I feel his hot member between my hips. He rubs it slowly up and down, across the taint, caressing the pucker. He rubs it three times. And then he enters.

I can, wide-awake and in an exceptionally dull American lit class, bring up the memory of Branden inside me. I can feel him when he isn't there, know his cockhead and shaft like a road map, or more like a sex toy—a well-used, deeply adored sex toy. If I'm careful, I can get near to orgasm just on muscle memory.

By all the gods and prophets, in this dream I feel him new again, sowing me with love, making my love grow.

I cannot say if I reached orgasm or how many times or how long between, because dream logic is its own thing. But I see his face so very close, peering down at me. His hair is sweaty and sticking to his forehead. He smiles so gently and says, "I love—"

But I cannot hear the end because steaming up behind him like a malevolent storm, there is some *thing*. A form solidifies before me.

A demon, a spirit, an evil djinn towers above us, back pressed against the tent's silken cloth. From a belt around its ample belly it pulls a massive knife, like a short-bladed scimitar. It grins madly and holds it skyward, then slashes down. And with a swipe and a snarl, it sweeps my sheikh away.

I am left to face the djinn. Its face I somehow know from somewhere once. I stare with fury and fear. I must save myself, myself and Branden. I lurch forward.

But suddenly I am falling through the sky, falling, falling until… I wake up.

WHAT WAS that? In the dark room all I know is panic. I can't hear Branden's breath or feel his solid form next to me. Where is he? Where am I?

And I realize I am alone in a hotel room in Rome, Italy. Branden is miles away in the Olympic Village, resting before his medal matches. We are both safe from evil djinns, aren't we? I lie awake, too buzzed to sleep, waiting for morning and to see my love safe in the day.

Intercepted missive 1001: Remember the little engine that could? Well, it did. Churn and cataracts, dontcha see? But a secret seen tells too much. Prepare for the pack attack.

CHAPTER 33
BRANDEN

NOW'S MY chance to earn some precious metal for myself. Not pure gold, maybe, but precious enough, made of bronze. I'm in what's called the repechage match of Greco-Roman wrestling, Division 1 of the light-heavyweight class. That's a mouthful of descriptors better explained by Google. Mainly, I lost my first match to the finalist of my division, but since winning the rest, I get to compete for one of two bronze medals in my weight class.

My opening match was against a Russian bruiser, already an international champ, and it did not go well. Let's say it was not the best six minutes (plus thirty seconds of half-time rest) I've ever had. Yuri will star in the title match tonight, wrestling a Mumbai guy of similar reputation, and we repechage winners will meet the gold and silver medalists on the podium. Up will go the mini flags, on comes the winner's national anthem. Sports page picture. The end.

I think I would have gone top two if I had stayed a middleweight instead of light heavy. Then again, my folks have been loud and supportive, really great when you're so far away from home. And Archie likes the musculature. I do look like a milk-chocolate version of one of those Nubian statues I saw in Sudan last summer. It's so good to have Archie here, even if we can't sleep together.

"Take care, my bomani," he says, "and kick that pale boy's ass."

My last opponent is from Belarus, speaks no English, and may have slipped in a few kilograms more weight than officially allowed. He looks rock hard. We shake hands, really squeezing tight. I refuse to be intimidated. The starter's whistle blows.

Like I hinted earlier, an Olympic wrestling match is two halves of three minutes each with a thirty-second rest period in between. Each of those periods can seem to be the longest three minutes in history. So I'm not going to give a blow-by-twist-by-takedown of this match. The opening of this battle involved a lot of avoidance dancing in circles, some solid grabs at waist and shoulders, and a few escapes. But no throws. Greco-Roman points come from those throws done by hands, arms, and chests but without using the legs—using the legs is okay only in freestyle wrestling.

So do I grapple with a supermuscular male in front of thousands? Yeah, sure. And do I get a chubby? You bet. And do I want to fuck this fucker? Not with a cattle prod. This is my opponent—not exactly the enemy, but nowhere near a love interest.

Especially after the asshole uses his right leg to sweep me off balance near the end of the first period and the referee doesn't call the infraction but awards points to pale boy. Everyone knows it's wrong; the crowd boos and my coach protests. But the half ends with me a point behind instead of up two.

I am steamed, stomping around and snorting like a bull while the coach tries to get me to drink water, calm down, and listen to him. And then it happens—what never happens in a public wrestling competition. I catch my opponent looking at my crotch.

So that's what intrigues him.

The second half begins, and we are grappling like a motherfucker when I pull off the one magic trick I know. He's taking a quick glance at what's swollen inside my lower singlet, and I make it jump. And he is stunned.

In that moment, I grab one of his arms, wrap it in my arms, and shove my hands into my armpits, a move called a Russian tie. I bend him over— he's trying to pull back—and I dive between his legs and flip us both, winding up with me on top of his shoulders, which I press into the mat. By my estimate, the ref is a good second late on calling my pin, but he has to do it anyway. Winner, Hickcock.

After the ref lifts my arm in victory, my opponent and I shake hands again, though I'm tempted to tap him on the fanny. I suspect it isn't often he get turned on and doesn't get his rocks off. (Those tales of athletes and rampant Olympic village sex? They're true. Luckily I'm a married man.)

I wave up at the folks and Archie. They are cheering like crazy, so they aren't hard to find. My coach and fellow wrestlers give me hugs—wrestling is a physical sport all right—and I head into the locker room to change.

Traffic is heavy in the large, well-appointed room that can't help but smell like man muscle. I decide not to shower—maybe I'll give Archie a musky surprise before I have to be back at the dorms. But I do something else, something I now know is stupid. When nobody is looking, I pull something out of my gym bag. I lean with one hand against a tiled wall. When I pull it down, there is a little spot glowing, hardly noticeable against the ceiling lights. A little present from the world's rare-earth team.

By the time I return to the gym floor, the Russian has decimated his competitor, and we are gathering for the podium. Dev, the Mumbai dude, seems very happy to be there, and isn't silver a reason enough to be happy? The Greek who won the other bronze smiles and throws an arm around my shoulders, and we step up to receive our medals. But the Russian looks worried. Strange. Russians usually just look pissed off. He peers down at me, a step below him. I think he's going to speak, but up goes the music and the flags. When the ceremony is over, but before I can move, he leans down and says in perfectly pronounced English: "Be very careful, my friend."

So what's up wit' that? Are he and his homies gonna roll me for my bronze? He steps away quickly, so I can't ask him what he means.

The folks and I said we'd meet outside the stadium, so I gather my gym bag, toss on my Olympic jacket, and head outside. There is no one there when I reach our rendezvous point. Not surprising; these arenas take time to get out of.

Or maybe it is surprising, because on a bustling Olympic events campus, no one is right here right now. Oh, now there's one person; I sense them passing on my right when I feel a sudden peck on my neck. The passerby doesn't pass but stops and grabs my right arm. What?

On my left, my mother appears, and Dad comes around in front. It's a group hug for us all, Archie of the quick kiss on my right. And we head into the city for all-I-can-eat spaghetti. (I've been starving to keep my weight down for the matches). A great late evening, plenty of Amarone wine, and they drop me off at the athletes' compound. Again, it's kind of quiet, empty. I turn and head up to my building and my room.

Great night, great morning, and I gather my bags, bronze medal placed protectively inside the suitcase. The morning's events have already started, and I'm going to meet Archie for whatever breakfast we might find. We're thinking about a rented room or a hotel to love in until closing ceremonies in two days.

I leave my bag behind the compound's check-in desk and head outside. Again, no one around at the moment. Again, an approach from the right side, but this time a sting, and the passerby grabs my arm as my legs turn to jelly and I'm in total darkness.

Intercepted missive darkside: Brand, Brand, whose got the Brand? Mutual (of Omaha) ensures hatred is in the market. Panic Amalgamated. *Sudan Slays a Sailboat* 'cause it has *No Gun to Shoot*. A three-fingered Aussie will let you know what's too close. Ow-wow. Hey, let's play the Korean way: Red light, Green light. Everybody RUN! Be afraid, my friends, be very afraid.

CHAPTER 34
TAHARQA

BRANDEN IS gone!

I get outside the athletes' compound, and he's not there. It's not like him to be late, at least not with me. I give a 360-degree turn and see no one. Finally, suspicions rising like soda bubbles, I go into the security area. And they have seen him. Yes! And they have his luggage here. Yes. And they have seen him leave with someone in a dark car. Oh no!

I run back outside, pull out my phone, and hit the tracker app. These wedding rings are such a blessed gift from Ahmed, indispensable and so precious, we will wear them to the grave.

No. Graves are not what I want to think of now.

The blip on my phone shows a location about three miles away. But how do I get there? I have no car.

Not far off the Olympic campus, there is a JUMP station, with several electric bikes waiting for rental. I have the credit card, and as I swipe and pull out my choice, I quickly consider and reject the idea of calling the Hickcocks. They are by now awaiting their own Chicago flight, and we decided last night not to see them off. We'd meet them at home.

If I ever get Branden home. Hold on, my bomani, your protector is on the way.

Branden

THE LIGHT is way too bright in here, and my head's pulsing is too big for this room. Whatever I got shot up with, it is not leaving a good impression.

I am lying down. Why am I lying down? Because when I sit up, my head spins so much I could vomit—if I had anything in my stomach since last night's wine. But I do sit up and stay.

"You are awake. Good." The Asian man saying this is across the nearly unfurnished room, leaning on a long metal table.

"What did you do to me? Where am I?"

His smile is apologetic. "I did not do this to you. And you are in Rome, not far from where we picked you up."

"You kidnapped me!"

He flinches at that, looks at his shiny black shoes. His legs, in dark dress pants, are crossed at the knee. His suit coat is stylish, and his tie, a deep red, sports a gold tie bar embossed with a gold star. Four tiny stars form an arc just to the right of it, like on the Chinese flag.

The face is Chinese as well, but not the accent.

"We do not mean to kidnap you."

"You have!"

Another flinch, "We do not mean to hold you."

"Then let me go!"

That sympathetic smile has become sickening. I wish I felt good enough to punch it out.

"You have information, very important information, that we need to know."

"Who is we?"

"We are a private enterprise. You would not know us."

"I would know you because there is no real private enterprise in China. And you're with the Chinese government."

He does not acknowledge or deny. He just looks at me.

"We need to know where it comes from."

"What? What comes from where?"

"We are aware of your antics." He calls the stratagem "antics"? "We know you have placed devices, small experiments, in certain places. Things like this."

He holds in his hand a perpetual light, likely the one I put on the locker-room wall. They must have pried a few bricks out to get it loose; I was very diligent with the dry-set superglue.

"I'm a college student. I don't know nothin' about that twinkly thing."

"We also know about the boat," he says. "The boat on the Nile."

"That's a movie," I say, "twice"

"That was *Death on the Nile*, and we don't want to mention that word, do we?"

All of a sudden, my bad James Bond movie repartee turns to ashes in my mouth. I have a good idea what he's talking about, a scary idea of what he might do to get it, and no idea at all of where the rare-earth fields are. I don't want to die on a humbug.

"Mr. Hickcock, if that's your name." He leans in toward me, hands on knees. "You can call me Mr. C." And I'm thinking, *How do you spell that?* Also, *Better than* Dr. No.

"Let me be honest with you."

"Please do. Especially that part about not kidnapping me."

He smiles. "Honestly, there is a lot of money involved. You should know. A future of almost limitless funds with, we understand, very limited expenditures, which we are willing to provide. In total. One hundred percent. That leaves a very large pie, and we see no reason to exclude you and your... partner or partners from having a slice. A significant slice."

"A slice would be good since I haven't had breakfast," I say, "but I'm a college student studying engineering, and an amateur wrestler. I don't know nothin' about pie."

"Oh, excuse my manners, Mr. Hickcock!" He rises, still smiling. "We should have offered you a meal. Negotiations always go better over food, don't you think? Please, let me order you something."

"I'd settle for a McDonald's breakfast."

"I'm sure we can do better than that. Coffee?"

"Sure." I can't stand the stuff.

"I will be right back."

And off he goes. The door swings closed, but I don't hear a lock click. I look around—not too fast because my head is still swimming. It's a very nondescript room, perfectly square, painted pale yellow. The fluorescents overhead aren't really throbbing. That must be my brain. Other than the couch I was lying on and the table he sat on, there is no furniture. I don't see an obvious camera setup, though those little GoPros can hide anywhere.

I quietly rise from my couch, carefully open the door. Down the hall one way I hear Mr. C talking, apparently in Italian and likely on the phone. Down the other way, another door. It looks like it could be an outside door. So I rush it.

And I'm outside! It's a regular Roman street, and a block away I see the Trevi Fountain. I may not have money for a cab, but I can get a cop up there. I start to trot along the way, when—

I'm grabbed from behind and a black bag is pulled over my head. Just before I'm jerked off the street, I shout one word:

"Archie!"

Taharqa

WINDING THROUGH traffic-clogged streets outside the central district, taking as few seconds as I can to check my GPS map, I finally get to the block where they are holding Brand. Or so I thought. The homing device is heading away from me. Damn it all to hell!

And somehow, as if sound can be pinned into the air, I hear him call. Even though I can't see him, I say in response "Branden?"

In front of me, a building door opens and out steps a well-dressed, very distressed Chinese man. He looks up and down the block, finally turning to me.

"*Hai visto un uomo andarsene da qui?*"

"*Non parlo Italiano*," I lie. I'm sure this guy is behind my man's disappearance. And from his behavior, he's as confused with this second disappearance as I am.

I climb back on my e-bike and circle around him as I head in the new direction of the GPS. Maybe this time I won't arrive too late.

Branden

SOMETHING IN that head bag must have made me dizzy, 'cause when they pulled it off, I find myself staring at a sunburned face showing too many teeth.

"Well, g'day, mate? How the fuck are ya?"

"Woozy as fuck," I say, shaking my head. "How the hell did I get to Australia?"

"Ah, you're not there, I'm just here. Mountain to Mohammed, eh what?"

"And why are either of us here? Is this another kidnapping?"

"Kidnapping? No, no! That's what that Chinese did to ya." He smiles again. The light on his teeth hurts my eyes. "We're just here to talk."

"Talk about what?" I'm still trying to shake the brain fog.

"Now let's not be coy, m'boy. Not somethin' you yanks are known for anyway. We're here to talk about the same thing the Chinese talked about—the rare earths." I try to look as blank as I can. I'm pretty sure the drugs are helping give that impression. "Say, ya didn't make a deal with them Chinee blokes, did ya?"

"Deal? My mind's too whacked to deal."

"Really, yank? Must be somethin' left over in the kidnap—er, transit bag. Sorry 'bout that."

"Not as sorry as I am."

"C'mon, yank, you can handle it. And I promise"—that big smile again—"the Land of Oz will make it worth your while."

"That would be good, if you hadn't got the wrong guy."

"The wrong guy, yank? I don't think so. See we been followin' yer tracks ever since that Sudan trade."

"What Sudan trade?" Holy hell, are they on to Archie? Do they have him in some other room? This space is as blank as the last one—pale paint, one door, too-bright lights, two chairs including the one I'm sitting on. I have no idea where my man could be if they have him. I had best delay and cover till I know for sure.

"The Sudan coast deal, y'know, 'tween the Canucks and the Saudi-Yank team. On that abandoned island."

"Canadians? Saudi-Yanks? Never met 'em." That's something I don't have to lie about.

"Then there's that jerry-rigged little sailboat ya had on the Nile. Permanent power, and a surprising little bomb ya put in it. My mate lost 'alf a hand trying t' grab it."

Jeez. Now I know what happened to our little love boat. And why Archie wasn't so upset about the felucca getting away.

"Then we lost what was left when the fuckin' Sudan prime minister had the whole area torched as a rebel act. Flushed all the metals away." He takes a deep breath. "And who was your partner on that little cruise?"

"I don't know where you get this. Who says anybody was on any boat?"

"We do 'ave our sources. And how about you on that Missouri rooftop."

In an ultimate caught-you-red-handed move, he flashes an 8-by-10 in front of me. Yeah, that's me, as cute as Brad Pitt in *Once Upon a Time in Hollywood.* We each went up on the roof. At least I kept my shirt on.

"Where'd you get that?"

"Wouldya believe some kid across the street woke up in the middle of the noight, caught ya in the act, and took a picture. He was gonna use it at show and tell, but we got to 'is mom first." He can see my surprise and anger rise. "Aw no, we din't 'urt 'er. Fact is, that kid's college is all paid for. We could make a similar deal with ya."

"I was on scholarship. My college is paid for."

"Sure, mate, and we can make it so ya can afford a lifelong vacation. We just need to know where the rare earths are."

"Rare earths are not rare. My chem prof told us so."

"Aw, c'mon, yank! Us Western nations gotta stand together, roight? Can't let those Commie blokes best us?"

I seriously consider asking about the Land of Oz's standing on fairness to the aborigines. But more seriously, I'm still fighting to get two thoughts together.

"I been drugged twice," I say. "I need some air."

"All roight, mate. Let's take a walk."

I nearly fall over getting up, and another man who had been behind me all this time steadies me. His hand has only three fingers. So sorry, mate.

The two lead me through an open office space that lets out onto a street. Not far off, I can see the magnificent ruin of the Roman Colosseum. The light is golden, a fine prenoon time for a stroll, and I breathe in deeply.

There's a flash in my vision. I see two steps ahead… a raven? Only for a second, but I swear a black bird had eyes on me.

Now three men approach us, all wearing hats, and they walk directly into our path. The central man, using his wide brim as a kind of mask, says tersely: "SAP. South Africa Police"

"What? Saps?" the Aussie says, "What the flamin' fuck, you callin' us names?

"Give it up, y'all," drawls the man on the left. There's cowboy Houston in that accent. "We're here for Mr. Hickcock. Will y'all kindly relinquish him, please."

I feel the Aussie's hand tighten on my left arm, but before my other escort can do the same, he is grabbed and smacked hard. I guess this is a no-gun-play crowd, a blessing for an innocent bystander.

The SAP cop grabs my free arm, and I'm the rope in a tug-of-war on a daylit Roman street. The tug doesn't last long. The SAP overpowers my Aussie mate like the Hulk on Loki. I am awash in a maelstrom of too many accents. Once I'm snatched, the winners put a sleeping mask over my eyes and drag me to a waiting car. Silent as it is, it has to be electric.

And as we pull away, like a movie screen in my closed eyes, I see Archie on a speeding e-bike, coming for me.

Taharqa

NOT FAST enough! Branden on the move again. I see two disheveled men watching their target move away. They turn and run back, then enter an empty business front as I bike past.

This ride is not good enough. The e-bike is about to run out of its sixty-minute time limit, and I am no closer to rescuing my beloved than I was an hour ago. I saw him for a second, but then the vision cut out.

In frustration I look all around me as if an answer must be written on the street. And I hear my vestal mother's voice: "Through father and mother, we deliver your power. It lies within and will awaken time after time."

I am resolute. I abandon the e-bike on the corner and make my way through multiple lanes of traffic to the looming, many-shadowed hulk of the Colosseum.

Intercepted missive 1111: In the shell game, the pea gets moved the most, found the least. Our tale grows curiouser and deeper, the stranger the danger. But get ready to grapple with mental magic more precious than Olympic gold.

CHAPTER 35
BRANDEN

"NO DRUGS, please!" I say as I am deposited roughly in what seems to be a leather easy chair. The mask is pulled off my face and I see the Electric Wizard. Dough-faced with tiny eyes and a wide grin, he looks at me like I'm one of his newest roadsters. He wears a black racing jacket over a T-shirt and jeans. He puffs on a cigar and leans back, so damn sure of himself.

"So, Mr. Hickcock, finally we meet."

"I didn't have you on my calendar."

"Hah, hah, quite funny," he says, not at all amused. "But you are a man on many entities' must-meet list."

I look around the room, which is occupied by all his minions, several chairs, and a large desk he sits behind. Too much muscle for me to wrestle.

"I didn't know college wrestling was so popular."

"Ah, the wrestling. It was quite good that you made the US team. We would have been hard pressed to arrange a meeting like this Stateside, you know—my former home nation and yours being bosom buddies and all that."

"You had the Texans. Isn't that where you're headquartered now."

"I would not trust Texans to retrieve a newspaper. I stay there for the taxes." He puffs on that stogie. "We are from the same nation now, you and I."

"I don't think that makes us friends."

"Politics and riches make all kinds of friends," he says. "We want to be your friend."

"Fine, then let me go get a hamburger."

"Your hosts have not been hospitable, I see. Well, I am sure we can treat you to a fine late lunch." He waves a hand and some minion comes up and exits the door oh so near me.

"So let us talk freely, as we do on X—" As he leans in, a sudden burst of church bells erupts, almost as if the room were inside the clapper.

"Moth-er-*fuck!*" The E-wizard shouts. "Must they ring that shit so often?"

"Sorry, sir," a minion speaks up. "It's the noon prayer."

"Let 'em pray on Friday like the real religions," he snaps. "Who picked a place so close to the penguin house anyway?"

"Sorry, sir."

"And did anyone find me a Jewish deli?" No answer. "Fuck you all." He snorts, then remembers me.

"As I was saying, let's be blunt: We have no interest in taking your rare-earth metals. Or at least not all of them."

"I don't have rare-earth metals."

"And I don't have fucking time for this. We know there are pure deposits of neodymium and dysprosium somewhere on this planet, and those deposits could make the permanent magnets in our EVs not only top of the line, which we are, but more powerful and longer lasting. We could finally send the petrol boys back to the desert. Let their Bedouin tribes bathe in the black stuff. Hah, hah!"

"So yes, we want those items, but we don't want anyone else to have them or know where we get them. You get it? A covert agreement. We pull out the metals we need, you and your people keep their secret hiding place. And of course we pay your people well."

"That would be nice, but my people live in a brick bungalow in Chicago. The metal they have is in water pipes."

"Very cute. I say—" Another burst of bells rattles the room.

"Jeezus fucking Christ!" he shouts. "How many fucking prayers do these cocksuckers need a day!" His rant goes on even as my food arrives. Coffee, cream and sugar, a Stromboli sandwich, and potato chips.

I admit I'm too hungry to think of much else, so I dive into the sandwich, sipping the coffee black in hopes food and caffeine will clear the mind fuzz. The sandwich is good—and gone in a few bites—and it is only after I finish the chips that I notice a strange taste in the coffee. Strange and frighteningly familiar. I spill the remainder on the floor.

"What the hell is in this?"

"That? A little chemical we use," he says. "We call it a truth serum. Works well, even with food. Works even better with, shall I say, motivation?"

A threat, and I should be scared, but I'm not exactly listening. I'm looking at the wall behind the EW where a dark spot appears. It grows and deepens until, rising in it, I see Archie's face, a raven on his shoulder. I know he sees me, and he smiles reassuringly.

"And what are you grinning at, Mr.—" Before he can finish that sentence, the door bursts open and in walk four men in suits. The shortest has a bald head, a well-toned body in form-fitting Armani, and his own brand of smile.

"Ellie! How are you?" he oozes. "And what's this? You have a guest?"

"He's *my* guest, you billionaire book merchant. Why aren't you off stroking your new rocket, Jeffy."

"Space jokes! How witty, especially from the guy who gives us Space Why." That smile is as cold as the coffee now on the floor. "And you know why I am here. This is Amalgamated business, and we in Amalgamated work together."

"I'm not in your stinkin' Amalgamated. I am independent."

"Except when you can't sell cars 'cause you don't have dealerships. My internet saved you."

"Your internet!"

"*My* internet. You poisoned yours with free-speech hate."

This could and probably did go on the rest of the day. Meanwhile, two Amalgamated Adonises come, lift me by the arms and drag-carry me out. I'm drifting into dope land, but I look back at the wall. Archie gives me two signs: Be quiet, and be patient. I believe he's coming for me. I believe in our love.

Taharqa

AGAINST ALL the jackals of hell, I will save my warrior. I'm still too inexperienced to project my form to him. As when I transported the Chaos Snake, I can only hang on for instants.

It breaks my heart to see him, so strong and yet powerless against greater forces. I must refocus my strength, restore my power. I lean back into my Colosseum shadow. I will save him.

The prophecy is clear to me now. This is truly my ninth ennead, the last test to triumph or to failure. Failure would be disastrous. No! Failure must be impossible. My infinite lover is in danger. I will save him.

What do I have to augment my power? The ring and the cellphone are useless: They leave me too late and too far away. In my pants pocket, I find one small piece of rare-earth metal, a mate to the amulet Brand must be wearing. And in the other pocket is a linen handkerchief. These will help. These must do.

Branden

THESE AMERICAN fucks got no shame. They pull me along through populated spaces, right across St. Peter's Square, and off to their waiting car. The arrogance of affluence.

And they don't even blindfold me, just take off around a few corners. I see us pass the Roman Forum, and not far away, we pull into a garage—a garage in Rome? The electric door rattles down, and they pull me from the car, perp walk me into a hallway leading to a room far nicer than any Hollywood movie set. And so silent you could hear a rat piss on cotton.

My newest escorts release my now-aching biceps, and I stretch and massage them. Soon enough, a different door opens, and in comes the well-built man I saw before. Call him the tech near-trillionaire.

"Please," he says, "be seated."

"I've been forced to sit through three kidnappings today. I'd rather stand for the fourth."

"Hear that?" He seems to be talking to people not in the room. Are we on a Zoom call?

"Three other abductions today," he continues. "As I told the Amalgamated board, we cannot wait for normal negotiations."

"Who is this we?" I ask. "Why do we have me on display here?"

"For someone so in demand, you act like you don't know your own value." He walks the room like a speaker on stage at a TED Talk. Is a camera following him?

"As for we, we are Amalgamated, the greatest assemblage of the world's wealth since Mali Emperor Mansa Musa." He smiles. Why do they always smile? "You could say we are the world." Music should play behind that.

"Very modest of you."

"In truth, I lie," he says. "Potentially the greatest assemblage of wealth in the world will be those who know where the pure rare-earth metals are. And that means you."

"Where do y'all get your false information from, the back of a comic book?"

"We have our ways, including the intercepted missives your people send out. We know you were in Detroit when the perpetual light appeared. And we've seen your picture on that Missouri roof."

I guess that moment was Instagrammable.

"Let's not play games. We're all Americans here; well, most of us. And no matter what the others offered, it's your patriotic duty to help us in this cause. As you have to know, rare-earth metals are the future."

"And it's my patriotic duty to give the future to America?"

"That's right."

"Just like it was my people's patriotic duty as slaves to create your American past, present and future?"

He frowns at that. No answer.

"Okay, let's talk money," he says. "How many billions will it take? We are Amalgamated. We can toss off billions like used diapers."

There it is again, the arrogance of affluence. I shake my head in disbelief. Only behind the tech near-trillionaire, I see that dark spot. And it isn't Archie I see, but a mist, a silent arm of fog sliding forward. I smile at its approach.

And there is a bang and some shouts and some sort of cans tossed into this palatial throne room. And it's gas! Some sort of knock-out gas, and I can't breathe, and I stumble. Archie's fog can't reach me, and I pass out.

Taharqa

I AM left coughing in retreat. These new invaders surprised us, and their gas invades my portal to Branden, nearly taking me out with my habibi. I am gasping, wheezing, the power in me overpowered. I fall farther back in the niche of Colosseum where I have been hiding. It protects me, but what protects Branden?

I do. Pharaoh Taharqa protects. Lion-headed Arensnuphis—this is a god's names, and it is now mine. I earned the gods' honor and their sanction, and gods do not fail. I must be them and strive like them and use the power that the gods placed in me before birth.

But what do I do? In all the years of apprenticeship, I spent my time mocking gods and the ones who believe in them. Is this my penance, to lose the only man I would ever love?

I will not allow even gods to make that happen.

I thought a less material approach, the gentle fog, would give me spare strength, only it makes it too easy to overpower me. We need power and reach, he and I. And quickly.

Think of what you learned and half forgot through life. Think of where power—where magic—comes from.

I carefully wrap my rare-earth piece in the linen handkerchief. Ancient magic and future science. Together there must be something to help us. I believe there will be.

Sorry, bomani. I will be there. In fact, I am there. I just need to touch you.

Intercepted missive climax time: Cry not for our heroes. What may seem lost can be found. Snakes alive! Evil must not live. What about the water?

CHAPTER 36
BRANDEN

NOW THIS room is dark, damp, odorous like some basement or a tomb. I am tied into my wheeled office chair this time, hands and feet locked into place. I roll my head to seek clarity, then drop it, almost asleep again.

"Wake him up," I hear, and there is a slap across my face. Motherfucker!

"Wake up, Mr. Hickcock." The accent is eastern European. Maybe Russian? "Wake up. It is time for you to talk."

"Talk? About what?"

"You play with us? We beat you on your wrestling mat, and we will beat you here."

I can't see a face, but a body moves in the gloom. Do I see epaulets? Military medals? A gold belt?

"Nothing to say?" He pauses. "Give him the shot."

That brings out my fear. "No, you can't do this! I have enough drugs in me to stock a pharmacy." No use—a hand comes from behind, pulls up my right sleeve, and jabs my biceps.

"Then maybe my injection will be the one that pushes you over the line. Now, where are the rare earths?"

I don't know where rare earths are—that's what I try to say, but my lips feel swollen and my throat rasps.

"Give him a drink." Those disembodied hands are back, pulling my jaw down and pouring water into my mouth, setting off a coughing fit. These fucks are really serious.

"Now, you will tell us what we need to know. If not now then later. We can lock you up"—I see a dark hole appearing, even in the darkness—"for as long as we want."

There is Archie's face, straining, determined. "The gulag is a black hole. No one will find you. No one will save you." Archie's hand reaches out and tosses—a black cat?

I don't think kitty will drag my carcass in like a dead mouse. So what is it doing here? What good is this, my love?

The cat, somehow unseen, starts to rub against my ankles. I can't pet you, little cat, but the soft fur and the purring seems to soothe me. I calm down. Better yet, I feel no drugs at all.

I look up, grateful for my man and his power. I see him hold out his hand again. It presents a handkerchief, a tiny square inside it. And the metal around my neck responds. I feel strong, stronger than I ever felt before. It is Archie's strength in me.

"Take him away."

The hands behind me have my shoulders, but Taharqa's strength is in my arms. I am pulled at, tugged on, even as I try to lean in my husband's direction.

I shrug my shoulders. The thugs holding me are tossed aside. There are guards in front of me, but they are too shocked by my new power to pull out their weapons.

My interlocutor gapes at me, frozen. I decide to give him my best imitation of a mad Hulk roar.

All of a sudden, bright light flashes down the length of this cavernous space. *Bam* and *brack*! There is the sound of automatic weaponry, a banging and a commotion like a movie firefight. Emerging from the light (Is it a doorway?), shouting men with rifles burst in. The gunfire sprays above the heads of my captors, but I figure I had better duck. There's no sign that Archie's magic makes me bulletproof.

One of the invading soldiers is silhouetted in the light. "Surrender the prisoner," he shouts, but he doesn't wait for an answer. He fires. I hear shouts of pain. I fear my own pain coming near. There is no place to hide except behind falling bodies. I try for Archie's image, but then I am struck hard on the side of the head. Archie can't reach me. It's lights-out again.

Taharqa

BY ANUBIS'S balls, how many of these bastards must we defeat? I had my beloved in my power, my Sebiumeker so near. He gained strength, purpose, clarity from the magic I sent him. So close! But he is pulled away again.

And in gunfire and violence! I pray he has not been shot. That blow to the head was more pain than he could ever deserve.

I will gather power again, but how? Think, Taharqa! Think!

Think of your ennead. What did you learn there? Use that.

First, no more shadow. Kush might hide underground, but Nubia's strength is in the sun god's light. Step forward and into the sun's power. Let my solar disk shine!

With the obvious, murderous intent of these latest monsters, I will have no more chances to take. I must free Branden now before they can harm him more.

Now what is the tool I need?

I tie the metal cube into a corner of the handkerchief. Linen cloth. With shaking fingers I tear the sacred linen into strips, then knot the strips together, metal cube at one end. Before each knot, I say the words: Heka! Heka! Djed medu!

Branden

OH, THE head swelling is for real this time, and the ache from my encounter with a rifle butt overwhelms whatever powerful feeling I might have had. Can this get any worse?

A rough hand pulls my head up, places something cold against my throbbing skull.

"I told you not to harm him!" A voice says. "Look at him now!"

I see the voice, or at least who it comes from. It comes from a thin, brown man. Middle Eastern? Desert military khakis. Combat boots. And I see who the voice is addressing. It is my old nonfriend, Rashid.

"Brando is not harmed," he says, "just a little bruised. Better he knows that we are serious, and that he is somewhere he cannot escape."

"We paid you well for this work, Rashid," the thin man says. "I wonder how many others have bought your services. But if you fail us, if we lose him, you will be the one who pays."

"Oh, we won't lose Brando, will we?" His grin is the worst of all, sharp teeth but missing humanity. "Brando will tell us. And if not, he will tell us of his Sudanese friend, who will eagerly talk to save his faggot lover."

How I hate Rashid. Let me count the ways. I try to spit at him from the office chair I am still tied to, but my mouth is not under my control, and all I reach is the brick floor between us.

"We must know where the rare earths are," the thin man says to me. "We know they are in East Africa, which means they are ours already. The Ottoman Empire ruled this caliphate, and we are active in our recovery of what was taken from us. Now, Mr. Brando, you must tell us what we rightfully ought to know."

I look up, woozy, in pain, lost to the thought I will not get out of here alive. I can muster only one word.

"No!" Then I whisper. "And the name's Branden."

Thin man looks frustrated. Rashid smirks, then reaches behind the leather bag at his side. He pulls out that dagger, almost sword length.

"Let us cut to the chase, shall we?" He comes closer. "Brando may need some… encouragement. A jolt of pain can loosen a tongue and be a godsend." I cannot look at him, but I know he is near. I look down at that wet spot on the granite floor. In it a hole appears.

"Let's see, let's see. Where best to cut?"

Rising from the hole is a snake. Slithering and undulating, a thin gray serpent raises up toward me.

"He wears sandals?" Rashid says. "How about he loses a toe."

The snake's hood flares out, two black spots on the interior. How nice. I'm going to die by cobra bite.

"Maybe the little toe."

In the corner of my eye, I see Rashid bending down to slice into my foot. But what I feel is on my calf: a tiny bump, an insertion. Is that a bite? This is the moment. But I don't feel pain or poison.

I start to shrink. Like a punctured balloon, all my size whooshes out. The ties binding me to the chair can't hold because I am sinking beneath them. Rashid's target, my right foot, recedes so quickly, he is cutting into the stone floor while I become small as a toddler on the edge of the chair.

But that's not all. Riding the snake's back like the cavalry, my lover Taharqa is spinning a knotted cloth above his head. He flings it forward and I hear both thud and grunt—the cloth/rope stretches out elastically and thunks Rashid on the temple. He falls forward, and his blade rattles to the ground.

In the next instant, the rope/cloth wraps around my Ken-doll waist. It pulls me in, and I slide down the snake's scales into Taharqa's waiting arms.

Nine bells toll in the cold room. We disappear, not into darkness but bright, glorious light. Behind us, the rest is not silence, but angry confusion, and the sound of rushing water.

Intercepted missive 2025: Fresh items from Roman newsmongers: Gunfire in Rome's catacombs! Blood and fresh bodies among the bimillennial dead. Someone muscled into a van, witnesses say. Tires scream on the street. Official silence. Climb down into a second news story: Four dead, mysterious. How does the River Tiber flood a room floor to ceiling? Do its gods know? Four bodies—three terrorist fiends and a Sudanese rat—sink like dead fish to the bottom. And the rest of the world spins round and round, chasing its own tales. Gods look down as gods join in divine intercourse. Tis a puzzlement, and a holy pleasure.

CHAPTER 37
BRANDEN

THE MAGIC world is a golden cloud, glowing. I am afloat in its warmth.

I am naked, comforted, caressed. At my feet, I see the snake. The asp weaves its way around my toes. That tickles. But the head changes, and the body sprouts fur and legs, and the snake is the cat. A purring, rubbing black cat is licking at my ankles, pressing its head into my shin, weaving its own path between my bare legs until it grows ragged feathers and it's a raven cawing raucously, flapping wings until…

It suddenly expands, rises, leaps. And the head is a lion, a golden mane and red, red tongue and sharp teeth. It's ebony eyes burn into mine, and I am frightened. I try to fight it off, but its paws/palms/sharp-clawed hands wrestle me. I twist away; the claws scrape against my chest, and I feel the sting. I am sure I feel the blood oozing, and that lion's tongue slathers over the flow. My eyes fill with tears. Surely I will be dying. But when I look down, I am sprouting hair. Long, dark hair, nearly a pelt of my own chest fur.

The beast has me now, arms pinned over my head, its own torso pressed down on my waist and crotch and hips. But this is not a feline body. It is a man in feline form.

I have been rescued from all this terror to be a were-lion's dinner?

I try to cry out, only to have that lion's muzzle pressed over my lips, the tongue plunged into my mouth. It's in my throat, probing and sliding. The taste is hot, flooding, and yet a hint of spice. It no longer feels like a muzzle. It is a mouth, a mouth I seem to know. It has a new name; it is named Arensnuphis.

The lion-man pulls back from my face, and I realize I cannot yell. I cannot talk. I only have gasps of breath, bits of whine, moans. The hair on my chest has stopped growing. The clawed hands no longer pin me, but I cannot move away. The torso holding me down breathes in, sliding its muscled skin over my open, vulnerable body.

A clawed hand presses against my heart, slides over a nipple, pinches with a pain so exquisite I arch my back to get more. Instead it pushes me up, or itself down, until the chimera's head has free access to my sex.

First the tongue licks at my aching cock—how long has it been swollen? The tongue wraps around it, juices and slides over it, and I am somehow harder and not relieved. The pointed tongue slips under my scrotum, soaking and stroking my balls, and I can't take it, but I have to.

I arch again, my hips rise, providing free reach into my most private hole.

The tongue goes there, covering my taint with wetness, taunting the opening with its raspy surface. I twist and bend. I want to go. I can't make it stop. I am ready and totally unprepared and it doesn't matter. I am going to be penetrated.

The beginning entry is a shock like a punch. Its member is so thick, my love hole feels frozen open. Yet inside, deeper, it slides effortlessly. My insides open like a relaxing fist. I feel the invader everywhere. It is fiery and loving, seeking nerve endings no one knows are there.

It's only then that the true fuck begins. He has me on his lap. His thighs and arms hold me up as he pumps into me. The movement is short, but I feel it everywhere. I mean it. This cock is massaging my heart.

The sex goes on. After a while I am flat on my back, my feet crossed behind his thrusting hips as he plows into me. Rhythm and reach. It is something I have never felt before, and it is as familiar as a recurring dream. It is my dream. And now I know, I know who it is. It is the pharaoh- god Taharqa, only Taharqa no more.

Arensnuphis, my eternal love.

Pharaoh, king, and god, I am taken by love, my lover pure and revealed and his true self. He is asp/cat/snake/lion/man/god of my life. Each stroke of his cock is a vow and a promise kept. Each moment locked together is our freedom.

Each feeling is a needle sewing me into him, tying him next to me. He says it took millennia for it to happen, and now I know our souls are one.

He pauses. Here, right in the middle, so deep inside me there is no place to hide, he stops. We kiss. His eyes hook mine.

"Sebiumeker, oh sweet, eternal love," he says, "before Taharqa ever was, my soul was wed to yours." He moves a bit; we gasp together. "Near ninety centuries past, we were made to be two as one. And now we are." A move, a gasp. "One being and a pair. Too human, but two gods." He bends into a kiss. My insides are burning and awash in love. "Sebiumeker, you are my partner now, forever Nubian, forever Kush."

How can I find words when so locked in love and lovemaking. But I must and will. I take his face in my hands. I lean up, which somehow takes him deeper, and we sigh as one.

"My king and god, I want no more than to be your shadow." A tear is sliding down to my ear. I laugh, making every feeling increase. "No matter what names they have called you, I know I am the lover-companion of Arensnuphis, and that is the greatest gift humanity and the heavens hold."

He smiles, begins his slow pump again. It kills me to wait, and I would die again and again to share love with him. His arms slide around to lift me, pull me to his chest. Our sweat is one. Our skin is one skin. My hands reach up, cling to him as we ascend, pump, and ascend.

And in this golden moment we are rising, rising. My legs cling to Arensnuphis, and I no longer feel fur, but his slick flesh and thrusting muscle.

"Sweet love," he shouts, "you are the only magic."

"Oh god, sweet companion," I moan, "your magic is love. Enchant me!"

"Well," he says, and he smiles, "you wanted to know what it's like to fuck a god."

His head, next to mine to kiss and nip at my shoulder, presses against my cheek. I feel feathers on his back.

Sprouting from his naked shoulders, black and strong, velvety wings spread. A span twice the length of our bodies and flapping gently to the rhythm of the fuck, it makes us soar ever higher. Arensnuphis is a bird, and his head appears above me. His image rivals the falcon Horus of the antiquity from which he sprang. Above, a gold disc of sun crowns his head.

My bird man is lifting us straight up, the wings driving us higher and higher. And my orgasm rises as well. The feeling in me, the feeling on me, all inside and out and around, itching and scratching and crying for release. Until I can wait no longer.

I open my mouth like I open myself. My prick reaches overload. And as I spew the hot fluids of this most momentous occasion, Anubis/Osiris/Horus/my Archie pulls in his wings, and we plunge like peregrines from the sky. These falcons fall at speeds topping two hundred miles per hour. We take that dive unafraid, breathless. Until, near the earth, we stop.

And I swear, falling in ecstasy, I saw a little red-headed dude, baseball cap askew, watching our descent with a huge approving grin on his bespectacled face.

I know this place. I saw photos of it at the national museum, and Rashid threatened to camel-ship me here during my time touring Sudan. We are at the sacred mesa of Jebel Barkal, inside the temple home of supreme god Amun (Amon, Atun). Egyptian or Nubian, at one time all the dynasties recognized this as the most holy home of the god who created ma'at, the universe, and more.

On a bed of woven dreams, wrapped safe in each other's arms, we are inside this lone mountain that reaches more than three hundred feet in the air. Outside, the sunlight gleams; the bluest sky holds not a trace of cloud. Inside we are warm, hot only for each other. There is the sense of wind on the skin, whispers in the ears.

"Holy orgasm, my god and mate, is this why people worship?" I ask.

Arensnuphis's face wrinkles disagreement. "I do not want worship."

"You have the powers of a god."

"I have powers, that is true. But I have one love. I don't want more."

Sebiumeker sighs, thinks, *And what about the stratagem?*

"It seems the world's not yet ready to share. You must be partner to the lion god of war who will lead Kush to victory once again. Until then, we will prepare and protect, plot and devise. And visit your folks."

"They'll like that."

EPILOG

IT'S ME again: Ahmed. Did you think I'd let you outta here without one more visit with the Ach-man?

No surprise that things carry on from here. I can't tell the whole story, but here are some highlights.

Our new-made gods, Arensnuphis and Sebiumeker, born Taharqa Nimiery and Brandon Hickcock, return to underground Kush once their consecrated copulation is through. No, it's not a magical trip, just a few ATV, train, and felucca rides to the Nubas. Not even a jaunt on a camel.

Queen Amanirenas throws one mean party of reunion on the evening of their return. Food and music, dancing and poetry—we Africans love our words. A speech in the Meroë language, one that is not yet translated today, commemorates the return of gods' choices to us. Linen cloth, beaten gold, and night-black feathers predominate.

As in Nubian culture, Abar joins the confirmation as queen-mother of the pharaoh-god. With a sweep of her hand, the room glows with grace. This is her power manifest, and she sits on the throned dais with the rulers—the Kush king, his American consort, and the Nubian queen—to make a quartet of leaders, sprung from ancient days, designed for today.

After some revelry, Arensnuphis stands in the mother glow and holds out his now-golden hand. As if written on his palm, he reads prophecy to the citizens.

"We have let loose a whisper," he says, "that will soon stir a whirlwind. Now is the time for Kush to move thoughtfully. As the world spins, we must check its progress, and even give it a push now and then.

"The stratagem remains, but changes profoundly. We know that many suitors have now turned to Sudan as a link to the possible location of untold riches they have bargained, kidnapped, and killed for.

"The stakes are high, but our skills are higher. Each of us on the dais has power we have not yet learned to use. With the guiding words in my palm, pulled from Thoth's hidden knowledge, we will reach our goals, our success, and our mission to save the world from itself."

A tintinnabulation of bells, augmented with drums, claps, and cheers, greets this message, and then the gig really kicks into high gear.

Even little old me gets some love, a few dance partners, and lots of smiles. We are on a roll; I just wonder where we're rolling to.

Sometime later in the evening, the god-boys pull me aside for a parley.

"Archie and me have been talking," Branden tells me, then he backtracks with a smile. "I mean Arensnuphis. We're gonna need some social media skills and some AI cover for our next tactics. Are you up for it?"

"Does a cyberbear shit in the digital woods?" I respond.

"We're going to do some bait-and-switch actions with our pursuers," Arensnuphis says. "I sense our efforts will need assistance from other nations, perhaps remnants of other empires of Mother Africa that have been forgotten in time.

"Also, we may need to jump into cryptocurrency despite the computer energy costs."

"Quantum computing might help with that," I offer.

"Perhaps, when it's ready for use," he says.

"Many things are ready," I say. "Ask China. And rare-earth metals can do fantastic acts and will do more fantastic acts in the future."

"Good. Oh so good," my pharaoh-god says. "Ahmed, we could not do this without you."

And I look into each of their faces. Yes, they love each other beyond bounds. But there is love there for little Ahmed as well. Now if I could just get some sex on the side.

"Stay tuned with us," Sebiumeker says. "We'll be blasting out of here with various devils on our tail."

And so it goes. Within days, when the party is over, our god boys will leave Sudan, no doubt observed by one international agent or several others. Their roles in the stratagem change, and new players enter the game.

Arensnuphis and Sebiumeker take a circuitous route, aided by some Arab guy's skill and manipulation of airline computer systems, till they settle in, of all places, Chicago. Yes, it's Brand's home, and his folks are nearby. But where else could you find a restaurant called the Meroë Sudanese and Mediterranean Grill?

To their own little world, they will be Brand and Archie.

As for our pursuers, I keep an eye out for the Chinese, the Aussies, the Russkies, the yanks, the near-trillionaire, Ellie of Space Why and why X, and any permutation of Amalgamated rampant on the scene. The Mideastern terrorists are claiming they have their own rare-earth stash, but we're all still waiting for them to produce some without committing enormous resources for meager gains.

That makes for a lot of rivals, so I've got a lot of eyes out. What's the name of that hundred-eyed god? Argus? So call me Argus Ahmed.

The players are on the field. The rules are to be made on the fly. A world of love, gods, and magic unleashed still has its story to tell. Stick around.

Intercepted missive 2030: The solution to the world and the destruction of the world all exist in the world. Need creates pleas; greed creates conflict; love creates the way. Four horsemen of the apocalypse ride fresh, hot winds: pandemic disease, pits of hunger, ancient hate, endlessly renewed war. Will we outride the riders? Will we learn to embrace one (solution) or the other (destruction)? Faithful, stay tuned.

Ahmed out.

GLOSSARY

WITH ALL the history, geography, and magic in this story, I tried to give contemporary references to unfamiliar words. My editors suggested (and I agree) that a glossary would help readers who might want or need more. So here is a list of terms, alphabetical but categorized as people, objects, locations, and magic or science. Spellings and definitions may vary between sources: Many of these words have had to survive changes over centuries and were written in no-longer-used languages. (Ancient Egyptian script left out the vowels.) I hope this summarization helps.

PEOPLE

Amanirenas: Kushite queen during the first century BCE. She successfully blocked Roman expansion. Darisis takes her name when she becomes qore.

Apopis: Demon of chaos often depicted as a snake. Enemy to Amun.

Arensnuphis: Kushite deity, "the good companion." Taharqa takes this name when he becomes a pharaoh-god.

bomani: Egyptian. It means "warrior."

Darisis: the name given to the sister-in-fate of Taharqa. She is renamed after her ennead.

effendi: Arabic. A man of high education or social standing.

habibi: Arabic. It means "my love."

qore: monarch of the Kingdom of Kush. I use this word for Kush queens.

Various gods: the names may be ancient Egyptian, ancient Nubian, and sometimes both. Powers are often similar, though there is a hierarchy. The main gods include Amun (or Aman, Amun Re, or Ra), the sun god and creator of the world, his great-grandchildren Isis, Osiris, Set, and Nephthys, and a great-great-grandson, Horus. Then there is Thoth, god of the moon and author of all wisdom. I mention the other Amun progeny in Taharqa's description of the ennead.

Other lesser god names include Anhur-Shu, son of Ra and Egyptian god of war, and Dedun, Kush god of incense.

Taharqa: the name given to the brother-in-fate of Darisis. And our hero, Archie.

Taharqa's teachers: the names are all from Egyptian royalty. I didn't follow
    genders listed in some descriptions. They include Amenemhat. Ankhaf,
    Ankmare, Ankhnesneferibre, Bakenranef, Djedkare, Haremakhet,
    Khamhor, and Nitocris.
Yuya: Egyptian courtier known as the "master of the horse." Rashid uses
    this name as a jibe to make fun of Branden's dismal camel skills.

OBJECTS

abaya: a long, flowing cloak sometimes worn by Muslim women.
bamiya: Arabic. Okra stew, but used here to represent the mix of reality,
    magic and imagination in works like this novel.
cartouche: an oval frame surrounding hieroglyphs that make up the name
    of a god or royal person. The frame represents a looped rope with the
    magical power to protect the name written inside it.
chador: a full-body-length cloth sometimes worn by Muslim women.
ennead: a set of nine. In ancient Egypt mythology, the Grand Ennead
    contains the nine main deities.
faience: glazed ceramics.
felucca: a small sailboat on the Nile River.
hijab: a head covering sometimes worn by Muslim women.
jellabiya: a long, loose-fitting garment, often made of cotton.
jibba: a long, open coat, often made of cotton.
kafthan: a robe or tunic.
kissar: the traditional Nubian lyre.
neme: a cloth headdress often depicted in Egyptian hieroglyphics and on
    statuary.
rabab: a lute-like musical instrument with a skin-covered resonator.
secondary school: British high school. Key Stage 4 is the school level for
    students ages fourteen to sixteen.
shendyt: the kilt often depicted in Egyptian hieroglyphics and statuary.
sirwal: wide-legged pants, often made of cotton.

LOCATIONS

Abu Simbel: Egyptian ruins originally built by Pharaoh Ramses II.
Ed Dueim, El Damazin, El Obied, Singa, and Rabak: towns in Sudan.
Jebel Barkal: a mesa and temple now in Sudan considered by the ancients
    to be a holy mountain dedicated to Amun.

Kemet: "the black land," from the fertile soil created by floods of the River Nile. Over the centuries it has been the home of Egyptian and Kush empires.

Kerma: the first Nubian empire, from 2500 to 1500 BCE. Now an archeological site and the location of Jebel Barkal.

Kush: the Nubian empire that at times ranged from the Nile Delta to near the confluence of the White and Blue Niles.

Meroë: the original heartland of the Kingdom of Kush. Now an archeological site near Shendi, Sudan.

Napata: once a capital area of Kush, now an archeological site near Karima, Sudan.

Nubia: from the word nuba, meaning gold, a region from the first cataract of the River Nile to the confluence of the White and Blue Niles. Home of the Kush empires.

Nuba Mountains: an area in south central Sudan.

Sahel: the region of Africa that transitions from the desert Sahara to the plush savannah.

Suakin: A former Red Sea port now mainly abandoned. Ruins of buildings made from coral dominate the area.

MAGIC AND SCIENCE

djed medu: words that are said to evoke magic. Literally "the words to be said."

heka: ancient Egyptian magic; also the name of the god of magic.

historiola: an incantation incorporating a mythic story.

Hu: used here as a way for the Nubians of today's Kush to identify themselves, it comes from the myth of the creation of the world. Egyptian mythology says creation is the result of Amun's masturbation, and that hu (spelled hwt since Egyptian language did not include vowels) was what he shouted as his seed was ejaculated, creating the land and all life.

ma'at: Amun's plan for the world and its humans

rare-earth metals: seventeen elements on the periodic table. I avoided most of the names in the novel, but here they are: scandium, lanthanum, cerium, yttrium, dysprosium, neodymium, samarium, praseodymium, terbium, europium, gadolinium, erbium, ytterbium, promethium, holmium, lutetium, and thulium. Promethium is radioactive and very rarely found on the earth's surface.

sa: an amulet or a hieroglyph meaning protection.

Read on for an Excerpt from
Love in Lockdown
by R Frank Davis

CHAPTER 1

Conner

THE YOUNG man is sitting on the curb, lonely as an abandoned calf, same place I saw him yesterday afternoon while the foul smoke rose. Did he sleep here? Had he worked here? The clinic is gone, burned down to rubble. Why is he still here?

His back is to me. I see dark curls, a black T-shirt, jeans, worn Nikes, light-brown skin. He seems so cold, frozen in sorrow there on a warm, late May day. Chicago is waking up; the world is waking up—one to its spring promise, one to its slaughtering past.

I can't let this dogie stay. Stranger or not, it ain't right. I climb outside my idling SUV and shout through my mask: "Hey! Hey kid! You all right?"

He turns, and above his mask, green eyes look back at me—eyes as green as mine but infinitely sadder.

"Not really."

"You connected with the clinic?"

"Used to be."

"Well, I can't leave you here, pardner. Let me give you a ride."

"Got nowhere to go." The next statement came without judgment, though it really should have had some. "Why should you care?"

"I'm on the clinic board. I care a whole bunch: about the clinic, about the patients, and about the staff." So that was a response to his judgmental side. Now to the hurting one: "Really, you don't have anywhere to stay? It's a pandemic."

"I used to sleep in a back room there." His hand flicked toward the scorched bricks and blackened metal. "It saved them on salary. I was mostly a volunteer."

Alone, homeless, young, and apparently broke. I should help. But can I trust him? There is no sign this fire has anything to do with my own dangerous predicament. But do I dare?

Right then my instinct strikes. It's not uncommon for me; I get an itching about something or someone, and it usually gains me a lot. Important lessons, best friends, major jumps in my career, a bout of love, all came with an instinctual feeling that this thing is right.

Well, the love 'bout damn near TKO'd me, the career is in a major slump, and my whole life got bucked like a raw-roped mustang. There's been loss, threats, murder. All those came out of instinct too. An instinctual insistence cost me work, love, and safety. A quiet, sad, frightening place to be in. So is this instinct, the first one in years, as damned as the last two?

Or am I horny as hell?

Time for scene analysis, Conner MacKay: First off, you're an aging actor/director on the canyon edge of "cast a younger Conner MacKay." Second, what you can see looks, honestly, luscious. (If it's wrong to say that mixing races leads to some of the most beautiful humans ever, I am sorry Halle Berry, Shemar Moore, and Henry Golding.) But third, he's a colt, someone with less than half your time on the planet, and you are pushing codger. On the plus side, in fourth, you're healthy, lean, and strong. (But oh, the gray hair! Especially the chest hair.)

And fifth, some madman out there is stalking you as sure as sunrise.

Still, you remember that youthful energy, the abandonment to physical pursuits and emotional connection. The world of new love. Splendor in the grass.

And what will you two talk about in this new world? He probably doesn't know who Warren Beatty was, or is. And I look at Megan, knowing that's no stallion I ever knew.

But if he's needful, I can help. And if he's open, we can see where that goes. And no matter what, we'll follow the campsite rule—always leave things better than they were when you found them.

Hell with it. Time to cowboy up.

"Come on," I shout, "let's get you outta here."

CHAPTER 2

Dante

NOTHING COMES for free. Yeah, I get it. But why do the bills come due so random, so costly, and so often so unfair?

All these questions. That's me. Hard questions: Why do police kill unarmed Black men? Why is a dangerous disease denied? Why, for so many, does raging hate feel better than a handshake or a warm hug? And the particular questions: Why did that White cop sit on that Black man's neck until that man was dead? How could children be snatched from their parents, left in cages, and nobody stopped it? How are gangbangers able to kill again and again? And how does a sane man comfortably ask—*publicly*—when he can start shooting Democrats?

But then I get lost in all my personal questions: Why did Dante Burke have to march downtown during a pandemic? Did Dante do enough? All he did was march downtown. Why didn't Dante refill his rescue-inhaler scrip before he left? Why, as we struggled to remain peaceful downtown, did violence march here—march and loot and burn on the only place I, Dante, have to stay? And why is Dante sitting on a curb for a night and a day with everything I own (that's left) in my backpack, staring at the smoking rubble of the neighborhood clinic where I used to work?

I chose this place, a health clinic in an impoverished neighborhood. I did it to pay my dues, to show my commitment, to use my self to help my people. But did I know my people, those of my people who did this?

I had left my well-respected state college at Christmas break, a semester before graduation, unable to bear any more of the relentless torrent of lies, arrogance, and pseudosuperiority being fire-hosed out of the too-very-White House. My anger wasn't from personal confrontation. I've spent most of my life sheltered behind one sandwich-board sign or another: cute baby, early reader, devilish eyes, nerdy student, smart collegiate, even mixed-race man. Being "more yaller than the sun" and having green eyes can do that for you.

But that December, some friends and I were walking near campus when a car of townies squealed by us. A hand out the window threw an egg, and my buddy was splattered. The idiots in the car yelled something, but their Midwestern/country drawl and the car's lumbering engine drowned it out. The egg hit my pal like yellow spit. We were all stricken.

And I was incensed, outraged because I was one of two brown faces in our group. Most likely a target, but not obvious enough to keep my friend from being slimed. I couldn't get it out of my mind. What had we done to draw this hatred? And what hadn't I done to confront it? I couldn't live with it on campus. I couldn't take it home, not to *her*, not even for the holidays.

So as an angered, confused, incited, gay Black man, I dropped out of my last college semester, sold back my textbooks, took my bus money and extended the ticket past home (in our careful little suburb) into the city. I wandered Chicago streets—not unfamiliar, but certainly not home.

Chicago is no place to be homeless in winter, so I stayed at shelters, tried single-room-occupancy hotels, maybe overstayed my welcome in a public building or on a commuter train car or two. Till I found this place, where they were looking for some spiff-up-and-take-out-the-trash help. Sounds basic, but at a public health clinic, trash can have a range of hazardous implications, so not everyone is willing to take the job. I was, and as I hired on, a thing called COVID-19 (known to a few who didn't see fit to tell the rest of us) was well on its way.

As January's chill blew into February, news stories about the coronavirus pandemic popped up like crocuses in the snow. I was working, learning new protocols to sanitize and socially distance, but I still had no place to stay. So some kind staffers let me use a back closet (and a broken-down examination table) "for the time being during the lockdown." "The time being" for front-line workers consisting of every day all the way up to today, through March to late May.

I had a role, if only a menial one, a task, and a place to do it. Working with people who care for people who (way too often) say they are way past caring. Smokers laughing till they cough up blood. Women with bruises on bruises: they nod their heads shyly but do not discuss their abuse. Children burned or broken and not allowed to cry. HIV patients expelled from their real families and their false friendships, and scared to death—death being more likely for COVID cases with underlying health issues. And old people, the grandmothers and grandfathers? We lost them to lonely tenements or to hospital emergency rooms, and then to COVID-19 itself.

I am Black, pale-skinned as I am, and I know that these things, day to day, drain my people. I have not experienced most of them personally, but I know that those who have, struggle for their humanity. And how, day to day, loitering outside their time-soiled doors and half-abandoned blocks, the thieves of their humanity wait. Sometimes my people laugh, but they never cry. Their anger and disappointment bend them and twist them upright, and then they explode, maybe over a videoed murder and maybe over a cigarette and maybe for no definable reason at all. And even if I know the injustice and see the explosion, I can't say I understand.

My people, sold from their African homeland to be taken, used, and abandoned here. And they go on, hobbled and unstoppable, making life from breath, sweat, and whatever is left over.

I exposed my health during a medical crisis to demand an end to a human-rights disaster: the dead-eyed-cop murder of Black people. But when I left the neighborhood for downtown, I exposed our clinic to attack. Why attack it? Because it contained drugs? Because there might be a bit of change in the till? Or because it sat at the back of a chain pharmacy and therefore was part of the corporate power structure? Was it angry retribution or advantage and opportunity?

Private property, acquired by injustice, is a justifiable target for protest.

Whether the assault on the clinic was to scream with rage, to punish the profit takers, or to grab drugs and money, the attackers trashed the building. And the fire totaled the pharmacy, clinic, and my illegal bedroom in the back. Gone from a community that has so little and needs so much.

I am sitting on a curb, gazing across rubble, nowhere to go. I am wearing my mask. I am smelling smoke, tallying costs—and seeing that the wrong people are often left to pay the bill.

I hear a man call.

Turning, I see his green eyes, like mine, but there is a White face under his mask. Wrinkles at the edge of the lids show the wear of life, yet the eyes are friendly. I hear that in the voice as well, which has a bit of Western twang. It seems welcoming, familiar somehow, and I bet that expensive leather seat in his car is comfortable. Our exchange of words shows his concern, his connection, his reason to offer help. But I need to be suspicious and not seduced. I have never been gay-bashed, never been raped, and I dare not walk into that now.

"C'mon, pardner," he shouts, "we'll rustle up some food."

What's happening? My legs instinctively push me up to standing. I'm a bit wobbly, and he moves to help me, but I recover without thinking. I head, stiff-legged, thoughtless, to the shiny, dark SUV; I open the door, feel the soft whoosh of the air conditioner, and climb in.

CHAPTER 3

Conner

DANTE BURKE, this dogie says. A good name, and proper. Dante is a first name, not a last. His voice is soft, his answers short. I can sense he is gay. He is not a threat; I can see he is wary and mourning and tired. He doesn't even answer when I ask if he's hungry. I pull into the next drive-through and order burgers anyway.

He seems to freeze when I hand him his sandwich, eyes peering over his mask.

Oh yes, the mask. "No worries, pardner. I've been self-isolating all along, and I even had a COVID test a day ago."

"But I've been in the streets, Mr. MacKay. The Black Lives Matter protests," the young man says. "I could infect you."

I pull my mask down. "I was there too, and I think we can chance it. We both need to eat, Dante. And please, even if I am that old, make it Conner."

He nods reluctantly and pulls off his mask, revealing a perfectly boyish face—early twenties, soft lips, prominent nose, high cheekbones, barely a hint of facial hair. It is a lovely face that only needs a smile.

Before he opens the burger box, he shifts the backpack that's on the floorboard between his feet. His hand shuffles around an outside pocket, pulls out an inhaler, and he takes a whiff.

"Jesus, Joseph, and Mary" I can't help but mutter.

"Oh no," he says, trying to reassure me. "It's just asthma."

"Just asthma is not 'just asthma' for a Black man. It can be fatal. And it's not 'just asthma' during a respiratory pandemic. It's a major health risk."

He looks a bit shamed by this.

"Hey, use your spray—and hold your breath this time so it has time to work. Then eat your lunch, and we'll find you a place to bunk away from viruses."

He starts to speak, but I stop him. "Use your medicine, pardner. This is no joke."

So he inhales the spray, holds his breath for a good twelve seconds. He unwraps the sandwich, snatches at a few fries and slurps some soda. He takes a third whiff, holds again, longer, then turns back to eating.

Maybe I'm imagining, but I can see his chest relax, his breathing settle. I remember a college roommate, so clenched in asthma attack he leaned out of our fifth-floor dorm window, desperate for air that was all around us but wouldn't fit in his lungs. Paramedics had to pull him, passed out, to the school infirmary. I never let that roomie travel without an inhaler after that.

Gonna have to watch out for this maverick. Half my age and still searching.

"I am so grateful we made the stop at burger-doodle," he says. Grateful; interesting word. And burger-doodle? An old Chicago radio jock used to say that. Where'd Dante hear it?

"I was two-full-days hungry," he continues, "and your reaction to my asthma was real and sweet, like a caring friend and not a correcting parent."

This is not a Black guy/White guy conversation across a color line. I've had those, even in Hollywood, and they are not as open and equal as this. He seems to be comfortable in this world. So what in holy hell is he doing working for a bed in the ghetto?

"So where are you from?" I say.

"Not here."

I let that sit a while. Obviously a wound he doesn't want touched.

"I'm not from here either."

"I could tell."

"Yeah?"

"Your accent. Kinda sounds Western." He finishes his fries, then says, "Conner MacKay. Why's that sound familiar?"

Uh-oh. A wound I'm sensitive about.

"Oh, I wouldn't say it's unusual. Maybe it was when my folks picked it, but seems like either and both are pretty common names these days. Soap-opera-star specials."

"No, not soap operas," he says, really studying me, appraising. "I mean, not you in them."

There's a pause, and I decide better to finish my burger, and as I chew along, it bursts out of him: "Cowboy!" And I wince.

"I'd visit my grandmother," he says happily. "She was always in the kitchen, and her TV was always on. 'For company,' she'd say. But it was always Westerns, reruns of Westerns. And the most recent rerun, *Wyoming*

Wild, had a young-guy star—real young, maybe thirty years ago—and it was you. Conner MacKay."

I gulp down what's still in my mouth.

"The last of the Western heroes," Dante says, and I wince again. "It's true. My rescuer, my hero, is the actor Conner MacKay, last of the TV cowboys."

"It was time," I say, recalling why that genre ended. "Those three decades in US history were too revered to be true. Finally, Westerns were being forced to show our bloody awful history: genocide and greed, betrayal and bondage, and then 'benign neglect,' with too much daily drudgery and casual killing behind all the imaginary bravado."

"That history wasn't your fault," Dante says, "and you didn't back away. You did that film about Native American truth and White lies. It was *way* successful. Won some Oscars. Wolf? Wolfing?" He is trying to guess the movie's name, but I'll be damned before I find the answer for him.

"Coyote!" he shouts. "*Coyote Moon*!"

So do I blush or brag? Correct the record or converse? The latter, at least for now.

"Still," I say, "it didn't take long for this country to switch their source of slaughter porn to police stories and ghetto crime."

"It's all magic, like *Harry Potter*," Dante says, which quite startles me. "Pecos Bill, Buffalo Bill, Wild Bill, Wyatt Earp: thrilling stories no more real than wizard wands or Apollo's arrows. That's how I see it. There's no sin in liking a good myth, long as you know it's not real."

I slurp at my soda, then say, "You really feel that way? That's kinda, well, open."

"I'm glad you didn't say 'woke.'" He smiles. Sweet dimples. "I like remembering the stories I watched: Steve McQueen's character was Josh Randall. The Virginian always wore black. Marshall Dillon had a jail janitor named Chester. And he wasn't Black."

"You're dippin' back way before my days, pardner." He smiles at me calling him a pardner. "You can stop the rewind at when Dr. Quinn still practiced."

"Those reruns didn't get much play on grandma's set."

"Neither did my show on most TVs."

"Oh, but I saw it." He settles back in his seat. "I remember you. I remember liking you. And I think they reran every episode twice."

"All twenty-six of 'em?" I suck on my soda straw; the sound lets me know it's as done as my first TV show, same as I'm done in Hollywood.

"I guess all." He stifles a yawn. "Yeah, I watched you a lot. Not as much as Robert Conrad, but then you never took your shirt off."

"Oh, I think I did. Once." I actually remember quite well, because they wanted me to rise from this riverbed and strip off my shirt. But they wanted me to shave my chest hair. We fought. Quite a bit. I won on a historical technicality—Western men didn't manscape.

"Whoa," I say. "*Wild Wild West* was thirty years before my show, and *Wanted: Dead or Alive* was ten years before that. Most folk your age can't remember the theme song to *Friends*."

"I like stories." He pauses a bit, yawns again. "Especially old ones. They have heroes, fun, danger, bits of history. They can leave out the dirty truths 'cause nobody remembers them. And they still give messages, morals, lessons that last."

"I remember now," he says. "I did see your chest. Your wet, dark-hairy chest. One show, after you got out of a river." He seems to drift a bit, get quieter. "Wanted a hairy chest like that."

That is flattering, except it's about something I don't quite have anymore. "The hair's not so dark now. It's been years."

"But it's not like you're ancient." I'm not so sure I like the way he says "ancient." Like I'm not, but not far from it. "I mean, you're a kind, friendly, older guy"—There it is! Older!—"who is going out of his way to help a stranger."

Yeah, but older.

He smiles again, drifting. I'm not sure he's not talking out of a dream.

"I bet it's a great chest anyway." He is drifting. "I like chests."

"That's truly sweet," I say. "And I like you, so you're not a stranger anymore, all right?" No response. "All right, Dante?"

His head droops over to rest against my right shoulder, and he is fast asleep.

Scan the QR code below to order

R Frank Davis (he/they) is a Black author with a romantic streak. He is also a believer in truth, reality, and facing the facts of American life. A local-newspaper reporter, big-city-daily editor, and managing editor of a prize-winning magazine over the last forty-five years, in retirement he has finally turned his efforts to creating his own realities through fiction. But that's not new; he's been writing stories ever since he could hold a pencil.

He may also be the oldest Dirty Old Man writing romance novels.

To be a good reporter or editor, one must have knowledge in many areas. Having an honors diploma as an undergraduate, a master's degree in management, an addiction to current events, and a great love of history, R Frank tries to tie what he's experienced to what he hopes readers will want in fun and intelligent ways.

Living in Chicago with his husband of ten years, he enjoys live theater and musicals, comedy and action movies, James Baldwin, jazz music, ee cummings, and hour-long walks, especially along the shore of Lake Michigan. As a single father, his greatest accomplishment was getting all three children educated, employed, and out of the house. He loves them madly.

Since becoming a published novelist, he has become very involved in social media, especially sites dealing with gay male romance. He is an advocate for "own voices" romances, BIPOC and interracial fiction, and authors who may not be well-known. He has two Facebook sites—RFrank Davis and RFrankly News N Views. He can be found on Instagram as rfranklie and on TikTok as rfrankly21.

As social intolerance, sexual freedom, and gender identity have become today's headlines, R Frank Davis is excited to tell tales of societal evolution, and to entertain readers along the way.

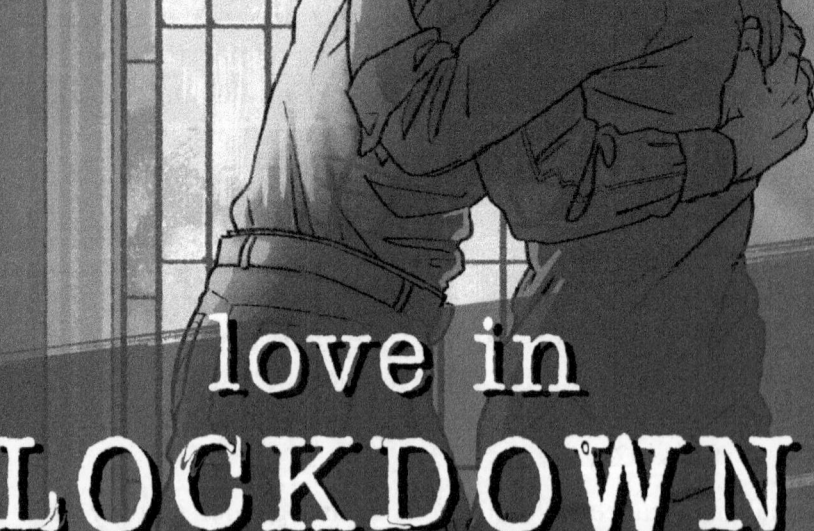

love in
LOCKDOWN

R Frank Davis

Conner MacKay is the last of the TV cowboys, but he's withdrawn from society—even before a global pandemic forces the world into quarantine. When he meets activist Dante Burke, though, Conner takes a chance. He can't leave a young Black man on the street in the face of a public health crisis. What kind of cowboy would he be then?

On the surface, Conner and Dante live in opposing realities: midlife versus youth, flush versus flat broke. But their politics, attraction, and close quarters bring them together until the heat between them grows into a burn almost too hot to handle.

Then old dangers breach their safeguards and threaten not their love, but their very lives.

Scan the QR code below to order

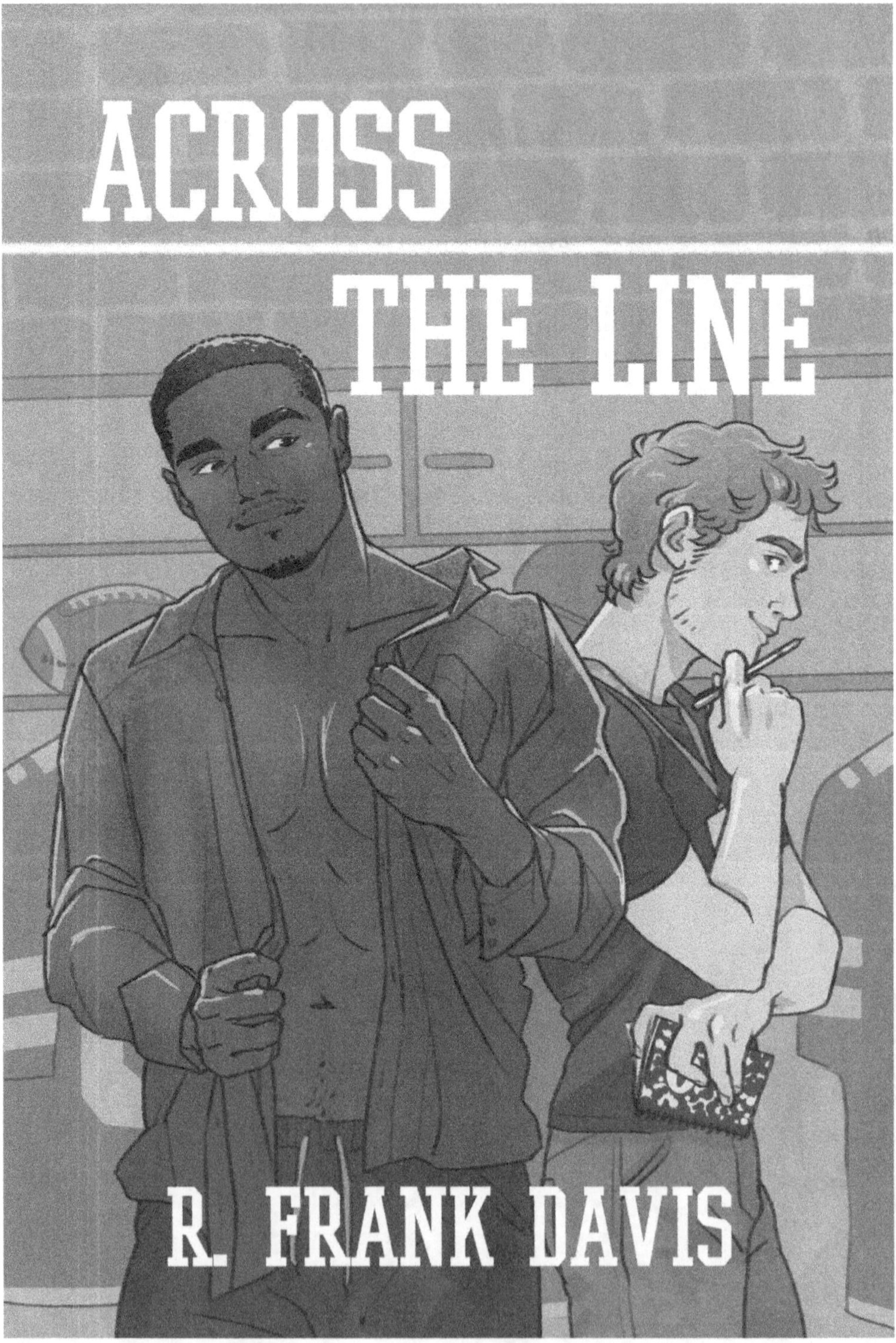
ACROSS
THE LINE
R. FRANK DAVIS

A chance meeting. A one-night stand. And then a pattern of them.

For Nigerian-born professional football linebacker Arikawe "Ade" Adeloyebe and Chicago newspaper reporter Rex Palmieri, not-so-casual sex is all they can have. Ade is closeted to protect his career, and Rex has to toe the line between his own job and his secret relationship with a sports celebrity.

Both men fall deeply in love, but misunderstandings, miscommunication, and outside pressure threaten to implode the relationship. Then a bounty-hunting scandal followed by a bloody gay bashing force Rex and Ade to face some hard choices. Can they tackle the opposition and cross the goal line to happiness together?

Scan the QR code below to order

www.ingramcontent.com/pod-product-compliance
Lightning Source LLC
Chambersburg PA
CBHW070526100726
47907CB00004B/1006